Burns So Bad

ANNE MARSH

Copyright © 2013 Anne Marsh

All rights reserved. No part of this book may be reproduced or transmitted in any form or by any electronic or mechanical means, including photocopying, recording or by any information storage or retrieval system, with the written permission of the author, except where permitted by law.

ISBN-13: 978-0-9910974-1-8

CHAPTER ONE

Jump thousand.

The familiar summer anthem of the smoke jumpers exploded through his head. Adrenaline flooded Rio Donovan's body as he anticipated the exhilaration of dropping through the air as he threw himself out of the DC-3's cabin and streaked towards Rail Mountain. Sixty seconds and two thousand feet.

God, he loved his job.

The plane pulled away with a roar, only half-drowning the whoops of his boys jumping out of the cabin behind him. Rio Donovan shot a sideways glance at his jump partner, angling his body away from hers. Christ, she was a cool customer. She watched the ground rushing up to meet them without so much as cracking a smile. He'd bet she'd already cataloged the burn area and mentally marked a half-dozen hot spots she'd rush to knock down as soon as they were on the ground. Gia Jackson was good. There was no doubt about that. She'd earned her place on Strong's jump team. So he had absolutely no business noticing how the jump harness separated her breasts into two teasing mounds. She was one of his boys too and... not going there. Fifteen hundred feet to the ground and his next job. *Focus, Donovan.*

Look thousand.

The forest fire beneath belched a big ass plume of dark smoke on his right, the sideways drift half-obscuring the small speck of burned over meadow he was aiming for. The drift streamers had to be down there somewhere, the red ribbons an X-marks-the-spot he wouldn't see for at least another thousand feet. The meadow swung crazily as the wind buffeted him hard, twisting him in a circle before he got the spin under control and his boots down because he needed to get horizontal, fast. Feet first, straight up-and-down. A holler tore from his throat. *Fuck, yeah.* This was living.

Straightening his legs, he dropped below Gia. He weighed more than she did and he'd bet it killed her that he'd make the LZ first. He loved how competitive she was. Beating her to the landing zone would be fun.

Reach thousand.

Still mentally counting down, he tightened his grip on the rip cord.

Pull thousand.

And yanked hard.

And nothing. Not a goddamned thing. The lines twisted around the drag chute, turning his backup into a mess of flapping nylon and rope. Cursing, he took his eyes off the ground rushing up to meet him and eyeballed the tangled mess. That was okay, he thought, his hands already reaching for the utility knife strapped to his thigh. Cut it away and pull the reserve chute. Plenty of time. Still, he didn't waste any seconds, sawing the sharp edge hard and fast through the ropes, because panicking was a luxury he couldn't afford. Every second closed the distance between himself and the ground and dying hadn't been part of his plans for today.

The tangled lines fell away, seeming to float next to him for a long second. He was bigger and heavier and the gravity *really* was a bitch. As soon as he pulled the reserve ripcord, however, he knew today wasn't his day. Or it was his last day. *Nada.* The reserve chute didn't fire and so now he was falling, not jumping, because he didn't have a working chute.

The ground spun again in a crazy 360 and there was no good way to land this.

No way to pull out and demand a do-over.

He'd auger. Pancake. *Die.*

Flashes of memories raced through his heads, bright pops of had-beens, the places and people he'd loved. He'd done his fair share of loving and he had almost no regrets there. All he prayed now was that Jack and Evan wouldn't let their adoptive mother see his body. She didn't need to carry that kind of memory with her. A thought and a prayer and then he watched the ground rising up toward him, because if he was going out, he'd see the end coming. He had less than thirty seconds to live and to start dying.

Rio Donovan was falling.

The sheer impossibility of that truth hit her, but Gia Jackson hadn't got where she was in life by refusing to accept the impossible. Her playful, sensual, Harley-riding computer genius of a partner who'd gleefully kicked her ass at every fire they'd jumped so far in this short season... was falling. To his death. His drag chute drifted away uselessly above him, tangled around a mess of lines, and she spotted no reserve chute. He'd have pulled the cord. She knew it. Instead of riding the toggles toward their landing zone, his big, leather-gloved hands were crossed over his chest. Gia couldn't make out his gorgeous face behind his protective helmet, but he was head up, feet down, barreling toward the ground in a one hundred miles an hour free fall.

No one, not even the legendary Rio Donovan, could survive that kind of hit.

She was his goddamned jump partner—and he hadn't called out or hollered. What the hell was he thinking? They were supposed to communicate. That was part of the plan. She'd enjoy rescuing his fine ass just so she could yell at him for the sheer stupidity of his giving it up move.

In order to do that, however, she had to get closer. She made a left-hand turn, curling up into a ball to drive her fall faster and close the distance between them.

"Problem, golden boy? " She had to yell to be heard over the wind's roar as she gripped the toggles. Snatching Rio from mid-fall wouldn't be a walk in the park. He outweighed her, plus she had to avoid tangling his arms and legs in her line.

Rio's head snapped up. "Technical malfunction," he drawled, like it was an everyday occurrence. His eyes stared into hers and this close she could just make out the long lashes he wielded like a weapon. She'd wondered before what it was like, seeing the world through Rio's eyes. If he felt it, he never showed fear. She loved that about him. Nothing ever seemed to scare him. God, to face life like that would be a miracle.

"Need a hand?" She maneuvered closer.

"I'm open to suggestions." His body hung there in the air relaxed, as if he wasn't hundreds of feet from dying.

She looked down, scanning for the first two sets of jumpers. Add Rio's weight to her own and she'd sink like a stone and getting too close to another chute would steal her air and drop them both on the other canopy. Killing three people today wasn't part of *her* plan.

"Grab on," she snapped, because she didn't have his kind of patience.

God. Of course he hesitated.

"My boobs and I will survive the contact, I promise," she snarled, correctly reading his hesitation. Now was no time to discover his inner gentleman.

Rio wrapped himself around her with an audible grunt. He might have said something, but she doubted it was *thank you*. Probably an order or a command, she decided, hauling hard on the toggles. There was no time to figure their descent out better. Face to face, he scissored his legs around her waist, pulling her tight. Despite two bulky jumpsuits and the yards of safety webbing, she swore she could feel the heat of him. There was definitely no missing his strength.

"Get your head out of my way." She craned her head, trying to see around Rio's helmet. He growled, but tucked his face against her throat. After all, now he was riding blind, trusting her to land them both safely. He might not have a choice, but she'd bet he hated the feeling. She liked being in control herself.

The ground spun below them, mixing up meadow with char and snags. The mountainside sprouted flames, first on her left and then on her right, as she faced them into the wind and steered for the LZ. The spotter in the DC-3 had warned the landing would be tricky. Sure enough, a blast of heat baked her face when she swung too close to the burn site and the air started to choke up with smoke. She adjusted her grip on the toggles, taking them westward.

"You sure about this?" he growled, sounding damned unhappy for someone who'd been about to die.

"You want me to dump your ass now?" she countered, correcting the chute's trajectory.

"Hell." His body tensed and she knew holding him was impossible if he decided to let go. "How much do you weigh, Jackson?"

She didn't take her gaze off the LZ. She was off the landing zone by twenty yards right now and hanging them both up in a tree—when Rio didn't have a safety harness—wasn't her first choice. A hundred foot fall would just kill him more slowly than the free fall.

"You're asking a lady her weight?"

She could *feel* his smoky chuckle in her ear. God. The things that chuckle made her think of were probably illegal in at least half the southern states. "You're no lady, Jackson," he said.

He was right. "I'm your jump partner."

There. The clearing spun into view again and she steered hard. The guys on the ground had *Oh, shit* written all over their pusses because they knew a problem when they saw it. They scrambled, pulling in their chutes and making room. She'd bet the lack of next steps was killing them, because unless they sprouted a giant trampoline out of their asses, all they could do was wait and watch.

And it was almost over.

"We the last in to this party?" Having a wingman was unexpectedly useful because she couldn't take her eyes off the ground.

Rio looked up, completely unconcerned. "Nope. We're going to beat the last two jumpers if you hurry this up."

"Got it." She did too. She wasn't letting him fall.

"Gia." She couldn't look at him now, but he had her full attention nonetheless. He made her name sound deadly serious. "You let me go if you can't land us both. Promise me."

Always a fucking gentleman. It was a good thing for him she played by a different code. She shifted, repositioning them, and the move pressed his chest against hers. *Welcome to my late night date fantasies.* "You're my jump partner. You don't fall on my watch."

That was the truth. Landing tandem—without a safety harness—was a high-risk maneuver, but letting him falling simply wasn't an option. He'd have done the same for her and they both knew it. That was what partners did. Too bad for him if he had an issue with her being female or having her girly bits squashed against his front. Rio was out of choices and he'd have to make do with her.

"Gia—" The way he said her name, she didn't know it was a curse or a prayer.

So she gave him the truth. "I'll kill you if you let go."

The final seconds were a blur of holding on and braking hard. The ground swung left-right-left in a nauseating arc as she picked a point over Rio's shoulder and drove them in. The muscles in her arms and back screamed at the doubled weight. But the chute held. *Rio* held. She bent her legs, getting ready to hit. Two broken legs would make her deadweight in this firefight. But as soon as her steel toes got close to brushing the ground, Rio pushed away, letting go and tucking into a roll. *Perfect as always.* Her boot clipped his shoulder—so sorry—and she caught his grunt as she slammed into the ground a few feet away.

He wasn't dead.

Hallelujah.

If she'd been more of a church-going, praying person, she'd have cranked out a few verses of something, but instead she ran, chute flapping, slowing her momentum to the litany of *thank Gods* in her head. The rest of the team moved in now that she and Rio were on the ground, whooping and high-fiving. Her head ran roll call, automatically taking stock of who had landed. Jack and Zay, Liam and Angel, Quinn and Van. Evan Donovan's big arm grabbed her as she tore past him, swinging her effortlessly to a halt. "Nice job."

Rio's brother made those two words sound like a gold star and a Purple Heart.

She grinned at him. "My pleasure."

Not dead. Rio took a moment to appreciate that glorious fact. Sure, he'd slammed his shoulder into the ground when he'd tucked and rolled, and Gia's boot had clipped his shoulder as the chute dragged her further up the field, but the landing could—should—have been so, so much worse. He inhaled sharply. *Control it.*

His back on the ground, his ass planted hard, he stared up at the blue sky. If he didn't inhale—which was almost an impossibility at the moment anyhow, as his lungs strained to get back up and working—he couldn't even tell there was a twenty acre wildfire to his right demanding quick attention.

Good thing he loved his job.

He could feel the steel-toes headed his way—he'd bet the entire jump team was either high-fiving Gia or headed his way to ask *What the fuck?*—so he did a quick inventory. He'd be sore tomorrow—nothing new there—but a quick twitch said both arms and legs worked. Which was nothing short of a miracle. Of course, Gia was probably the most stubborn person he'd ever met, which was another miracle given the ability of his two brothers to hang on and not let go, and she'd made it damned clear that she wasn't letting him fall.

Gia.

Letting go of Gia was the hardest damn thing Rio had done lately—and not because he'd been afraid of dying, but because she smelled like lemons and outdoors. He had no idea if she knew that, or if the scent was just Gia, but he got a contact high immediately when he was around her and those seconds wrapped in her arms were pretty unforgettable.

For many reasons.

He pushed himself into a sitting position, waved off the incoming team members and eyeballed the clearing. The last two jumpers were down, pulling in their chutes and pointing their boots towards the flames, ready to get to work.

Usually, he did the rescuing. Being on the receiving end was a new sensation, but hardly one he could refuse when the only other option was dying. He wasn't fatally stupid. He definitely owed Gia. So what did it say about him that he'd noticed how her breasts felt pushed up against his arm when he was in the middle of *dying*? He was fairly certain he'd remember her accidental touch for pretty much forever, which gave a whole new meaning to memories to last a lifetime.

He'd nearly died.

Shake it off, he reminded himself. Although the fire came first, some things needed to be said. She'd had his back. And his front. He was fairly certain though that Gia hadn't been thinking about getting his rocks off while she'd steered them both to the ground. That had been his problem. He wanted to believe the insta-chemistry was an adrenaline-fueled response to almost dying, but he suspected it was more than that. He'd felt something for Gia from the moment she'd joined their team.

Once again… shake it off.

Halfway across the LZ, Gia popped her helmet off and clipped it to her belt. Despite the distance, it felt like some magic string connected him to her. She took a few questions from the rest of the team as she yanked off her helmet, but then she strode off, clearly ready to get down to the business of fighting fire. While he sat here on the ground like a dumbass, dazed and confused. What the hell was wrong with him?

He picked himself up with a grunt, unbuckling his jacked harness. When he got back to base camp, he'd go over the entire pack. Misfires happened, but he didn't like it. He'd packed that chute himself and Jack had checked it. Every inch of that line had been neatly and precisely folded. Just like always.

As if he'd heard Rio mentally call his name, Jack strode over. He'd got his chute off and his game face on. "What the hell happened up there?"

He slapped Rio on the back, his hand lingering a moment longer than usual. Apparently, Jack had done the math too and realized just how close to dying Rio had actually come.

"Malfunction." *Christ.* He relived the moment when he pulled the rip cord and nothing happened.

Jack looked like he was entertaining the same thought. He jerked his head towards Gia, who was rolling up her chute. "She bailed your ass out."

"Sure did."

Jack frowned. "We'll go over your chute when we're back at base."

His oldest brother approached safety with the kind of focus usually reserved for national security matters. Maybe that was because of the way they'd grown up. They'd been three young boys who'd met up on the streets of Sacramento and then stuck together. Given their youth, life had been hand-to-mouth, carving out an existence for themselves where they could. It had been Jack's idea to take the last name Donovan. One more thing they could all share, he'd pointed out, and Rio and Evan had agreed. Even when the fine state of California had eventually tried placing them in separate foster homes, the Donovan brothers had stuck together. Always. After one too many runaway attempts, the three boys had been sent as a package deal to Strong. They and Nonna had been a family ever since.

The concern written all over Jack's face wasn't a surprise, but Rio preferred to ignore it. It wasn't as if he didn't care about safety—after this last little free fall he *absolutely* cared—but he'd never gotten quite so worked up about it. He preferred to move forward. Dwelling on the past never helped.

Jack lent him a hand sliding the harness off. Rio didn't need the assist—the chute lines were the issue, not the buckles—but Jack clearly needed to do something.

His brother paused, gear slung from his hands. "Are you hurt?"

No and that was another mark in the miracle column. "Not so much as a scratch. If you tell Nonna, I'll kill you."

Their adoptive mother didn't need to know she'd almost lost one of them today. She understood the risks of what they did. Smoke jumping wasn't for the faint of heart and, sometimes, good men got hurt. He was just damn fortunate he hadn't joined their number today.

Because Gia Jackson hadn't let go of him.

"We're starting in five," Jack said. He didn't ask again if Rio was okay. They needed all hands on deck to knock down this fire and Rio had no intention of sitting this one out to commune with his inner self.

"Got it." He turned around, scanning the clearing. Gia was on the side nearest the fire. Of course.

"She's good," Jack said quietly.

She was. She was also the first woman they'd brought on board. It wasn't that the Donovans preferred to keep the team all-male—although it certainly made certain logistics like suiting up simpler—but there just weren't that many women interested in jumping out of planes into the very center of a forest fire. And then hauling a hundred-plus pounds of gear around with them while they shoveled dirt onto twelve-foot flames. Maybe women were simply smarter than men. He grinned. Jack's fiancée, Lily Cortez, would have agreed with that statement.

He strolled over to Gia, not sure what to say. The DC-3 pilot had dropped a crate of supplies for them and she was checking out a chainsaw. She'd tugged off her gloves, one caught between her teeth, her fingers flying over the tool. Gia definitely knew her stuff.

"Hey," he said, squatting beside her.

She set the chainsaw down on the ground and rocked back on her heels. "You ready to roll?"

"Always."

"Good." She nodded and reached for her glove lying on the ground.

When his hand shot out and grabbed it first, she looked up and glared at him. "Are we playing keep away now, Donovan? Because that's real mature of you."

"Thanks," he said roughly.

"You're welcome." She made a give-it-up gesture with her bare hand. "Return the glove."

He winced. "You saved my life."

Some things had to be said.

She huffed out an impatient breath. "Does this mean we share some kind of psychic bond now, or you're going to pull a Robin Hood and stick by my side until you've returned the favor?"

He shook his head. "Not in my plans for today, no."

"Good." She smiled, a lazy, happy stretch of her lips that warmed him up inside. This was why he generally opted for pissing her off rather than pleasing her, because he felt the effect of her smile straight to his toes. With a really, really long detour in certain parts in the middle. "Can we go back to fighting the fire?"

He held the glove open for her. She stared at him for a moment and then slowly slid her hand inside.

"Would it kill you," he asked, "to say *You're welcome, Donovan?*"

She thought for a moment. He kept his fingers loose around hers because, hell, they were practically holding hands out here in the forest and he was pathetic. In the month since she'd joined the jump team, he'd yanked her up and down a dozen hills when everyone was scrambling with the gear. A helping hand was also standard practice getting in and out of the DC-3. But this was different somehow.

She shrugged. "Okay then. You're welcome. Now can we go fight the fire?"

"You bet." He stood, pulling her with him.

When they were both on their feet, she looked at him and then down at their joined hands. "You can let go now, Donovan."

He did. She was right. They had a fire to knock down. Part of him wished she'd call him Rio. Not Donovan and not partner, but by his name. He wasn't interchangeable with his brothers.

"Thank you," he said again, starting for the fire. "For catching my ass. That was above and beyond. I owe you one."

"I'm not expecting a fruit basket." She sounded irritated. "Or joint accounting." She waved an arm impatiently toward the rest of the guys. "That's our team right there. We jump together. We fight together. We *stick* together. If you're dumb enough to fall out of a plane, I catch your ass. You'd do the same for me because that's how it works. I'm one of your boys."

One of his boys? Like hell she was.

She shoved past him and stalked off toward the fire.

Christ. She was good. And her speech showed true management potential. He'd have to talk to Jack about giving her more responsibilities on the jump team. Unfortunately, though, he still had a problem, because there was no way he saw Gia as just one of his boys. He had a feeling he wouldn't be able to help himself. He'd held Gia and he wouldn't be forgetting the feel of her anytime soon. Hell. Lusting after a team member was every kind of wrong and he damned certain didn't look at Mack or Zay or Joey that way. So he had no business looking at Gia like he wanted to strip her jumpsuit down those long, long legs and follow his hands with his mouth.

Gia Jackson was off-limits.

CHAPTER TWO

Ten hours later, it was dark and past time to take a breather. Although the twenty-acre wildfire was mostly contained, knocked back behind the lines the team had dug, the surrounding area was red and black, lit up like a parking lot. The jump team sprawled on the ground, debating the relative merits—or lack thereof—of dinner. The MREs they'd packed provided calories, but not much in the taste department. Gia was no cook, but this stuff sucked.

Her body had aches and pains in places she hadn't known she possessed. A long soak in a Jacuzzi followed by an hour with a massage therapist sounded ideal, but definitely wasn't an option for tonight. Instead, she wriggled her ass around the small hollow she'd excavated in the ground and stretched her boots out in front of her. Hell, just getting off her feet was bliss.

Rummaging in his pack, Evan Donovan produced a bag of marshmallows and someone else grabbed a handful of sticks. Evan had a sweet tooth—and a team of hungry jumpers. Five minutes later, everyone had a piece of sweet gooey goodness speared and toasting. Five minutes after that and the stories started coming.

For a while, Gia was content to sit back and listen. Since she preferred her marshmallows burnt black on the outside and heated to volcanic temps on the inside, her turn over the fire had lasted just long enough to catch her goodies on fire.

Joey swung his stick wildly to illustrate a point in his story, narrowly missing her head. Par for the course for him, since the team's youngest jumper didn't do anything by half measures, whether it was jumping, fighting or simply talking.

"Hey," she protested. "Until there's a bottle of shampoo in my future, keep that thing away from me."

Going with the short hair had been a smart move. She'd chopped the mane off five summers ago because hair got in the way during a jump. She hadn't mourned the length even if she routinely woke up with a raging case of bedhead. Wash and go was practical out in the field, and she didn't have time to mess with ponytail elastics. Plus, she already had to work twice as hard to pull her weight on the team because her biology put her at a disadvantage. God hadn't equipped her with the balls—or the muscle—to cut line the way Rio did.

When fire season ended, however, she went back to U.C. Davis and her graduate degree in meteorology. That fun fact had amused the shit out of the Strong jumpers. Joey in particular was convinced he'd wake up one morning and spot her face on his television. TV didn't interest her anywhere near as much as weather patterns did, but there was no persuading Joey of that.

He shrugged, his marshmallow making a return pass. "Worried about your good looks, Jackson?"

Mack leaned in and handed over another marshmallow. "You gonna read us the weather?"

She'd weathered—har har—endless jokes about being the weatherman. She didn't have the classic good looks or the polish the job required. And she didn't have the interest. She wanted to do more than talk about the weather and spit out tidy sound bites for tired commuters and families planning weekend getaways to the beach. She wanted to analyze weather conditions behind the scenes, be the person issuing the forecasts and alerts.

She also wanted to jump.

It didn't matter that she had a heart that sometimes bordered on busted, or that her PSVT was arguably grounds for sitting out the season. Forever. The PSVT was a heart arrhythmia she could work around and she needed to jump. B trumped A every time. The first day she'd gone out a plane bay, wind roaring in her ears and fire waiting for her on the ground, she'd known. This was her calling. *This* was what she loved.

As the marshmallows heated up and disappeared, the guys started talking, trading chitchat. War stories at first. Fires fought, fires lost. Who'd hiked in, hiked out or bunked down in the shake-and-bake, holding the fire-resistant shelter in place as the fire roared overhead. Twenty-acres became two hundred, then two thousand in a familiar game of one-ups-manship. First, the fire stories, then the Penthouse letters to the forum. She had no idea why the bigger the fire, the bigger the dick, but clearly there was a connection.

Jack flashed her a grin from across the fire and she felt her own answering smile. She loved the rough-and-tumble un-PC crew. Her guys were honest to a fault and—for most of them—missing any kind of a verbal filter. Jack's fiancée appeared to have taught her man something, because Jack had stopped sharing when the conversation took a right turn from fighting fires to fending off the females.

Joey started telling some impossible story involving a fire truck and the fire chief's twin daughters and pretty soon good-natured laughter greeted each new addition to the tale. He didn't believe his bullshit either, but the team egged him on, demanding deets. Which Joey added.

Or made up.

Gia needed to write a book.

The rest of the team sprawled on their packs, popping the tops on the MREs. Catching five or ten minutes of rest because they all knew the fire wasn't done with them. Evan fished a squashed PB&J out of his pocket and Rio leaned over and snatched it playfully.

"Man, you've got to work on Faye's cooking skills."

Two slices and a slap of peanut goodness sounded way better than the MRE Gia had forced down. Any meal that came in a poop-brown plastic bag was definitely no Wolfgang Puck special.

"That sandwich is my own stuff," Evan grumbled, slapping a hand on Rio's shoulder. Rio rolled with the blow, but he let his brother pluck the sandwich from his hand. "You think Faye should be cooking because she's the girl in our relationship?"

Rio's answering laugh crinkled the corners of his eyes. "Shit, no. I think she needs to cook because I *know* you can't. The two of you are gonna starve, unless you decide to move in with Nonna."

Rio's contagious smile had Evan grinning ruefully. "Faye wants us to have our own space, but those Sunday dinners are a lifesaver."

Rio always could make anyone smile.

Stop it.

Attraction in the workplace was a no fly situation. Sex with someone Gia worked with? An even worse idea. Sure, her team was parked around a campfire, shooting the shit and sharing sexcapades. The topic of conversation was about as far from PC as words could get, but the conversation wasn't mean-spirited either.

And it meant that her fellow jumpers saw her as one of them.

She wasn't having sex with a co-worker, and definitely not one of her boys. After all, she knew *precisely* what kind of no good, love-em-and-leave-em nonsense those boys got up to. Exhibit A? Tonight's stories. If she slept with a jumper, she would become irrevocably a girl in the team's eyes and then she didn't jump again without a fight. They were good guys and they had hearts of gold—but they were *protect and defend* to the core. She'd end up the girlfriend waiting at home and, as much as she loved being a woman, she was also a jumper. This was what she did and she was good at it.

Rio Donovan was damned pretty however, bona fide eye candy, and she wasn't going to deny herself a look.

It was just touching that was off-limits.

"We need another story," Joey demanded when conversation finally lagged, speaking around a mouth of marshmallow. He looked like a five year-old demanding his companions flip the television to his favorite station.

Mack grinned and settled back. "Bedtime stories are the best."

There was no doubt in Gia's mind what kind of story her boys wanted. This wasn't toddler time at the local library. All heads swiveled towards Rio, even Jack and Evan looking interested.

The request didn't faze Rio, not in the slightest. He eyeballed his audience and sprawled back on a pile of packs like a modern day pasha, all sexy confidence. "A story?"

Mack snorted. "Or tell the truth if you dare."

"You and Mimi still dating?" someone asked.

Rio looked disappointed. "You're asking me to kiss and tell?"

Last summer, Rio had taken up with Mimi Hart, the local bartender and proud owner of Ma's Bar. That was the camp gossip, backed up by a handful of Facebook photos. Gia was fairly certain the pair hadn't survived the year. At any rate, she hadn't spotted Rio and Mimi together since she'd joined the jump team. Since Rio didn't strike her as the subtle type, she figured he wasn't slinking around with Mimi on the side. No, if he'd been dating the other woman, he'd have been up front and open about it. There was a lot to be said for Rio's blatant, unabashed sensuality.

While the team grumbled, Rio looked over at her. It was just a look, she told herself. Nothing different from the way he'd looked at her every day for the past month. A small smile tugged at his lips.

"You up for a story, Jackson?"

Two could play this game. "Sure." She grinned back at him. *Give as good as you got.* That was rule number one in fire camp. "I'm always game to hear the same old same old."

A chorus of wolf whistles filled the air. Her guys always enjoyed a little friendly one-ups-manship.

"You think you can tell a better story?" Rio asked.

"Absolutely." Right on cue, every head swiveled her way. "We are talking about sex, right? I think my subscription to Cosmo is still valid and I'm fairly certain I've got all the working parts. Fact or fiction—you decided."

Rio smiled.

She watched his face, wondering if he'd break first in this mental game of chicken they were playing. Probably not—Rio never quit, never gave an inch when he wanted something—so she was on the hook for a hot bedtime story for the guys. Looking at him was pure pleasure. His dark gold hair was buzzed short to his scalp and, at some point during the day, he'd pushed his aviator glasses on top of his head. Dirt and five o'clock shadow streaked his jaw, but his eyes were focused on her face. She had no idea what was going through his head, but that was Rio. He was all smiles and grins on a real pretty surface, but he kept his thoughts and real feelings hidden.

Finally, he grinned. "Ladies first."

"Someone better buy me a beer," she said. Mack tossed her his canteen and, uncapping it, she swallowed. After a day in the field, the water tasted copper and flat. God. A beer would be pure genius right now.

"Once upon a time," she started and her audience groaned. Someone hollered something about a ban on fairy tales, but she kept right on talking. "There was the girl who we'll call Gina, to protect the innocent."

"You claiming to be innocent?" Joey tipped his canteen toward her and she winked, settling back against her pack.

"Now Gina was paying her own way through grad school and those tuition bills packed a wallop. She figured she needed to get a gig in addition to teaching because she was pretty damn sick of Ramen noodles."

"So she hooked up with a bunch of smoke jumpers." Someone hooted. "Becoming a weatherman comes with a stiff price tag."

She didn't want to talk about the weather.

Not when she could be out living it on the frontlines.

Grinning, she plowed ahead with her story. "Smoke jumpers are ugly ass bunch—present company included—and our Gina was looking for something a little prettier. So she put her on dancing dress and this pair of five-inch stilettos..." She mimed sliding a pair of fuck me shoes on her feet, holding out her ash-covered steel-toes. "Just like mine here. A real sexy number."

"This isn't Miss America," Evan groused. "You don't have to show me your shoes."

"You watch beauty pageants?" Mack leaned in. "Hell, man, the swimsuit part is okay, but a shoe parade on the boardwalk?"

"How come you know about it then?"

"I got sisters. And a mother and way too many aunties." Mack grinned and swiped a marshmallow. "Other than that, I'm pleading the Fifth."

"Well our Gina wasn't running for Miss America. She was looking for something a whole lot less nice."

"Did she find what she was looking for?" Rio eyed her and she told herself that was *not* a shiver she felt chasing down her spine.

"She sure did. She took herself down to a strip club her friends told her about and she got a job dancing weekends there."

Mack frowned. "Are we in fact territory here—or fiction? Because I'm just saying—knowing which would help me visualize this better."

Gia grinned at him. "I'm not telling, but if you were standing in line outside the club on a night she was dancing, you'd better be slipping the bouncer more than twenty bucks to get and park your ass in the good seats, because Gina could dance. She had this little school girl skirt and stockings that came up to right here."

She sliced a finger across her Nomex-clad thigh. Yep. Every eye in the house followed that move. Sex had that effect on her boys. Even Rio was watching.

Which was the whole point if she was being honest with herself.

She wanted him watching her.

Rio was playboy naughty. Gia got that. He didn't mean to hurt anyone, but he'd never slow down and stop. That heat between them, it burned so bad and the bad was both good—and not. She could have him and the erotic possibilities of that had her hormones going wild. Unfortunately, her head saw the other outcomes just as clearly. She couldn't sleep with him without jeopardizing her place on the team. He and his brothers owned Donovan Brothers. That made him her boss. Worse, he was protective. She'd seen that over and over in him. If he became her lover, he'd want to protect her. Keep her safe. And there was nothing less safe than jumping out of a plane into the heart of a fire.

That was also true.

The radio picked that moment to squawk, interrupting her Cosmo-inspired masterpiece. "Base to jump team, come in."

Evan cursed and grabbed the mike. "Jump team to base, we copy."

"Playtime's over, gentlemen." She flipped them a two-fingered salute and turned her attention to the radio. The chorus of groans was quickly hushed by the update from the command center. The winds had picked up and the fire they'd believed knocked down had come roaring back for round two.

So much for the rest break. They'd be working through the night. She shoved to her feet, reaching for her pack. As she headed for the trail, falling into single file behind Joey, Rio's hand circled her wrist—touching her, against all the rules they didn't talk about—his thumb rubbing over her pulse. Which wasn't speeding up, damn it. She couldn't play his kinds of games.

"That true? What you said, back there?"

That sexy rumble had her walking faster.

"Every word of it," she said. "Now move your ass, golden boy. We've got a fire to catch."

CHAPTER THREE

The hangar's loft was the unofficial landing zone for orphaned and surplus gear, a handy place for the jump team to store their shit and the unofficial *leave me alone I gotta talk* spot for the team. Gia wasn't the only one who had issues calling home.

She flopped onto a pile of gear bags—sweet Jesus, those things weren't pillow top mattresses—and eyeballed the hangar. Home sweet home. Signing on with Strong's jump team for the summer didn't feel crazy at all. In fact, being here felt damned right. For the first time in her life, she was living life on her terms. For three months, she had nothing but flames and planes to look forward to it and she wouldn't have swapped it for the world.

In two months, she'd head back to Davis and her off-campus apartment. She'd finish her degree and starting hunting for what her parents called a *real* job.

The loft smelled like old smoke and it wasn't difficult to find the source. The chute packs sported plenty of burn marks on the packs, as did her boots. It didn't get much more real than this. The fire that had scorched the team's collective ass earlier this week didn't know that it was a play date in her parents' opinion, her last-ditch effort to outrun their genuine concern for her health and well-being.

Nope, the fire didn't give a rat's ass.

Fire burned, chewing through whatever fuel it found, and if she was too slow, she'd be fuel and not firefighter.

She was good with that.

Her parents weren't.

Damn it.

She punched the familiar number into her cell. Too bad the reception here was absolutely stellar. After a couple of minutes of obligatory chitchat—and, hey, they discussed the weather too—her mother segued into her favorite topic.

"Why would you want to jump out of a plane and into a forest fire?" Her mother clearly would never voluntarily walk to the edge of an open plane bay and hurl herself outside into the open air. Her mom's idea of a plane ride was the Expedia special to Hawaii. "That's dangerous work, honey."

No kidding.

The silence stretched on for a minute.

"I love it," she said finally, because her mother clearly was waiting for some kind of a response.

"But you love your graduate program," her mother pointed out. "You could work in the lab for the summer. It has air-conditioning. You'd get a byline on a journal article. Or," the enthusiasm kicked up a notch in her mother's voice, "I'm sure you could still take that television station up on their internship offer. You could be on *TV*., Gia."

Been there, done that and scored the commemorative bumper sticker. Her college internship had been informative. Reading the weather on pt. wasn't a bad gig, but it was safe. Boring. Not how she imagined spending the rest of her life. Take your pick.

"I jumped last summer," she pointed out.

"Exactly why you should try something new this summer!"

"I loved it," she continued doggedly. "This is what I want to do."

Blessed silence filled the air for a moment, but Gia knew her mother was simply regrouping. Sure enough, her mother went for the big guns.

"You could get hurt. What happens if you have an attack while you're out there surrounded by fire?"

"I won't."

"You can't know that for sure."

Unfortunately, her mother was right.

"And I've got a special pocket in my jumpsuit just for my pills. I jumped last summer and didn't have any problems."

"I worried about you every day." Her mother meant it, too. She'd have spent Gia's dream summer wondering if her daughter was gasping for air on a forest floor somewhere, while Gia had been jumping head over heels out the plane and into love with the whole job of smoke jumping. Last summer, she'd still been a lowly trainee, though, and she'd only gotten in a handful of jumps with the Arizona jump team she'd assisted. This summer, however, she was on Donovan Brothers' payroll and summer had already started heating up with plenty of jump time for everyone.

"Please don't," she said, knowing that two words couldn't stop her mother from doing what her mother had spent a lifetime doing already. There was no cure for that and her mother had the best of intentions. It was just that Gia was done with living in her mother's protective cocoon. She was twenty-four. She was an adult. She didn't need to be bubble-wrapped like the glass angels her mother took out of storage precisely once a year to be hung carefully on the Christmas out of harm's way.

She loved the freedom of the jump followed by the deafening roar of the wind in her ears as the forest swung in a crazy patchwork quilt of burned-unburned beneath her. The rude jerk of the chute snapping open and the slow, slow glide to the ground followed by a balls-out fight to slow the flames was her idea of the perfect day.

Yep.

She *loved* that part of her new job and if that made her crazy, so be it.

"Gia—" Her mother sighed and there was an ocean of feeling in the sound. Frustration. Love. And, yes, fear. Gia couldn't lie and say her job was safe.

"I don't want to read the weather on TV," she said quickly. "Not ever. That's not what I planned on doing and TV station jobs aren't that easy to score anyhow. I don't think they'd want me."

She wasn't a hair and makeup girl. That was for certain.

"I love you." Her mother said those three words like they made all the difference. And they did. Gia wanted to smack her head against the loft's wall, but the words were out there. Her mother loved her. Her father loved her. The whole family of aunts and uncles, nephews and nieces, loved her. And that meant she was supposed to stay home where it was safe so none of that love was at risk.

She'd felt less trapped in a box canyon with the winds shifting and the flames licking at her boots.

"Mom—" She had no idea what to say.

Joey's head popped up in the loft's entrance. "You coming with?"

Reprieve.

"Look, Mom, I've got to go. I'll call you again. Later." Much, much later.

Unfortunately, their conversation would just be a replay of the same old same old. She'd already said everything she could think of and none of it was enough to buy her freedom.

After a firefight like Rail Mountain's seven thousand acre bonfire, the jump team liked to unwind at Ma's. To call Strong a small town was an understatement—the place boasted one main street, with a handful of one-of-a-kind local businesses that included the bar. The place looked like pretty much every other hole-in-the-wall she'd decorated in recent years—a long, polished bar, plenty of stools, and a very nice flat-screen and pool table in the back. Tonight's on-call jumpers were nursing Cokes, but the rest of the guys had already ordered several rounds of beer and tequila.

Gia straddled the stool, nursing a shot of Patron with a side of lime. The jukebox pounded out one of her favorite country tunes and some of the guys had already got up to dance.

She could get up and join them.

She loved dancing even if she wasn't particularly talented in that department. Once she felt the beat and let the music wash over her, having two left feet didn't matter. Joey executed a particularly complicated twist-and-turn, accidentally pinning his partner against his chest. Mack shoved away with a laugh and Gia smiled. They were good guys.

Mimi leaned over the bar and Gia checked the level in her glass. Nope. She was still good.

"Holy hotness," Mimi said.

Gia eyed the jump team whooping it up on the floor. "You have a particular example of hotness in mind, or should I just be skeeved that you have a thing for my coworkers?"

Apparently, Mimi did have a thing for firefighters.

Mimi laughed, a raspy, happy sound. "Honey, are you truly that blind? You work with some of the hottest men around. You have to know that."

Of course, but they were all off-limits. That thought had her banging back the rest of her tequila and nudging the empty shot glass across the counter toward Mimi. "I work with them. You try that for a week and see how much sexy is left. Cursing, farting, peeing in the bushes—I promise you, cutting line is not romantic."

Liar.

Mimi obligingly poured another shot of Patron, waving away the fiver Gia offered. "On the house. You're a minority of one."

Gia bet that meant the other woman wanted something and, sure enough, Mimi reached beneath the bar and pulled out a calendar. Gia bit back a groan. Evan Donovan had plenty to answer for. His fiancée, Faye Duncan, had shot a charity calendar. Usually, Gia was all for helping out the less fortunate but, in this particular instance, Faye had done so by convincing the smoke jumpers to strip down to their skivvies. Or less.

Mimi tossed the calendar onto the bar. "I have it on good authority," she said, "that there's a sizable female contingent out there enjoying Strong's toy catalog."

That calendar was like late-night as-seen-on-TV products. Looking away was impossible. Gia's fingers reached for the calendar and started flipping, even as her brain put out a cease-and-desist order.

"I can't," she groaned, but did. Mack made a real fine Mr. March. Which she didn't need to know. "My eyes are burning."

"Be glad you weren't here then," Mimi said darkly. "Faye is all about equal opportunity. You'd have been stripped down and Miss July."

Since *no way in hell* seemed like the wrong response for a charity project, Gia turned the page—and came face to face with September. *Fuck*. Make that *Rio*.

Rio straddled a chair, his jump suit unzipped and pushed down to his waist. Cut. There was no other way to describe the man, because his stomach's sculpted planes and lines redefined *six-pack abs*. He leaned forward in the photo and damned if Gia didn't want to pretend she could reach in and touch his sun-bronzed skin. She imagined most people would be plenty happy when September rolled around and they could hang Rio on their wall for a month. She winced. If she was honest, she'd count herself in that number.

"He's mighty fine." Mimi traced Rio's picture with her finger, with a small smile that said she was making a very happy trip down memory lane.

Two could play the gossip game. "I heard you two are dating."

Mimi laughed and removed her hand from Rio's picture. "Your gossip's out of date. We spent some time together last summer, but Rio and I haven't dated for months."

Relief probably wasn't the safe reaction, but that was all Gia had. The look on Mimi's face said she'd suspected as much too, and Gia hated being transparent. She drained half the shot glass and sucked on her lime while she considered that.

Mimi surveyed the bar and sighed. "It's not like there's an active dating scene in Strong. My good parts are drying up."

"I'll drink to that." Gia raised her shot glass to toast that statement. When she banged the empty back down on the counter, Mimi topped it off.

"You got a ride home tonight?"

"I'll find one." After four shots of tequila, she had no intention of going anywhere near her truck.

"I'll take you when I close up. Just tell me one thing." Mimi leaned closer. "I heard you saved Rio's fine ass."

A new tune was starting on the jukebox and the bar had achieved that cheerful, slightly out of focus haze that meant no more tequila for her. "His chute malfunctioned."

"Uh-huh." Mimi eyed her speculatively. "Four thousand feet above a man-eating wildfire. Tell me the part where you snatched him out of the air."

Gia had no idea what kind of story Mimi wanted. The simple truth was, she wasn't so good with girls. Guys made sense. "I got close. He grabbed on. We landed."

Mimi made a face, so clearly Gia hadn't told the story right. "Way to ruin the story. You sure he wasn't crying like a baby or hollering with gratitude?"

Gia pretended to think for a moment. "Positive."

"Well that's a bummer." Mimi shook her head. "That boy owes you. You should collect."

"Excuse me?"

"Come on. You've heard the stories, right? Person A saves Person B's life and B has to spend a lifetime at A's beck and call until he's returned the favor? The Moor Azeem in *Robin Hood? Mulan? Puss in*

Boots and *Shrek*? Any of this ring a bell?"

The thought of Rio *owing* her should not have her girly bits heating up, but she could think of all sorts of things her smoke jumper could do to pay her back. And none of them involved animated cats or ogres.

"He's a good guy," Mimi offered, watching her face. "And he's fantastic in bed."

Too much information.

"He's my jump partner." She flipped the shot glass over, shaking her head when Mimi gestured with the bottle of Patron.

Off-limits.

Mimi raised a finger, gesturing wait-a-minute as another customer down the bar beckoned for a refill. "That's a waste of a mighty fine man, but your loss. Here. Try this."

"I shouldn't." She had the day off tomorrow, but nursing a hangover headache wasn't in her plans. Still, her fingers curled around the chilly sides of the short glass.

"That's true for lots of things." Mimi grinned, turning away to do the refill drill down the bar. "Drinks. Men. Life."

Rio leaned against the wall, glad for the first time for his years working covert ops. Those two tours had taught him how to blend into the shadows when he wanted. It probably put him in stalker territory, but right now those skills let him watch Gia without freaking her out.

Gia.

His nemesis and fixation had her feet hooked around legs of the barstool, her thighs spread ever so slightly to keep her balance. By his count, she'd down four shots of tequila, so she probably needed that assist. Gia usually wasn't a big drinker, but the whole team was unwinding some and she simply wasn't big enough to soak up too much alcohol. When Mimi slid her an icy-cold glass with a wink, he heard Gia laugh despite the steady blare of the jukebox. Because he was standing too close and watching her too much.

She wrapped her fingers around the glass, raising it to her nose for a suspicious sniff before taking a big slug. He definitely wouldn't have pegged Gia for a whiskey sour kind of gal. He'd have guessed a fruity daiquiri, with one of those little pastel umbrellas and a cherry because she had a real feminine side she tried hard not to show the team.

Rio tried hard not to think about tongues and cherry stems.

Or about kissing the icy froth off her upper lip, because Gia was uninhibited in her enjoyment of her drink. She also looked damned hot out of a jumpsuit. For tonight's agenda of drinks and dancing, she'd paired faded jeans with a sleeveless blouse that buttoned up the front and tied in a knot at her waist. When she shifted on the barstool, she gifted him with a peek of suntanned skin and flat stomach. To take his mind off *that* sexy possibility, he shifted his eyes down her long, long denim-clad legs until he hit a pair of cowboy boots. Gia rocked the strong and sexy.

As soon as she set down the glass, she slid off the stool and headed for the dance floor. The move had been only a matter of time. He still didn't know that much about Gia—she'd only been on their jump team for a matter of months and the job interview didn't allow the kind of personal questions he was meditating on—but he knew she loved to dance. Plus, there was her alter ego "Gina." He'd liked the hell out of that story. He only wished he knew if it were true. In moments, her hips and arms were swinging as she flashed a contagious smile. The guys certainly welcomed her with open arms and, within minutes, she was twirling back and forth between Mack and Joey.

Eventually, when he got tired of watching, he stepped onto the crowded dance floor, cutting in smoothly. Two well-aimed steps and he stood between Gia and Mack. Not that she'd noticed.

Which was part of the problem.

About the only time he had her eyes on him was when they were three thousand feet in the air or fighting fire. He'd always be a firefighter—and he suspected Gia would be too—but that wasn't *all* he was. Because fuck if he didn't want Gia to look at him and see a man.

He moved in and Mack flashed him the bird. "Wait your turn."

Like there was any hope of that.

The music howled, the cowboy singer loud in his praises of Saturday night honkytonk, and Mack vined, the dance move setting his steel-toes tap-tap-tapping. He must have seen something on Rio's face—or was just plain feeling charitable—because Mack sashayed back, leaving room for Rio to step up.

Gia spun back, laughing. *Gotcha*. Unaware that he'd joined in the fun, she slammed into him. Déjà vu.

He steadied her with his hands on her hips, savoring her warmth through the faded denim. Flexing his fingers, he repointed her in the right direction, waiting for her feet to rediscover the song's rhythm.

"Wow, Donovan." She blinked at him "Give a girl some warning, would you?"

Damned if he didn't want to kiss the surprised look right off her face. Or put it back there for a whole different reason.

Mack slung a hand around her waist, dragging her back into the line. "Cut the man some slack, Jackson. He just wants to make sure you appreciate he's been working out."

Gia's eyes dropped down Rio's body and he felt her passing glance like a lover's hand wrapping around his good parts and squeezing in all the right ways. Predictably, his dick sprang straight to attention, leaving him rock-hard for his jump partner. Which probably was a testament to how long his current sexual dry spell had been.

Nothing more.

Mack danced Gia down the line. Rio hadn't planned on letting go, but his fingers slipping away from her hips and maybe—although he wouldn't admit it—brushing her ass. He didn't want to dance, but he did want to get his hands on Gia. Since dancing was the only way to do that right now, he tucked his thumbs in his belt and let his feet find the rhythm of the country song.

Rio was a good dancer. He'd always excelled at anything physical.

Gia was—enthusiastic.

She sashayed back up the line, not quite to the beat, laughing and calling something over her shoulder to Mack. Rio was fairly certain her parting shot had included at least one obscenity. His partner had a potty mouth. Her eyes, though, were happy. He thought about that for a moment, but that was the right word. And Gia enjoying herself was a sight to see. He was used to seeing her tightly disciplined and focused, with eyes for nothing but her LZ and the waiting fire.

Except when she had her arms around him. Of course, she'd been rescuing his ass—if he was being fair, which he wasn't inclined to be, not right now—and her options had been hold on tight or let go. Since he still wasn't a fan of freefalling *sans* chute, he was glad she'd decided to hold on.

The problem was, that almost embrace had him imagining other scenarios where she held him wholeheartedly.

The fundamental problem with line dancing was that no one needed a partner. There was also not much in the touching department. Trading Ma's in for a Regency ballroom and a waltz had never seemed like a better idea.

Snagging her wrist, he pulled her into line next to him.

"Dance with me."

She shot him a look—as if he'd forgotten what they were doing—but she popped into the line beside him as Bob Segar belted out of the jukebox. He could have told her that he'd known where she was and what she was doing the entire summer. But that would have been creepy and the last thing he wanted to do was drive her away.

Because he wanted to pull her close.

"Tush push!" Mack bellowed. Joey sent up an answering whoop from his left and then the whole line exploded, boots stomping the floor as the team swung into action to the mellow tones of the sex and Segar's voice rasping nostalgically.

Heel toe heel heel. Right foot, left foot.

Mimi had invested in bar stools, not dance floor, and thank God there was no space to spare. Each time Gia scooted, her hips brushed his. When her hands swung up, clapping enthusiastically, her fingertips brushed Rio's chest. Thank God for small spaces.

One and two and three and four—

The tush push shoved her ass and hips forward and then back. Thanks to the limited dance floor her sweet curves brushed his front. His arms enveloped her as he clapped over her head. That was as close as he was getting to holding her tonight, unless his luck changed. He didn't want to need her like this, to spend every minute plotting to get closer. That wasn't how he rolled. Wasn't who he was. He didn't *do* need. Except when he was around Gia Jackson.

She grooved, her body finally catching up with the music, swinging her hips in one sexy circle. He danced along, because, really, watching the faded denim pull tight over her hips and ass was no hardship at all.

Cha-cha forward. Back. The blood in his dick thumped out a drumbeat all its own, reminding him that his sexual dry spell had gone on for far too long. Off-limits, he reminded his southern parts. He could dance with her—he just couldn't sleep with her.

One, two, three four. His thigh brushed hers as she missed the count and stepped early, hopping on one foot to rediscover her place in the line. *Five, six.* Her fingers bounced off his hip as she moved.

The heel of her boot planted itself on his toes. He grinned and leaned in. "You're a lethal weapon, Jackson," he growled against her ear.

Tipping her head back, she smiled up at him. "Suck it up, golden boy. You've got a pair of steel-toes."

Her hair brushed his cheek—because he might, just might, have angled his face towards hers—and he sucked in a deep breath of coconut-scented Suave.

Seven, eight.

He could have kept dancing all night.

Gia collapsed in the booth, resting her feet. The damned cowboy boots were nowhere near as comfortable as they looked, even if the red leather had screamed *Buy me* when she spotted the pair on Macy's sale rack. She considered slipping them off underneath the table but decided against it. Riling Mimi up with a health and safety code violation probably wasn't prudent if she wanted the bar's owner to give her a ride home.

Plus, Mimi's tequila packed a punch.

If she took the boots off, her body might assume that was a memo to relax completely and go to sleep. Not her best plan. She'd heard that was how Evan had met his soon-to-be wife. Faye Duncan had given in to the tireds in Ma's and Evan had scooped her up. Gia didn't want a diamond ring or a trip down the aisle herself, but Evan seemed happy enough. He'd pulled Faye out of the line and he was slow-dancing her to a tune only the two of them could hear, his big arms wrapped tightly around her.

There were worse fates.

Maybe she should try dating again.

There were other pretty fish in the sea besides Rio Donovan, and surely her hormones could pick an alternate man. He couldn't possibly be the only one to get her all worked up. Evan bent his head and kissed Faye, Gia looked away. Was being a great kisser a family thing?

Not going there, she reminded herself.

The bar was a happy blur and she could feel herself relaxing for the first time in weeks. Of course, maybe that was because she wasn't pussyfooting around her jump partner. She had to do something about the way he looked at her. Other people were starting to notice. The problem was, she liked the way it made her feel. It probably didn't mean much of anything—Rio loved women, loved touching—but she warmed right up inside when his dark eyes slid over her and then paused like he'd found something he liked.

Had *he* fantasized about kissing her?

Once again, so not tonight's problem. She munched a few peanuts and curled up in the booth, her head tipping back against the booth. Five minutes. She'd close her eyes for just five minutes and then—

"You're not driving."

Gia's head snapped forward with a jerk. She blinked sleepily up at the big body blocking her view of the bar. Yep. That was Rio leaning in and cutting off her exit route. "Of course not. I'm not stupid or suicidal."

He didn't touch the opening she'd handed him. Instead, he tucked a hand beneath her elbow and gently tugged her forward. "I'll take you home."

Newsflash. He still looked at her like he wanted to eat her up.

Her girly bits were fine with that.

Her head? Not so much.

"No need." She pulled back, waving a hand toward the bar. "I'm bumming a ride from Mimi."

"I'll take you," he repeated. "The bar doesn't close for another hour and you're asleep sitting up."

True.

"You're on my way," he continued. "Hell, we could drive to my place and you could walk home. Your cabin is six down from mine. But, if you ask nicely, I'll stop the truck in front of your door."

He held out his hand and grinned at her. His other hand swiped her purse from the table.

She thought about the offer for a minute, more to prolong the moment than out of any true hesitation. It probably counted as sad and pathetic that her dance with Rio was the closest she'd gotten to any action lately. Or that she liked the way he held her hand now.

"An offer I can't pass up? I'm in." She slid out of the booth, brushing against him as she stood up.

Most of the jump team had left while she'd been holding her snooze fest in the booth, and only a small handful of regulars propped up the bar. She caught Mimi's eye and waved as Rio steered her toward the door. *Don't need a ride* she mouthed and Mimi shot her a thumbs up.

It was just a ride, but she appreciated the vote of confidence.

Rio didn't say anything else as they crunched their way across the parking lot gravel. The night air cleared her head some, although she still was better off riding shotgun. Rio's truck was a big black sleek beast—parked next to hers. She hesitated, but she'd come back for the vehicle tomorrow.

Rio reached around her, popping open the passenger side door. The heavy weight of his hand burned into the small of her back as she grabbed the roll bar and swung up. He was probably afraid she'd fall on her ass in the parking lot. She considered the possibility and decided it was still on the table.

Damn tequila.

Rio's truck was a mid-range with plenty of power. The tow rig said he meant business, but all the stuff in the back was neatly organized in milk crates. That he'd labeled, for crying out loud. She didn't know anyone even made label makers anymore. That kind of organization effort was superhuman. She tried not to stare while she buckled up and got comfortable. Moments later, he dropped into the driver's seat and started the engine. While she pretended he was the Strong taxi service, he drove them out of the parking lot and down Strong's one main street, headed for the base camp where the jump team had a row of summer cabins. Since she didn't need to provide directions, she had plenty of quiet time to stare at him.

His hands on the wheel, big and sure, effortlessly guided the truck down the road and over the occasional rut. He drove well, like he did everything. Which got her to thinking about what else he might do well.

And that was trouble she didn't need to borrow.

As soon as they reached the cabins, she opened the door and jumped down before Rio could come around and get the door for her. She could feel him looking at her, but this wasn't a date and she didn't wait for a guy to lend her a hand when she had two perfectly good ones of her own.

There was probably a bad sexual pun in there, she thought muzzily as she fished in her purse for her key. Maybe she should borrow Rio's label maker, because the bag needed a CDC intervention and her key was definitely not surfing the top layer of crap.

He plucked the bag from her hands and, wouldn't you know it, found her key immediately. At least she wouldn't be sleeping on the porch.

"Home sweet home," she said. "You didn't even make me walk."

He grinned and bumped her shoulder with his, subtly steering her towards the porch of her cabin. She hadn't bothered turning the light on before she'd left, so the front was pitch black.

"I can be a gentleman."

"So I've heard." Sometimes. The whispers promised Rio was a wild man in bed. The stories he told around the campfires were nothing compared to the rumors. He was big. He was bad. He was a damned Donovan, with the sensual creativity and drive to match. He also liked being in charge, if what she'd heard was true. Very, very much in charge.

Gia didn't give up control.

But Rio tempted her.

He fell into step beside her, heat radiating from him. Yep. Definite temptation.

"You shouldn't listen to gossip, Jackson."

He'd called her *Gia* earlier. Now she was clearly back in the partner bucket.

"But it's really good gossip," she pointed out and clomped up the stairs. When she jabbed at the lock with her key, she missed. Definitely too much tequila.

"Let me." His hand closed around hers and took the key away.

That sounded perfect. There were all *sorts* of things she was ready to let him do.

"Okay." She leaned in toward him.

The key snicked in the lock and he opened the door with a flick of his wrist. "Gia? You might prefer sleeping inside." A grin tugged the corner of his mouth. "As opposed to on the porch."

When he smiled, she wanted to run her tongue over his bottom lip until he moaned. *Bad libido.*

"I'm not ready for bed," she said and placed her hand on his chest.

He looked shocked—and that made her giggle. And move closer. She could feel the hard pounding of his heart trapped beneath her palm. "A man with your kind of reputation shouldn't be so easy to shock. I'm disappointed."

"Can't have that," he drawled. Bracing one hand against the doorframe, he snaked the other hand around her waist and drew her towards him.

Rio tightened his arm around Gia's waist and swung her into the shadows. They weren't entirely alone—no one ever was at base camp—but darkness created an illusion of privacy.

Arousal or tequila had pink flushing her cheekbones, and when she shifted her head, her chopped-off hair brushed the line of her jaw the way he wanted to.

"I'm kissing you now," he warned. To hell with what he should or shouldn't do. This was just a kiss and one kiss couldn't possibly hurt.

And he was the king of rationalization.

"It's about time." She grinned and leaned back against the cabin.

He wanted her leaning into him, wanted her begging for more, so he gently thumbed the blouse away from the smooth skin of her shoulder. The soft fabric snagged on his calloused fingers then fell away. *Hell yeah.* He cupped her tanned shoulders and pulled her towards him, done waiting.

She deserved sweet, but he didn't give it to her. No, he pulled her right up against him and wrapped an arm around her waist to keep her there. The move pressed her breasts against his shirt and, even through the layers of clothing separating them, he could feel her.

Her nipples were hard. That was the one coherent thought left in his brain as he covered her mouth with his. She wanted him. And he could take advantage of that. He brushed his lips over hers, capturing her small gasp.

"See?" He whispered the question against the corner of her mouth. "Kissing."

Her response was half-sigh, half-gasp, which he decided was all permission. He threaded a hand through her hair, tilting her head back. And kissed her. A raw, hot, possessive kiss. He thrust his tongue into her mouth, familiarizing himself with the taste of her. He kissed her thoroughly, leaving nowhere untouched, and she moaned, opening wider, letting him take her mouth so completely, he wasn't sure where he ended and she began. His own heated response shouldn't have been a surprise—hell, he'd started this and had the hard-on to prove it—but at some point their kiss stopped being an exercise in sensual dominance and became something *more*. Something he had no intention of stopping because, Christ, Gia Jackson could kiss.

~

Rio lifted his head and she wanted to groan in protest. To draw him back to her, but he had *that look* on his face. The one that said he wanted to do some more talking instead of more kissing.

"I don't play nice in bed." His eyes didn't move from her face as he warned her, and yet she felt undressed. *Naked.*

"Maybe I don't mind." Leaning forward, she curled her fingers around his right arm. He had powerful biceps, probably from all that sailing he did. In fact, there was nothing soft about him, just a strangely attractive masculine power leashed beneath the skin. He could do whatever he wanted and she wouldn't be able to stop him. That should have scared the piss out of her because she wasn't ready for his kind of sexual games. But this was Rio. When push came to shove, he'd always do the right thing—and doing the right thing meant not hurting her. She believed that with everything she had.

"You should." One hand braced against her door, he leaned into her. Now even going forward wasn't an option. She was going to stay put until he let her go. "You should turn around, go inside and lock that door. Otherwise, I'll be coming after you. I'll have you naked and underneath me so fast, you won't have time for regrets."

Right now her only regret was that she'd decided he was off-limits for tonight.

"Maybe I don't want to play nice," she said, echoing his earlier words, and tugged him towards her. She knew her lips were swollen and damp from his touch, but the erection punching the front of his jeans promised he wanted more of her.

Instead, he stepped back. Suddenly, she had all the options in the world. Left, right, forward or backward. She had her pick, and all she wanted was Rio.

"Go inside, Gia. Dream of me," he growled, tracing her lips with a finger. "You want us to stay professional, it's up to you, because I'm warning you right now I plan on doing everything I can to make you want me, sweetheart. The next time I hold you, I'm taking what *I* want."

Got it.

She leaned up and brushed his lips with hers. "Good night, hotshot."

Rio spent the night *not* sleeping, so he was a cranky ass bastard the next morning and he knew it. After Gia had gone inside, he'd gotten back into his truck—reluctantly—and driven the short distance to his own place. Too much tequila for her, too much Gia for him. Unfortunately, he wanted more and that was a problem.

She was on his jump team for Christ's sake.

Now, pulling up at the hangar to kick off the workday, he parked the truck harder than he needed to. Spitting gravel was vaguely satisfying, but a ten-mile run was just what the doctor had ordered to shake things straight in his head. Or his dick. Grabbing his duffel, he strode inside.

His dick was definitely the problem.

Jack was just stepping out of their makeshift office holding the week's jump list. Slipping up behind his brother was child's play. Jack got in the zone when he was working and backing a Mack truck into the hangar probably wouldn't have broken his concentration as he pinned up the list. Sure enough, Jack clearly hadn't heard him coming, because he jumped when Rio's hand landed on his shoulder.

"Son of a bitch." Jack slapped at Rio's hand. "You've got to stop with that Ninja stuff. You're taking years off my life."

It wasn't his fault his brother's ears weren't what they should be. Or that he was possibly walking around in a daze of happy love and sex. Reuniting with Lily Cortez had been good for Jack. Rio liked the spark of happiness he saw in his eyes. God knew, the Donovans had gotten a rough start in life. They'd formed their own family as young boys lost in the foster care system, eking out a few rough years on the streets before they'd landed with Nonna. Nonna had been their first happy ending, taking the three boys under her wing and raising them with love. Now, it looked like both Jack and Evan had found second happy endings with the women they loved.

Which was great.

Rio was happy for them.

He just had no intention of joining them on the monogamy and marriage train. So he looked over his brother's shoulder, trying to read the list, and shrugged.

"You should listen better," he said.

"Right." Jack speared the eight-by-eleven with a red thumbtack. "I'll get right on that. Or you could try scuffing your feet."

They had this conversation regularly. Jack would complain about Rio's super stealth skills. Rio would dodge the underlying question and counter with his own slurs at Jack's hearing and general agility. On the best days, their bickering degenerated into an impromptu wrestling match.

So, no, he wasn't answering the unspoken question. Jack didn't need to know where Rio had spent the years Jack had been working for the U.S. military. Not only would that have violated several direct military orders that he didn't give a crap about, but it would have dragged Jack into the dark world of covert ops. There was no reason to share the ugly memories.

Erasing them would have been first on his to do list but, since that wasn't possible, he atoned when and where he could. Drugs ripped apart families and destroyed lives firsthand—so when his country had asked him to step up and take part in a war on drugs, he'd been all in. He *couldn't* walk away from that fight because he knew firsthand what happened when that product left the site in Colombia, or Mexico or Humboldt,

California. A match might take care of the immediate problem, but the growers always rebuilt elsewhere and the pipeline was still in place. So Uncle Sam had taught him how to go in and take care of the problem.

Permanently.

There was no reason to share ugly memories with Jack, especially when knowing just a few of the details were dangerous enough to get a guy killed. Needing a distraction, he examined the list pinned to the board. Despite being one of the team owners, he didn't get into the daily ops stuff. That was Jack's bailiwick and his brother was a logistics wizard, which meant this week's jump list was a surprise.

He scanned it twice just to be certain. Jack hadn't paired him with Gia. That was definitely a mistake.

When Jack tried to slip by him, he body checked him against the wall.

"You've got a typo on your list."

Jack shook his head. "I don't think so."

"I jump with Gia."

"Not this week." Jack twisted, almost breaking free, so Rio stuck out a foot and tripped him.

Hitting the floor hard, Jack hooked an arm around Rio's throat. Rio rolled, pinning Jack beneath him. Checkmate.

"Every week," he said.

"Rio—" The warning in Jack's voice was clear.

"Do you have a problem with my jumping with Gia? She saved my life. She's damned good at her job."

"She is." Jack rolled, breaking free, his left foot clipping the back of Rio's knees.

"So I want to jump with her."

"That's not what you *want*," Jack said. Rio considered the implications of punching his brother. Friendly wrestling on the floor of the hangar was one thing. Bruises were another. For one, they'd have to explain bruises to Nonna and then there would definitely be hell to pay.

Rio settled for a few minutes of hand-to-hand, wrestling with Jack until long minutes later they broke apart panting.

"I've still got it," Jack said with satisfaction, letting his head thump against the floor.

"Go again?" Rio wasn't entirely sure he could lift his head, but he wouldn't give Jack the satisfaction of admitting that.

"Sure." Jack flopped an arm weakly to the side. "Christ. You killed me. And I need my energy."

"For Lily."

Jack grinned. "Absolutely. You have any idea how much planning goes into a wedding?"

He had absolutely zero desire to know. "You asked her," he pointed out. "Weddings are a definite side effect of engagement rings."

"She's worth it." Jack sighed happily. "If she wants the whole big white dress and church thing, she gets it."

The new rules in Jack's universe were simple. What Lily wanted, Lily got. In exchange, Jack got Lily. From the besotted look on Jack's face, his brother thought he'd got the best of the bargain. As long as Lily made Jack happy, Rio would welcome her into their family. Or try, he admitted. It had been him and his brothers and Nonna for so long that letting some else in close seemed strange.

Okay. Worse than strange. Completely wrong.

But he'd figure out how to do it before the July wedding or how to fake it, because Jack and Lily were now a package deal and he wasn't losing his brother.

"She's going to want kids," he said.

The thoughtful look on Jack's face should have warned him, but his brother's next words floored him. "I'm not opposed." Jack grinned. "Making kids is good too. The family's getting bigger, Rio."

Best of luck with that. Rio couldn't imagine having a kid of his own. Ever. He wouldn't have the first idea of how to be a dad. So instead he circled back to *his* problem.

"I want to jump with Gia," he repeated.

Jack turned his head toward him and cracked an eye. "I know, but I've got a problem with that. The way you look at her isn't professional."

He knew how he looked at her. Like he wanted to eat her up. He didn't particularly like feeling this way, but he couldn't *not* jump with her either. If that was the only way he could get close to her, touch her, he'd take it. He was almost as pathetic as Jack.

"I haven't touched her." Kissing, he decided, didn't count. Not really. He certainly hadn't done everything he wanted to, and it had been a one-time aberration due to too much tequila on her part followed by slow dancing. "She's my teammate, Jack. My jump partner."

Jack looked pained. "Is that *all* she is? Tell me you don't want to get horizontal with her."

Having a conversation about this was not something he wanted to do. "She's on the team. That makes her off-limits. You don't have to tell me that because I'm not five. I understand the rules."

"It's harder for her. She's jumping with the guys. We all pretend she gets an honorary dick with her chute, but at the end of the day she's a girl. If you look at her and see breasts, what stops the next guy on the team from doing the same?"

"Newsflash," Rio growled. "Most workplaces are co-ed these days and you don't see the employees going at it like bunnies. It doesn't matter whether Gia's male or female. She can jump and she can do the job. When I go out the plane, I trust her to have my back. I think she proved she can handle it. Change the list."

Jack closed his eyes and let his head thump against the floor. "This won't end well."

"You forgot to invite someone to the party," a throaty voice said from the door.

Hell. *Gia.*

Jack groaned. "When Gia sues for sexual harassment, I want it duly noted that I had the best of intentions."

"Me too," Rio drawled.

She looked hot, and the fact he knew that probably made him an equal candidate in that lawsuit. Today she'd gone for urban waif or suburban homeowner on a DIY kick. Her ripped-up jeans were faded almost white from washing, but she sported the usual pair of steel-toes. Now that he thought about it, last night at the bar had been the first time he'd seen Gia wear anything other than work boots or running shoes. He'd liked last night's cowboy boots. Almost as much as he liked the white tank top she rocked now. There had been a shower in her recent past and her hair was slicked back wet. She was sun-bronzed, strong… and he couldn't tell what she was thinking. A small smile played around her lips as she tucked her thumbs in her pocket and she leaned against the doorframe.

"I appreciate the vote of confidence and the loaner penis, but everything else is nobody's business."

Jack didn't hesitate, but Rio had never made the mistake of underestimating his brother. "Got it."

She eyed the pair of them calmly. "We're a team, right?"

Jack nodded, still clearly their self-appointed spokesman. Which was fine, because Rio really had no idea what to say.

"We are," Jack said.

"Then no worries." Gia smiled. "As far as you're concerned."

"Come on," Gia said, spinning on her feet.

Rio should walk—run—the other direction. She was team. She was one of them.

She was also *his*.

He had a primal need to mark her, take her. Learn her from the inside out. He didn't need a consult with Evan and Jack to know that he had absolutely no business thinking this way. Unfortunately, no part of his body—from his head to his dick—appeared to be on board with the company policy.

Jack elbowed him. "She's talking to you. I'm off the hook."

Rio had no idea why Jack got the get-out-of-jail-free card here, but damned if he didn't bound to his feet and follow her out into the parking lot like a tame puppy. He could practically hear Jack laughing.

Gia didn't hesitate. She walked over straight to her truck and opened the passenger-side door for him. "Get in."

She'd clearly been back to Ma's to collect her truck. He wasn't surprised she'd left it there—Gia didn't do stupid or irresponsible, and driving after drinking tequila would have qualified on both counts—but he'd bet she wasn't happy he'd seen her like that. Gia didn't let her guard down often.

He didn't budge. "Field trip?"

She shot him a look. "We'll get it out of our systems."

He opened his mouth. Closed it. He definitely needed "it" defined before he put his foot in his mouth.

"Well?" She looked at him impatiently and jingled her keys. "Are you in or out?"

The way her gaze traveled down his body and settled on his dick, she wasn't talking about her passenger-side seat. Not really.

"We need to talk," he said weakly. Christ. Who was the girl here?

She smiled. Slowly. Like she was humoring him and didn't care that he knew it. "Okay. Get in. We can talk while I drive."

He probably should have asked where they were going—for all he knew, she planned on driving down to Death Valley and dumping his ass out on the sand to roast—but he was pretty much ready to go wherever she wanted. Because, holy Christ, Gia taking charge was unexpectedly sexy. All that direct bluntness aimed his way and he had an erection that wasn't going to quit anytime soon.

Which she knew.

Because she'd checked him out.

He got in the cab while she walked around and climbed in the driver's side door. Gia's truck was a mess, the seats half-hidden beneath a pile of flannel and an extra pair of steel toes. The woman also had enough tools to stock a small Home Depot. He shifted the junk so he could buckle up and got comfortable in the seat.

After tossing her bag on the backseat—which only added to the organizational carnage when half the contents spilled out—she hopped in, flipped the key in the ignition and peeled them out of the parking lot. When she turned on the radio, however, she surprised him again. She apparently liked the same country crap his brother liked. Which explained her enthusiasm for last night's line dancing. She drove as enthusiastically as she danced too. He'd jumped out of a dozen helicopter bays with her and watched her wield a chainsaw with cool expertise but he hadn't, as far as he could remember, driven with her before.

And Gia drove fast.

Straight up the highway, like a shot from a gun speeding toward some unseen target.

Hell.

He white-knuckled the grab bar above the door. It was just possible she'd mistaken the highway for the Indy 500. "Are we in a rush?"

Because he had plans for tomorrow that dying would put a kink in.

"You can drive next time." She flicked him a small smile and he had no idea what she meant. But he definitely liked the idea of her on the back of his Harley. Taking her riding had all sorts of possibilities.

All too soon, she pulled off and killed the motor. She didn't rush into speech, though. No, she sat there, running a finger over the steering wheel, listening to the ping of the engine cooling down.

"So," she said eventually.

"Yeah." He didn't know whether she'd brought him out here to have her wicked way with him, or if she was finally in the mood for conversation.

She unbuckled her seatbelt and turned toward him. The foot and a half of black vinyl between them was nowhere near enough space. Not if she wanted him to keep his hands to himself.

She took a deep breath.

"You need to stop staring at me."

He wasn't sure what the right answer was. Hell. Apparently everyone but him knew he had the hots for her. Well, he knew too, but what he hadn't known was that it was written all over his face. He reached for his seatbelt and punched the release mechanism.

"Let Jack change the jump rotation," she suggested.

He shook his head. "That's not going to solve this, Gia."

"Okay." She inhaled again, like she was getting ready to clear a forty-foot jump or wrestle sharks barehanded. "I like jumping with you." She probably wasn't imagining the same verb he was. *Jumping* was clearly a synonym for *fucking* in Rio-land. "I don't want another partner."

"Good," he cleared his throat.

"God." She stared at him. "You're supposed to be good at this."

"At what?" He definitely felt like she was having a conversation without him.

She waved a hand impatiently. "Talking with girls. Seduction. All this romance crap."

"You want romance crap?" *From me?*

She shook her head. "I want sex, Rio."

"You want sex." Rio shoved a hand over his head.

"Guys ask for what they want," she pointed out. "And you did grant me the honorary dick and all back there at the hangar."

"You want sex," he repeated. Apparently, he hadn't seen that coming, despite kissing her goodnight on her porch. Maybe that was simply standard Rio operating mode: drive the girl home, kiss her senseless, retreat before he had to go any further.

"You're not a guy. If you were, I wouldn't feel like this." He sounded certain. Good to know his interest was all-female. She didn't need anymore competition for Rio's attention.

"So?"

"You really want me to answer a question like that?" He looked like he was torn between a laugh and a growl. It was a good look for him.

Her heart sped up a beat looking at him looking at her and it wasn't her PSVT kicking in. The conversation she'd overheard kept replaying in her head, but she'd kind of gone past the point of no return and that was fine with her.

"Yes," he said. "Yes, I want to have sex with you."

"Are you busy now?" she asked and he laughed.

"I think you kidnapped me," he pointed out. "Did you plan this?"

"Nope." She opened the truck door and swung down. "It's your lucky day. If you get your ass in gear."

She probably should have planned ahead, but now she was acting on instinct—and something much, much more basic. Tiptoeing around Rio wasn't working out for her. She had a job to do and she had to be able to concentrate. That was her excuse anyhow, when the truth was that Rio Donovan was not only gorgeous, but he was lethal to her peace of mind. She looked at him and she thought about sex.

It was really that simple.

Slamming the door, she marched around to the back of the truck and lowered the tailgate. One quick shake and she had a blanket tossed in the bed. "All aboard," she gesture and Rio laughed again.

She loved his laugh. The sound was as warm and bold as the man.

"You're direct," he said, but he came around to her side.

"Is that a problem?"

She told herself she wasn't holding her breath.

"Absolutely not. Tell me what you like in bed and I'm a happy man."

Their impromptu bed probably didn't qualify as romantic, but Rio didn't want romance and neither did she. When she looked up, the trees made a green canopy overhead shutting out the sky and the air was filled with that sleepy summer buzz of insects and God knew what else. She didn't care. Right now, she wanted Rio and she'd decided to take what she wanted so… she'd turned over a new leaf. Got started on the new and improved her. Hopping up into the truck bed, she patted the space beside her. The moment felt awkward and yet not. So screw it.

She also wanted to kiss him, so she'd start there. Clothes could come off later.

"I haven't had sex in a truck since I was in high school." He dropped down onto the truck bed beside her. "I could be rusty."

She wasn't worried. "Just shut up and kiss me."

He pulled her onto his lap so that her legs straddled his hips, her groin notched against his. When she stretched, there was no missing the heat or the strength of him. Or the way his fingers curled over her hips. She rocked slightly and he groaned.

"This needs to take more than five minutes, Gia."

She grinned. "You have a reputation to live up to, hotshot. I'm expecting way more than five minutes."

He shook his head. "You're a tough customer."

He leaned up and his mouth captured hers, gentle but inexorable. His lips brushed against hers like he was tasting her. Slow with the sweet promise of more, when she wanted the speed and the heat, the pure adrenaline rush of Rio Donovan.

"I'm sorry you overheard my conversation with Jack," he whispered.

"Make it up to me."

"I promise." He kissed her again, harder and deeper, wrapping himself around her and pulling her down onto his body. The last time she'd been this close to him they'd been falling a hundred miles an hour toward the ground. She didn't know where they were headed in such a rush this time, but it felt right. He explored her mouth and somewhere, somehow, their kiss changed. Became more. Her hands slid up his arms, locking behind his neck and pulling him to her as she met him touch for touch in a blaze of sweet heat that threatened to spiral out of his control.

Good. God.

Rio's mouth was perfect. She opened for him, angling her face so he could stroke deeper, and he did. She broke away, panting.

She wanted *more*.

More kisses, more tongue, more Rio.

Reaching out, she tugged on the hem of his T-shirt. "You're taking too long."

Her fingers slid beneath the edge, finding hot, masculine skin. God. He felt incredible. Her fingers moved lower, bumped against the hot tip of his erection, and he sucked in a breath.

"I take it you believe in providing incentives," he said dryly and hauled the T-shirt over his head. *Definitely her lucky day.* His stomach was all hard, sculpted ridges, and she didn't know whether to look first or go straight to the touching-and-licking portion of the day's agenda. He wasn't waiting for her to decide, however, because his hands went to the waistband of his jeans. Unsnapped, unzipped and then shoved the denim down his thighs. Her throat went dry.

Sweet Jesus. He went commando. That figured. He was also sporting one hell of an erection. Thick and veined, his fully erect penis had her reaching for him. She was *so* done being hands-off.

"My turn," he said, and she heard the sensual warning loud and clear in his voice.

Thank God.

She reached for her boots, unlaced and toed them off before flopping on her back, giddy with relief. This was going to work. He wanted her. She wanted him. The giggle that worked its way out of her throat surprised them both. Who knew having Rio could be both sexy *and* fun?

He pounced, wrapping a sun-bronzed arm around her waist and taking her down. She hit the blanket, and he swung himself over her, his knees parting her thighs as his chest and shoulders blocked out her view of the sky. Trapped. In the best possible way.

"You still have too many clothes on," he growled.

He kissed her, and who knew just kisses could make her so hot? His lips rubbed and pressed, his mouth slanting deliciously over hers as he devoured her like she was his favorite flavor. She didn't want to close her eyes because the fierce concentration on his face as he penetrated her mouth made the erotic burn build and build, but the sensations were so good, and she was lost, lost, lost in him.

Her eyes drifted shut, drinking him in.

Wickedly sweet.

His hands were plenty busy as he kissed, running down her shoulders and back. He didn't break their kiss as he pushed the straps of her tank top down.

"Gia?"

"No questions. More doing," she urged.

"It's your turn to kiss me."

With another hard, hot nip of his mouth, he stripped her tank top off and she wrapped her arms around his back, exploring until she brushed the top of his ass. His hands discovered the waistband of her jeans and popped the button open. Two seconds later, and the only thing standing between them was her bikini panties.

Not much coverage there, she thought happily, her brain fuzzy with heat and lust. His fingers brushed over her belly and played with the lacy band.

She arched against those teasing fingertips, stroking herself against him and feeding the unfurling pleasure. *So good.*

So very, very bad.

The pleasure paled in comparison to the man rising up over her, fiercely intent on her body.

"Jesus," he whispered roughly, pulling back. His fingers left her stomach, and his palms brushed her shoulders. "We shouldn't do this."

"Probably not."

The problem was, she wanted to. And it wasn't just because his large, hard body felt so good next to hers. She definitely wanted the man inside her. Her hotshot was a heartbeat away from pinning her to the blanket, his eyes alight with the thrill of the challenge. He braced himself over her, all his attention focused on her as if she were uncharted territory he fully intended to explore.

To take.

Her hand lifted, tracing the strong line of his jaw and the sweet rasp of stubble beneath her fingertips. Rio wasn't polished, but neither was she.

She slid her hands over his face and behind his head, tugging him closer. A new heat burned inside her, heat and an undeniably sensual craving for the man watching her so intently. Learning her. She wanted to take him, run her hands over those broad shoulders and down the hard muscles of his back.

First, though, she had to get him to kiss her again.

Because he stole her breath when he worked his mouth on hers, and who needed to breathe? She knew the moment he lost control. He rolled, putting her beneath him again and threading his fingers through hers. The truck bed dug into her back as Rio's legs pushed hers open, his erection rubbing against her intimately. The bright shock of pleasure sent her arching up into him.

"Be sure, Gia." The words came out hoarse. "We can stop right now, if this isn't what you want. If it's too soon for you."

Hell, no, she didn't want to stop. Or wait. "Shut up," she said fiercely. "I'm waiting for you to kiss me."

"This doesn't change anything." His eyes moved over her body as one hand released hers to cover her shoulder in a slow, sensual caress. "When we go out on a call, when we jump—this changes nothing. We're jump partners, you and me."

"Absolutely not," she vowed. "This is just sex."

He grinned and dropped a kiss on the end of her nose. "Really, really good sex."

Not yet. She skimmed a hand down Rio's abdomen, loving how he stilled then pushed himself against her fingers. "I might have *some* ideas on how to manage that," she said and palmed him.

Died. He'd died and gone to heaven, which was not a place Rio had ever expected to visit. He knew his limits.

But Gia started to stroke, and he about jackknifed off the truck. Her palm was warm and smooth as she fisted him, moving slowly down as if she had all the time in the world and was enjoying the journey. Then she added a second hand, covering every inch of him that she could reach and keeping up that steady, mind-blowing rhythm. She might be in no rush to get where she was going, but his dick had other ideas. Hell, his whole body was on board with what she was doing.

Her fingers danced over his shaft like she was playing a goddamn flute, and he groaned. Rubbing her palm over the hard, aching tip, she spread the moisture she discovered down the length of him. Up, then down again, each tug a hot, erotic draw on his balls.

He'd never hold out. She watched him, keeping her eyes on his face and not on his dick. Happy, like this was a test and she was getting it all right. He sucked in air, fighting for control. Her fingers rubbed, finding a particularly sensitive spot beneath the swollen head, and his hips arched off the blanket.

"Gia," he warned hoarsely. Each touch brought him closer and closer to the edge of no return, and this wasn't how he wanted their first time. He wanted her delirious with need. He wanted to love her and love her, to give her so much pleasure she couldn't think.

So no way he'd come before she did.

The panties had to go. Damned if he didn't like the way she looked in pink lace, but she'd look even better naked. Pulling back from her wicked hands, he reached for the scrap of nylon.

"Those panties should be illegal," he said hoarsely, liking how the lace looked in his hands as he cupped her ass and lifted. She laughed, and the happy sound shot straight to his balls. The scrap of a bikini tied on the sides with little loops of ribbon. With one hard tug the strings covering her hips came apart in his hands.

Hell, yeah.

"Lift," Rio ordered, his voice harsh.

Biting back a dazed whimper, she did. He tugged her panties free, tossing them over his shoulder. For a long moment, he did nothing. Just looked at her. She wanted kisses. More touches.

She reached for him.

"Nuh-uh," he said, pinning her hands to the blanket. "This is my turn. Right now, I'm enjoying looking."

"Take a picture," she growled, "and enjoy it later."

He laughed. "You're beautiful. I could look at you all day and never be done. But..." he leaned forward, his mouth so close she could feel each word on her skin, "...I could be convinced to hurry up."

His mouth started a slow, hot glide down her body she was so onboard with.

His hands cupped her breasts, first just the curve and then stroking her nipples. The gentle pinch that followed sent pleasure tearing through her. Too much. Too fast. *Not enough*. Rio's mouth descended, kissing a wicked path from her stomach to where she burned hottest.

"Open up for me, sweetheart," he rasped, running a hand along her thigh.

She did, and her reward was his finger rubbing through the swollen folds. "You're going to taste sugar-sweet," he said.

She heard her own raspy groan as he pressed a small, first kiss against her burning clit. She shuddered, crying out louder. Fiercer. His hands on her were a welcome anchor in a maelstrom of pleasure. She wouldn't fly apart. She wasn't alone here.

"Let's make you feel even better."

He didn't ask. No, he just touched. His tongue pushed through the sensitive folds in a bold, erotic demand. She'd had oral sex before, but the way Rio commanded her body was new. And sexy as hell. He knew exactly what she needed, and he planned on giving it to her.

Over and over.

He angled her thighs wide, pinning her open with his shoulders. Yes, please, she thought happily. The position gave him full access to her body, and the delicious heat of him had her coming off the truck bed.

"Nuh-uh," he said, tapping her clit. "No moving."

There was no question about it. He was in charge. She should have minded, but God it felt so good. When his mouth covered her again, spearing her opening, she groaned. He growled and started at the bottom, licking his way to the top of her slit. Working through her folds as he tasted every single inch of her.

"Much better," she gasped out, and he just took her higher. Rolled his tongue back and forth over her clit in wicked circles, spreading her juices around the sensitive skin until she felt the orgasm trembling just around the corner.

Foil tore, and he rolled down a condom. "I'll always keep you safe," he said, and she heard the promise in his voice.

"Not from you," she breathed, and he grinned.

"You know what I want from you." He pressed her thighs apart firmly, notching the blunt head of his erection against her opening.

He wanted sex. Hard and fast. "God yes," she groaned.

He nipped her ear. "Good. We're on the same page."

He had no idea. She couldn't take much more of this, but her body had other ideas. She had to come. Was reaching for the pleasure point. He pushed the heavy head inside her and waited for her to adjust to the impossible fullness, the girth of him.

And to tease her.

"Good?" The word was more demand than question.

Oh God, *yes*. She nodded, her head banging against his shoulder.

"Hang on, sweetheart." He pulled back, pushed in, not stopping until he was seated all the way. *Double yes*. He stretched her, opening her wide. Wet sounds of skin moving on skin surrounded them.

A sudden pinch made her gasp, but then he was through and in. He tensed but she didn't see what he had to complain about. He hadn't been the virgin here.

"More," she groaned, arching up to meet his next thrust.

His face tight, he palmed her hips, sliding one big hand under her ass. The other curled around her hipbone, pressing her forward to meet the downward thrust of his cock.

"You drive me crazy," he rasped. "Are you okay?"

"Shut up." She dug her nails into his shoulder. "Move."

"Soon," he promised.

His hand found her clit and tapped the side lightly. *Heaven*. She arched up and he slammed into her, his finger skimming the tight nub. Pulled back and did it again, his finger finding each slick, sweet curve as he pushed in deeper still.

Holding still? Impossible. Her hips slapped his, their bodies fused together, his forehead resting against hers. It was sexy as hell, this closeness. No space at all between them. His mouth explored her forehead, her cheek and throat, planting raspy, open-mouthed kisses against her skin, as if now that he'd had a taste of her, he couldn't have too much.

She was *so* on board with that.

Locking her legs around his hips, she dug her bare heels into the small of his back as each hard stroke rammed her into the bed of her truck. He pulled out—the sweet, rough friction making her squeeze him tight—and her body followed, arching up into his. In. Out. A primal rhythm that picked up speed as he rode her towards the edge.

"Gia." He growled her name, and she came undone.

"Yes…like that. Rio!" Her heart pounded along with her words, hammering out the heavy pleasure beating through her. She exploded, melting around him, milking his dick and taking him with her.

"Fuck. *Gia.*" His harsh breathing filled her ear as he buried himself inside her body, his voice low and desperate as he followed her over the edge. She loved the way her name sounded like a needy plea and a hoarse shout, how in this moment he held her too tight, so very close, and there was no more space between them. Hip to hip, breast to chest. Cheek to cheek.

She wanted to look up and watch his eyes as he came, wanted to pretend that there was nothing more than a condom between them and that a relationship was still in the cards for them. He was a good man, she thought, wrapping her arms around him.

Bad boy on the outside, good man on the inside.

Rio rolled, pulling her on top of his chest. Gia probably had ridges permanently tattooed on her backside. And that wasn't the biggest problem. Nope. *That* was the unexpected V-card she'd given him.

"What the hell was that about?"

The words came out of his mouth and he froze. *Real smooth, Donovan.* His only excuse was that nothing about Gia Jackson screamed *virgin*. She was brash. Bold. And wonderfully, deliciously sexy. He didn't have any complains. He just didn't know why she hadn't told him—or why she'd picked him to be her first.

She met his eyes. Didn't duck her head or play dumb, but that was Gia for you. "You noticed."

"Of course I did." Wasn't the whole virginity thing supposed to be special? Because he damned sure would have made sure her first time was special if she'd given him a heads-up. Candles. Compliments. Hell, even a fucking bed would have been an improvement.

Instead, he was reduced to repeating the obvious. "You were a virgin."

She looked thoughtful. "You were a virgin once."

"When I was fifteen," he growled. "That was years ago. You, on the other hand, were a virgin until about five minutes ago."

She shrugged. "They were good minutes."

He agreed with her there. Everything about this afternoon had been spectacular. Hell, Gia could throw him in her truck and take advantage of him seven days a week if she wanted. He was totally onboard with that.

She rolled her eyes. "Don't be such a pansy about this, Donovan."

"Rio," he growled and she smiled. She knew she was pushing his buttons all right.

"I'm only discussing this once," she said. Now she definitely sounded annoyed.

"Once is enough." While he waited for her answer, he traced his hands down her spine and shifted. The bed of her truck was no Sleep Train special and something was poking him in the ass.

"I'm picky," she announced. "I wanted my first to be the best and, from what I've heard, you're that. *Rio*."

He definitely liked the sound of his name on her lips. They could go back to being Jackson and Donovan when they returned to base camp. Right now, however, they were off the clock and off the grid. Since he'd just been inside her body—deep, deep inside—he figured he'd earned first name status.

"Besides," she shrugged. "Being the last virgin on the jump team seemed like overkill to me. Unless you think Joey is still holding out?"

He wasn't debating whether or not Joey had done the deed. He'd rather bleach his brain—and he recognized a distraction when he heard one.

She'd always been one of the boys.

She'd told erotic stories right alongside them.

"I thought," he shoved a hand through his hair. "Hell, I don't know what I thought."

"That I wasn't really a woman, Rio? Or that maybe I just preferred girls like the rest of you?" She shrugged. "Men tell stories, Rio. You should listen to yourselves sometimes. So I told stories, too. I thought it was time to get some hands-on practice."

"Really good stories." He grinned up at her. So, okay. She didn't want to make a big deal out of this. They'd had sex and they'd leave it at that.

That was okay with him.

It really, really was.

He ran a hand down her back. Gia had a really, really nice back. Her breath caught in a sexy little hitch as he touched her, which was even nicer. So he did it again. Maybe he could convince her to stay longer.

She raised a brow. "If you ask nicely, I'll give you a ride back to camp."

Or not.

"You'd leave me stranded out here?"

She sat up and reached for her bra. "Jack wouldn't be surprised."

He didn't want to talk about his brothers. Clearly, their moment was over though, so he carefully shifted her off his lap and reached for his own clothes.

CHAPTER FOUR

Driving back was damned awkward. The mood in the truck's cab was all morning after, except that it was afternoon and neither of them had gotten any sleep.

Nope.

That had been no siesta they'd taken.

Instead, she'd taken Rio. Or he'd taken her. Both ways worked.

She could feel his eyes watching her and it was too bad he hadn't come with an instruction manual, because she had no idea what he was thinking. He sprawled there like they hadn't just been naked together in the back of her truck, his hands on her. In her. And his tongue...

The truck jerked right and she corrected her course. Getting them both killed would definitely spoil the afterglow.

"Problem?"

He had no idea. She wasn't sure what she'd expected, but this awkward drive home wasn't it. The bubble of anger was welcome. Something that was finally familiar. Rio had entertained women before. Surely, he could come up with some kind of conversational chitchat to fill in the silence. She'd take anything. A compliment. Next steps. The fucking weather.

Weather she could do.

"There's a high pressure front moving in. That will force the winds through the canyons and raise the fire danger. We'll be jumping by the weekend."

Her analysis met with dead silence. Clearly, the wrong thing to say right now. *Jesus.* No wonder the guys called her the weatherman.

"Do I make you nervous?" Now he sounded interested—and pleased. He was definitely a guy.

"Do I look nervous?" she countered, fixing her gaze drilling into the asphalt. Waves of heat shimmered, cooking the summer air over the highway until the light bent and tempted her with illusion.

"You look beautiful," he said and there she had it. Her compliment.

She snorted. "Pull the other one."

"Did anything I said or did back there make you think otherwise?"

"Sex goggles?"

"That's tequila." She could hear the smile in his voice. "And trust me, I find everything about you desirable."

Alrighty then.

Time for a change of subject. "Do you think we've fixed our chemistry problem?"

He smiled, a slow, lazy curl of his lips that definitely should have been illegal. She knew, because she looked. She considered pulling the truck over and having her way with him again but that smacked of desperation.

"Are you asking me if I'm going to stop looking at you when we're out in the field?"

Was she? She stared at the ribbon of highway like the answer was painted there between the neat yellow lines.

"Sure," she said finally.

He laughed. "I doubt it. I like looking at you."

That was definitely heat flushing her face. Damn it, she didn't blush. Of course, she also didn't flirt or have hot sexual flings either.

Apparently, it was her summer for new experiences. She hadn't thought much beyond getting Rio in her truck and then getting this itch she had for him out of her system. He leaned towards her and her body hadn't got the memo that Rio was a one-time treat to herself.

Her body definitely wanted more.

"I'm going to stare right back," she warned, because if he got to look, so did she.

"Deal," he said and settled back in his corner. That was too bad, because she'd been enjoying his proximity. That little smile played over his lips again and she had a feeling she'd just agreed to something dangerous.

Eyes on the road, Jackson.

"You think no one's going to notice?" Her voice sounded throaty. Maybe she had an inner sex kitten after all.

"Honey, of course they're going to notice. They already have." Rio didn't sound concerned.

"That's why I told you to stop staring," she pointed out. Outside the window, a billboard flashed by advertising U-pick fruit, the sheriff's car parked behind the faded boards. Welcome to Strong, California. Orchard-fresh apples *and* a speeding ticket.

"I tried."

"Not very hard."

"And you dragged me into your truck and had your way with me," he said happily. "Now I've got your permission to look all I want."

She tightened her fingers on the wheel and slid him a quick sideways glance. He was looking at her right now, a hot, knowing stare that made her feel like she was bouncing up and down on the front seat of her truck. Naked. Surprisingly, that wasn't a bad feeling at all.

"You don't mind if the others find out?" She felt like she should add more words to the question, but what? *About us?* Were they an *us?* Not thinking about anything more than getting her hands on

Rio's hot body had been shortsighted.

"You're not my dirty little secret," he said dryly. "Although Jack's definitely going to make a case that I'm not acting professional."

"Is that what you think?"

He shrugged. "It's true. Technically, I'm your boss. We're on the same team and we're working together. Sex is usually a recipe for disaster in the office."

She took her eyes off the road and looked at him. "I didn't hear you complaining. Are you going to fire me?"

Peek snuck, she turned her attention back to the road. There was something about a man in steel-toes that revved her engine. Rio was a delicious package all wrapped up in faded denim and those boots were just the icing on the Rio cake. She loved the way he'd let her turn him inside out. He hadn't wanted to give into this *thing* they felt for each other, but he had. Having that kind of power over a guy like him was a heady rush.

He shook his head. "Hell, I should give you a raise."

"I'm not stopping you."

"You'd kick my ass, Gia." He laughed. He was right, too.

She eyed the speedometer. Two miles until Strong. Too bad their afternoon was almost over. She had a sudden urge to take the back roads and spend the rest of the afternoon just driving around with Rio.

"I don't need presents," she agreed. "I pull my own weight."

"It was a joke." She could feel his eyes on her. "But that's part of the problem, isn't it? I know the jump team matters to you and, God knows, I don't want to fuck that up for you. I don't know how the rest of the guys would feel if they knew for certain we were…"

He trailed off. Yeah, Rio. Finish that sentence. Because, honestly, she had no idea what they were either. Teammates, absolutely, but she'd also like to think they were friends. Maybe not besties, but they'd had each other's back and that counted for a lot. Were they lovers? Friends with benefits? Picking a label was hard and he was right anyhow. She didn't want to jeopardize the camaraderie and acceptance she'd earned on the jump team. Not for sex, no matter how great.

She took a deep breath.

Take what you want.

Don't wait for anyone to give it to you.

"I want to see you again," she said. "You can be my dirty little secret."

Strong appeared and disappeared outside the truck, all three streets-worth. Ma's bar and the general store flashing by in seconds. The hangar was no more than a few miles away.

Would he?

Or wouldn't he?

He didn't say anything right away and, since she was new at this, chances were she'd misread him. Maybe one afternoon was enough for him. Just because he'd been happy to let her have her way with him today didn't mean he wanted a repeat. She'd heard the campfire stories and, even dismissing ninety percent of what she'd heard, the other ten percent said Rio didn't stick. He loved. He left. Mimi might count as a relationship, but she wasn't sure.

And did she really want a *relationship* with Rio?

"I've never been anyone's dirty little secret before." She couldn't tell whether he was amused or simply thinking about it.

She parked next to his truck and shook her head. "You don't know that."

He opened his mouth. Closed it. Clearly, she had him there.

She jabbed a finger towards his truck. "And here you are, delivered safe and sound."

"Are you kicking me out?" Now he definitely sounded amused.

She took the keys out of the ignition, although she had no idea where she intended to go. Away. That worked for her. "I brought you back," she repeated.

"Gia." His husky voice saying her name made her shiver. Damn it.

Reaching out, he trailed a finger down her bare arm. "I'd love to be your dirty little secret."

Having Rio as her secret was fun.

Sexy as hell.

And yet... something was missing. She wasn't sure what it was, but maybe dirty secrets took more than two nights to mature. Whatever. Rio came to her or she went to him—she wanted to keep their relationship even—and the sex was great. Keeping her hands off him when they were at work was a challenge, but she figured she'd get used to it. Or they'd burn themselves out and go back to being just jump partners. Option B was far more likely than that first one.

The third morning, when she opened her cabin door, she discovered Rio had been playing Secret Santa. He bought her a prickly cactus with a fleshy red flower smack on top of the spiny barrel. Jesus. She didn't want to know why he thought of her when he saw that thing, but not only had he, but he'd transplanted the poor thing from the florist's shop to her front porch. The small card announced *Made me think of you* in a dark, slashing stroke. He had beautiful handwriting.

If he wanted to swap bouquets, she'd play. She'd whacked down armloads of goldenrod with her machete and dumped them between the sheets of his bed. *For my golden boy* she'd scrawled in magic marker on his pillow.

Her handwriting was nowhere near as precise as his.

He got the message, though, or maybe he just believed *thank yous* should be said in person, because she woke up and she definitely wasn't alone. Rio's weight pressed her deep into the mattress. Shifting, she curled her legs around his hips. *Hello.* Something soft stroked over her skin. He'd brought flowers to share. How very nice.

"Gia," he crooned, drawing the spray of goldenrod down her throat. Jesus. That shouldn't have felt so good. Maybe it was because she was still half asleep.

"I did *not* give you a key," she protested sleepily.

He smiled. "You gave me flowers. And you sleep with your window open."

She bent her head to the side—which was about all she could manage with one big ass smoke jumper lying on top of her—and examined the bedroom window. "The air cools down at night. I wanted to take advantage."

He made another slow pass with the flower, pulling back some so he could explore her body. "I put the screen back. Maybe you could focus here, Jackson?"

The flower teased a lazy circle around her left nipple.

"My bed's occupied," he continued, "so I came over here to thank you."

The flower moved right and her breath caught. God, he was good.

"All my fault," she agreed happily. "Take your clothes off and I'll make it up to you."

"Promises," he growled. His mouth followed the flower, tracing a hot, damp path over her collarbone. His hair was damp from recent shower and he smelled like some kind of cologne too. All put together, while she was her usual messy self. Her tank-top had ridden up over her stomach and the pair of striped boy shorts she'd pulled on before falling into bed weren't Victoria's Secret.

He'd have to make do.

She shoved the sheet down with her foot.

"You bet," she said and proceeded to show him how very, very good she could be.

CHAPTER FIVE

They needed to work on Rio's definition of *secret*. The man had *dirty* down pat, but the keeping his silence thing wasn't working for him. He kept looking at her. In public. Despite the current heat wave, no new fires had been reported and that meant no jumps. Instead, the jump team was busy with training routines and equipment checks.

After a week, she was probably fortunate he hadn't taken out a billboard to announce the change in their relationship. She'd already checked Facebook, just to make sure, but the man's status stubbornly read *single*. There were no incriminating photos of him and her, nor did he write on her timeline. *That* would have had the whole team talking. As it was, she suspected that everyone knew. Jack definitely did, and what he knew, Evan knew. Evan had driven back to Strong when his R&R was up and then *he'd* started shooting her looks.

As long as no one said anything, however, she could pretend.

She was good at that.

Today, however, Rio had made his intentions of running by her side clear. He'd kept his mouth shut for the first three miles, letting her settle into the rhythm of the run, but now he was clearly gearing up to talk. At least she knew his cardio endurance was good. "You okay?"

"Never better." She kept her eyes fixed on the trail. There was one hell of a dip coming up and she had no desire to bite it.

He made a sound. "Gia—"

Her heartbeat picked up, a familiar fullness clogging her throat. There was no telling which moment her mis-wired heart would pick to backfire, but this was apparently one of them. Maybe. She focused on calming her breathing. Having a PSVT attack in front of Rio wasn't an option.

"I think we should renegotiate," he said from behind her. "Go public."

She flipped him the bird. "You make us sound like a stock trade," she called, hoping he'd write off her breathiness to the uphill run.

He mumbled something, but she didn't turn her head.

Instead, she counted heartbeats. *Onetwothreefourfive.*

And it didn't work.

She still wasn't ready to discuss what they'd done. She put on a spurt of speed and beat him to the dip. After that, it was single file for the remaining three miles and he didn't have a chance to ask his question again. Honestly, she didn't know what she'd have said. Thanks for a good time? Call me if you're interested in a repeat later tonight? Because she hadn't been signing up for a relationship or even serial sex. No, if she was being honest, she hadn't thought beyond finally, finally going to bed with Rio Donovan. Somehow, she'd imagined that once (or twice, thrice, or even a dozen times) would be enough and they'd go on with their lives.

See? That was her big mistake right there.

The trail crested, the forest spreading out beneath them in a dense canopy of treetops. To go with the bright, hot day, the weather report had promised thunderstorms at night. The whole area was bone dry, waiting for one well-aimed lightning strike to set off a wildland fire. Business would be knocking at the jump team's door before long.

Thinking about incoming fire calls was safer than thinking about the man dogging her heels. She started down the trail, digging in to slow her descent.

"You don't even know what I want to talk about," he called.

She could guess, so she picked up the pace.

Seeing Rio every day she came to work—after spending the night in his arms—made it impossible to forget the reasons getting involved with Rio would be an epic fail. Mentally she ran through the list, losing herself in the steady rhythm of her run. First, Rio was playboy naughty. Gia got that. He didn't mean to hurt anyone, but he'd never slow down and stop. This heat between them burned so bad and the bad was both good—and not.

Hot sex was definitely not something to dismiss and he'd been her first.

She'd had dessert before she'd eaten her vegetables.

She could live with that, and he'd made it clear that a repeat wasn't out of the question. Unfortunately, her head kept pointing out the other outcomes just as clearly. Sleeping with him publicly—and she didn't mean in the voyeuristic *look at me* sense, although inviting eyeballs on their relationship felt just as intimate—would definitely jeopardize her place on the team. They'd more or less gotten away with it so far, but he and his brothers owned Donovan Brothers and that made him her boss. Worse, he was protective. She'd seen that over and over in him and she'd already spent a lifetime trying to fight free of an over-protective family. If he became her full-time lover, he'd want to protect her. Keep her safe. And there was nothing less safe than jumping out of a plane into the heart of a fire.

Been there, done that, and she was still trying to get off the family guilt ride. No way she invited more in the form of hooking up even semi-officially with Rio.

Bursting out of the trees, she spotted the finish line for their run. Covered with pornographic graffiti and ancient love stories, the battered picnic tables were a welcome sight. She put on a final burst of speed, nothing but the air sawing through her lungs and the burn in her muscles. Forty yards between her and happy collapse.

Rio tore by her with a whoop.

She had just enough time to think *shit* and then her chest tightened, her heart sprinting into overdrive as she lunged for the picnic table. Now wasn't the time for a PSVT attack, but the disease was the ultimate party crasher.

Breathe.

She'd taken her pills that morning.

Rio ran, fists pumping, feet chewing up the distance between him and the goal. The harder he ran, the less he thought about the woman dogging his heels. Gia was no quitter. He didn't turn his head, didn't give her any ground, but he knew she was right there on his six like she was out in the field. Slapping a palm down on the table, he turned and fist-pumped.

"Winner!" he crowed.

Gia hurtled towards him and he caught her, swinging her to a halt. Flushed and determined, she sucked in air, trying to catch her breath. Lust slammed into him. She was fucking gorgeous.

And she'd loved him and left him. Quite literally.

"Christ, Rio." She leaned into the picnic table.

In addition to sexy, she looked tired. And winded.

He frowned.

Gia usually ran circles around him. "You okay?" he asked.

"You bet," she said, but she didn't meet his gaze. Instead, she stepped away from the table and started walking, shaking out her arms and legs. While he thought that over, he went over to his truck, reached in the bed and snagged a bottle of water. Dehydration he could fix.

She ignored him when he held out the bottle, pacing faster with her fingers on her pulse and a frown on her face. She'd run the trail as hard and fast as ever, but she was definitely winded.

"Out of shape, Jackson?"

She plucked the water bottle from his outstretched hand. "Never."

He looked her over because her barely there running shorts and jogging top demanded a second glance. Every other inch of her body was bare, sun-bronzed and sweat-slicked and he had to agree with her about the shape she was in. She looked glorious. Hotter than any fantasy woman he'd ever conjured.

Maybe she'd pushed too hard.

"I should make you drop and give me twenty."

She grimaced. "Be kind."

That was also not like his Gia. She pushed herself—and she'd gut any man who tried to cut her any slack because she was a girl or tired or even plain having a bad day. Gia didn't do excuses. Before she could stop him, he reached out and pressed two fingers against the pulse beating in her throat.

"Jesus, Jackson."

Her resting rate had to be pushing two hundred beats per minute.

She shoved his hand away. "I'm fine. I pushed too hard at the end."

That was possible. But Gia had run that trail dozens of times. She'd trained in the off-season. If she'd been middle-aged and out-of-shape, he'd have bought the excuse she was selling. But she wasn't. And he didn't.

"Gia—"

She ignored him, dropping to the ground to stretch out her calves. He crouched beside her. She didn't want to admit that she had a problem, and yet she clearly did. He didn't know how or why, but something was up.

"I ran too hard," she repeated. Her eyes flashed, demanding he back the hell off. And that was the thing, wasn't it? He might be her jump partner, but that was all he was. He didn't have the right to hound her about how she felt unless it impacted the team. And her brown eyes were looking daggers at him, promising instant death if he didn't drop the topic.

Maybe she had run too fast.

He hesitated.

She sighed and held her wrist out. "Check me now."

He wrapped his hand around her wrist, tracing the soft skin with the pads of his fingers. Finding the vulnerable patch where the pulse that beat in her wrist almost undid him. He pressed two fingers against the vein and forced himself to focus. Her heart still raced, but the mad jackhammer beat had slowed.

"See?" she said. "I'm fine."

No, she probably had a bridge somewhere that she wanted to sell him, but he couldn't make her talk if she didn't want to. If she said she was fine, he had to believe her. And it was possible she'd simply had a bad run.

While he weighed that possibility, is pager buzzed madly. "We've got incoming," he said.

Gia's head came up. "Fire?"

She sounded like he'd offered her favorite flavor of ice cream.

He nodded. "Jack just called the whole team in. It's a big one."

"Can't wait." Gia hopped off the picnic table. "I'll race you back to base."

The DC-3 reached the jump site thirty minutes after takeoff. The plane's interior was no luxury limo ride; the team sprawled haphazardly on the floor of the stripped down interior. Seats were for pansies, Jack had ruled, and no one had disagreed. Without the seats, there was more room for cargo—and a clear path to the door. That worked for Rio.

Today's fire call was a bad one, with the incident commander calling in Strong's jump team as backup for a team that had been on the ground forty-eight hours and counting. More hands were clearly called for, along with fresh supplies. Sure enough, as the plane circled, Rio got his first look out the open door and, no shit, the caller hadn't exaggerated. One big ass fire was chewing up the wildland beneath the plane. Fifty, sixty acres and the weather forecast called for the wind to pick up, which would only push the fire further faster. Right now, though, the smoke was a dark column punching up into the blue sky.

Mack was the day's spotter and he'd picked out the landing zone from earlier aerials. Fortunately, the drop site was a clearing right on the edge of the fire, a mercifully big tree-free area, reducing the risk of snags and hang-ups. Unfortunately, the site was parked at the top of a steep gulch. That was never good news. While Rio craned his neck, mentally marking visible hotspots, Mack conferred on his headset with the pilot and then aimed the drift streamers out the door.

Mack flipped a bird towards the ground. "Bombs away."

Mack's face revealed no trace of humor, but he seemed to have his shit together, so Rio wouldn't hassle him. Today. He was fairly certain though that Mack was nursing a big-time case of PTSD.

Silently, the two of them watched the streamers go down. Nice and straight, which meant there was no crosswind to worry about at the moment, although the wind could and did shift like a bitch. Even at fifteen hundred feet, the flames chewed up the mountainside in an audible welcoming choir.

Whatever Spotted Dick, the pilot, said must have gotten the mental thumbs-up from Mack, because he motioned for Rio and Gia to take their positions in the door. Gia bounded over as the plane banked hard, coming back around for the jump pass.

Mack eyed the two of them; the jump list had spelled out the first pair in the air, but not the individual jump order. "Ladies first," he decided.

Rio and Gia would be first on the scene, radioing the ground conditions back up to the rest of the team. They'd make the call whether it was safe for the rest of the jumpers or not.

Gia stuck her tongue out at him and promptly swung into the open door, arms and legs braced, before he could retaliate. He'd watched her jump dozens of times, he reminded himself. This was just another day in the office, so his heart had no business kicking his heartbeat up a notch when she leaned her head out the door and eyeballed all that open space. As soon as Mack slapped his hand on her shoulder, she launched herself out the door with a whoop.

At least this time Mack didn't follow with *bombs away*.

Rio got himself into the open door fast. It was fifteen hundred feet to the ground and she wasn't landing without him.

Or that was his plan at any rate.

He shot out of the door when Mack's hand hit his shoulder in the familiar jump sign. Head down, he tore towards the ground, the wind roaring in his ears. *Back in the saddle, baby.* He'd wondered if his head would play games with him on this first jump since the malfunction, but he was good. Bad luck, Evan had ruled after going through Rio's chute pack. And now he'd gotten right back on the horse. He eyeballed Gia, marking her progress, but she'd already snapped her drag chute and gotten her feet down. She was right on target to put down nice and easy in the center of the clearing, so he spared a glance for the fire. Holy shit. There was nothing nice and easy about that.

Their LZ was on top of a ridge above a densely wooded slope that ended in ponderosa-studded forest sporting twenty-foot sheets of flame. They'd need to pay careful attention to conditions on the ground. The terrain was steep and, if the wind shifted, they ran the risk of getting overrun. He got his feet down, head up.

The drag chute popped, yanking him back and up. *Business as usual.*

Jump thousand.

Look thousand.

Below him, Gia pulled her cord and her chute deployed. He banked left slightly, not wanting to run the risk of tangling his feet in her lines.

Reach thousand.

He wrapped his hand around the rip cord and prepared to pull.

Wait thousand.

The ground closed in. He'd been in office buildings that were further from the ground. Four hundred feet between him and a terminal ending.

Pull thousand.

The chute deployed perfectly and he steered towards the LZ. The canopy bucked and everything was good. Gia hit the ground textbook perfect, already running and rolling her chute.

Check your canopy.

He eyeballed his chute—it was open and not tangled, so he'd definitely improved on his last jump. Being wrapped tight around Gia hadn't been a hardship. He liked holding her and Gia had steered them both in like Super Woman before depositing his sorry, falling ass safely on the ground. So now he also owed her. Big time. That part, he didn't like. He preferred to operate on a cash-and-carry basis when it came to his life. He didn't owe anyone.

Except now he owed Gia.

His steel-toes hit the ground and he ran hard, running out his momentum. The chute hit the ground, but Gia was already there, chasing his ass and gathering up the surplus nylon. The DC-3 banked overhead and headed away from the drop site. Spotted Dick would make another pass over the fire to do re-con while Rio and Gia assessed the site from the ground. If everything checked out, the rest of the jump team would join them on the ground.

"Ten minutes and they'll be back, ready to jump when we give the go-ahead," he said and she nodded. That left them just enough time to do a quick on-ground assessment. If conditions weren't right, they'd pull the plug on the impending jump and hike out themselves.

They turned as one and headed towards the fire.

Smoke poured up the sloping side. The first order of business once the team landed would be building a fire break. They needed to clear a strip of forest ASAP or that fire would burn right up the hill.

Sheets of orange flames chewed up the grass, but Gia didn't hesitate. She waded right in.

"Hey." He swung her to a halt with a hand on her arm. "Where are you going?"

She looked at him like he's crazy. "For a beer."

Lame question. He shut the hell up and fell into step beside her. Settled for kicking down the small flames that licked at their boots. She frowned, but she didn't say anything. He could feel it coming though.

When they reached the edge of the ridge and peered over, he was ready to call it a day. That was definitely a new flavor of hell down there. Embers and burning debris peppered the ground around them, warning that the fire had no intention of staying put forever. That kind of ground hid unseen gullies beneath all the tall brush that hadn't burned in years. Ten, maybe twelve, feet tall, he estimated, which would make even the basic act of walking almost impossible. You'd have to cut your way through because nothing had burned here for decades.

Beside him, Gia nodded. "Okay. Let's go radio the guys. It's a tall order, but we can knock this down."

He took a second look at the fire. "I don't like it."

"We're not picking out paint colors. Give me specifics."

"The wind's shifting," he pointed out. When they'd jumped, the smoke column had been more or less vertical, but now the tip had hung a left.

"Anything else wrong with this site?" she asked dryly.

He had a list as long as his arm. Number one, however, was the wind. While they'd stood here arguing, the wind had picked up. The drift streamers on the ground danced restlessly. If the wind hit just right, feeding oxygen into the fire, the whole damned place would explode into flames and they'd be looking at area ignition.

"It's not safe." He needed a second opinion, an escape route... Hell. He didn't know what was up with his sorry ass but, clearly, he didn't want her to do her job. No—he wanted her safe and they were standing face-to-face with fifty acres of wildfire. He wouldn't get what he wanted today.

"That's why we're here. To *make* it safe," she pointed out.

"You want me to make you recite the ten standard firefighting orders?"

Those orders were the mantra, rule book and Bible for any firefighter on the ground. Following them kept good men safe and had done for fifty-plus years. Which was the point. The Forest Service didn't want to lose any more firefighters.

She eyed him. "As long as you remember that the tenth order says we fight the fire *aggressively*, Donovan."

"And safety comes first," he pointed out. "That's in the rule book too."

"Fuck off," she said amiably. "This is my job and I'm doing it. What's wrong with you, Donovan?"

"You," he snapped, giving her the truth. "You don't think, Gia. You rush into dangerous situations."

"I'm doing my job. That means taking a risk sometimes."

"No," he repeated. "Your job is what I say it is."

She stepped into him, her hand shoving his chest. "Bullshit, Donovan. I'm a smoke jumper. I fight fire. Really nasty, really hot fire. So that makes this fire line all part of a day's work. You know it. I know it."

He stared at her, because keeping his mouth shut right now was the only prudent course of action.

"You know what your problem is?"

He was certain she'd tell him.

"Surprise me," he drawled.

"Sex." She rocked back on her heels. "But here's a newsflash for you. Having sex with you doesn't make me incompetent or the little woman—so you stick your alpha male bull crap up your uptight, over-protective ass. Sex doesn't make you the boss of me."

"You liked taking orders just fine," Rio growled.

Gia considered planting her Pulaski in his thick skull, but there were probably laws against assaulting her boss with the razor-sharp hand-tool even if he was asking for it.

"We had a deal," she snapped, slamming the Pulaski into the ground instead. See? She'd get a start on cutting line and get her frustrations out at the same time. That was practical.

Because what Rio didn't get to do was to change the terms of their deal. Sex wasn't supposed to change anything between them. It was supposed to be fun, not a game changer. From what she'd heard, Rio Donovan should have understood that very well. Hell, he hadn't had a relationship that outlasted a fire season.

"Remember that conversation?" She prompted him when he didn't answer right away. He was staring at the low flames chewing up the forest floor. She squinted, following his gaze. Sumac and scrub oak, yucca and manzanita all hung on for dear life to the mountain slope in a thick, almost impenetrable web of branches. Getting through the tangle would be almost impossible.

He moved, putting a few feet between them "We didn't talk."

It was too hot to get much closer to the flames. The day was going to be a scorcher too. The thermometer had read 75 when they'd taken off. Once again, however, he angled himself until he blocked her access to the flames. Standing between her and the fire was definitely not part of the deal. She hooked a boot around his ankles and tugged until he was sprawled on his ass. Only then did she step back into position. "Careless of you, Donovan."

"I said: Sex changes nothing, right? You. Agreed." She punctuated each word with a stab of her finger.

"I was busy. You distracted me," he accused.

"Why does it matter?" The sex in her truck had been fantastic. She couldn't have asked for better. Hell. She was fairly certain he'd set the bar so high that she'd be disappointed the next time she picked a lover. She'd been pleasantly sore afterward, deep inside her body, a primal reminder of where he'd been and what they'd done together. She liked it, which probably said all sorts of things about her.

He swung around and stared at her in frustration. "We had sex."

"I was there," she reminded him. "And it was fairly unforgettable."

"Fairly?" He growled the word and she bit back a grin.

She wasn't grinning a moment later when the ground gave way beneath her, sending her backwards down the hill.

CHAPTER SIX

Gia pinwheeled, jamming her fingers into loose rock to halt her downward plunge. She cursed like a trucker and his heart took up residence in his throat as time did the slow-down-speed-up thing. Rio didn't know what he'd do if he lost her, but it wasn't an option. Since she'd joined the jump team, he'd been pussy-footing around his feelings for her. He still didn't know what they were—only that desire definitely had a starring role on the list—but he wasn't losing her. Not to the fire, not to an accident. Not ever and particularly not now when he was finally ready to find out what this thing between them was.

He jammed his Pulaski into the loose shale and descended after her.

Twenty long seconds later, he reached her. She was sitting up. That was a good sign. She wasn't *standing* though, and that said it all.

"Talk to me," he said. If she could talk, she hadn't cracked a rib or punctured a lung.

"I jammed my ankle." Tight with pain and frustration, her voice made it plenty clear that Gia did not appreciate her current situation. "Goddamn it. I didn't see that coming."

"That's why it's called an *accident*," he pointed out. "As opposed to an *on purpose* or *suicide*."

"Try *stupid*," she groused.

Dropping to the ground beside her, he ran his hands down her arms and sides. She didn't shrug away, but he could sense her impatience. A check-out after a slide like the one she'd just taken was standard operating procedure. She was dirty as hell, wearing half the hillside, but all in all the damage seemed to be limited to her right ankle.

He probed her ankle carefully and she hissed. "Bedside manner, Donovan."

"Rio," he said and pressed lightly. "Can you bend it?"

"Maybe." She tried and succeeded. Except she bit her lip, her gloved hands flexing on her thighs, the whole time. He needed a medical pickup.

"Yes," she said, her eyes on his hands. "I can move it."

She sounded relieved. Apparently she'd had her own doubts.

"Not broken," he said, not trying to hide his own relief. A broken ankle out here would be a challenge.

"I should buy a lottery ticket," she muttered.

She was probably right. She'd slid a good thirty feet.

Overhead, the column of smoke no longer punched straight up. Instead, it bent slightly at the top, as if a southwest wind had joined the party. Mack had guesstimated the wind speeds in the area at maybe twenty-five miles per hour. If that wind dropped, however, and hit the ground, the wildfire could explode. The wind would sweep through their gulch and funnel the downslope fire towards them.

"Rio?"

He liked the sound of her name on her lips, although he decided he'd prefer to hear her moan his name when he had her in bed. An *oh, Rio* as in *more, Rio* and *yes, please, Rio*.

She tried to tug her ankle away and he held on. Carefully.

Hurting Gia was the last thing he wanted to do. Not that he

routinely went around with the plan of inflicting bodily harm on others—although there had been that incident with the Big Bear Rogue hotshots earlier this summer—but Gia got special treatment. She was in a category all by herself.

"Let me look at your ankle."

When he reached for the laces on her boot, however, she stopped him. "Don't."

He shook his head. "Don't be a baby, Jackson. Let me see the damage."

"It's not that. Look behind you." She nodded and he looked up. Holy. Hell. The wind had shifted all right, sending smoke and flames boiling up the hillside.

She grimaced. "I'm going to need that boot on. If you unlace it and my ankle swells, I'm going to be running barefoot. I don't want to do that."

One of the first rules of fighting fire from the ground was to remain aware of situations to watch out for. Donovan Brothers ran a safe operation. Every man—and woman—on their team knew the eighteen watch out situations. He had unburned fuel between himself and the fire, winds picking up, and terrain that was rough as hell. Worse, their current location had all the makings for a really, really bad flashover.

She shoved to her feet and he had to let her. He knew that. The ice-cold sensation was back in his stomach, because the fire behind them meant business. All he could think was: thank God the jump team hadn't landed yet. Because this was the kind of set-up where no one went home alive.

Gia started limping away from the flames. "The fire's going to outflank us."

He knew that too.

He wished with everything he was that she was wrong.

But she wasn't.

Instead, he followed right behind her. Her face paled after two steps, her teeth worrying her lower lip. Shit. She'd definitely done a job on her ankle.

"Drop and crawl," he ordered. "Save your ankle. I'm going to grab our packs and get a better view."

He could see her, he reminded himself, and their lives were on the line. Leaving her—temporarily—was the only way to keep her safe. He sprinted rapidly to the top of the ridge, his boots digging into the loose shale. And got his first full-on view of the fire. The fire downslope was moving steadily towards them, a wall of super-heated flame and gasses.

Definitely fuck-you territory.

He ran options in his head and came up blank. The fire was making a run up the hill, it had plenty of fuel even without the pick-me-up boost from the wind. He and Gia had a ridge that required mad monkey skills to scale and a canyon that was going to suck in air and flames. They'd definitely been dealt the losing hand in this round.

He hoped like hell that other team had been dropped on the south side of the fire, because anyone over here was looking at a barbecue. Swiping his pack from the ground, he searched for open ground. The flames crept steadily up the hill now, and his head picked this time to remember stories of blowups that had consumed thousands of acres, taking down good men and women. The Mann Gulch fire had killed thirteen firefighters in minutes. No one had successfully run from that fire, bad ankle or not. A fucking cheetah or Olympic sprinter would have died right alongside those firefighters.

"Time to shake and bake?" she asked calmly, crawling over the ridge's crest.

He shook his head. "There's too much fuel here. The fire won't pass right over us. Do you trust me?"

That was the million dollar question right there.

She eyed him, calm and composed. Like they weren't minutes from dying because the fire shelters were designed to hold off the heat and flames for brief periods of time only. After that, the glue melted and... he so wasn't thinking about that right now. The only small mercy was that a lungful of superheated air would probably kill them before the flames did.

"What do you have in mind?" she asked.

"I'm going to set a backfire." He could burn out the fuel. In the few minutes they had before the fire overran them. Gia couldn't run, not on that ankle.

"Do it. Do you need me for that?"

He shook his head, getting out his lighter and turning his attention to the ridge's unburned expanse. He only got one chance to get this right. "See if you can tape up your ankle in case we have to run."

She didn't reach for the portable first aid kit. Instead, she got on the radio, calling in to the DC-3 circling overhead. "Unsafe conditions on the ground. Repeat: do not jump."

The fire was a thousand yards and closing fast.

He set the lighter to the dry grass. A fusee would have been better, but Spotted Dick hadn't dropped the supplies. That would have come after the jump team landed—and then the entire team would have been in jeopardy. His flames licked through the dry grass, happily chewing up the fuel. She fell in behind him, using her Pulaski to move the dirt and build a safety zone. When the downslope fire reached them—nine hundred yards away now—the bigger fire would suck the flames of their smaller one towards it. Everything in its path would scorch and leave nothing else to burn. That was their new safety zone.

"Are you sure about this?" She eyed his lighter doubtfully. The burnt-out area was awfully small, the wall of flames racing towards them impossibly high.

"Trust me," he repeated. "I'm not going to steer you wrong, Gia."

He stepped through the flames and onto the blackened ground. She didn't look happy about it, but she followed.

"I should have brought my bikini. This is swimsuit weather."

He grinned. "You've got to warn me, because I hear Facebook

calling."

She made a face.

Embers and debris started raining down around them. Four hundred yards and less than a minute to show time. He could hear the branches creaking and hissing now, the air around them thick with smoke.

"Deploy," he ordered because he was the senior jumper and that put him in charge. "We're going to count ten and then cover."

Hands icy cold despite the searing outside temps, he watched as she yanked the shelter from her pack and cracked open the packaging. She stepped in, feet pointing at the flame sweeping toward them. Cover her head too soon, and the heat could rapidly become unbearable inside the protective cocoon. Wait too long and—fuck, he didn't really want to imagine becoming a crispy fry right now.

Jack had waited out a firestorm, sharing a single shelter with Lily. Ben Cortez, Lily's uncle and Strong's fire chief, had always said that the shelters were a last resort. The older man was right. Rio could see the fire coming, could feel the heat rolling towards them. He and Gia were out of options.

"Get down," he ordered and she promptly did, hitting the ground like a gigantic silver inchworm. He ran his eyes over her shelter, checking for gaps or problems, but she'd deployed textbook perfect. Thank God. Resting his hand on her where her shoulder should be, he squeezed gently. There would be no one to check him but she was the one who mattered here.

He eyeballed her one last time before dropping to the ground between her and the oncoming fire. She could kick his ass later. He was bigger. Hopefully, his body would give her one more buttress against the heat. His heart gave an unexpected leap. She'd be okay. He refused to imagine any other ending to this jump.

The fire roared towards them now like an out-of-control semi. Less than a hundred yards, he guessed, but now he was running blind, unable to see what was coming. Pulling his shelter into place, he tamped the edges down under his gloved fingers. If the fire didn't blow over, if his escape fire hadn't done its job and chewed up the available fuel... well, what happened next wouldn't be pretty. And it might not even be fast. The shelter's glue would melt and then he'd be next. Working fast, he followed out the ground beneath his face and turned his nose and mouth into the shallow space because in seconds he'd want that cooler air. Badly.

Christ.

Had he done enough?

Had he missed something?

The fire hit and he stopped thinking and just reacted. Held on and held on...

CHAPTER SEVEN

When Rio tapped Gia's shoulder in the all clear sign—and it had to be Rio's hand on her shoulder, because who else was out here?—relief hit her hard. She'd never deployed before, although the procedure had been covered heavily in training and the jump team practiced the maneuver at least once a week. Jack Donovan was a big believer in muscle memory and apparently he was right. She'd known exactly what to do.

Three and a half minutes of hell. Of not knowing whether the shelter would hold or if the backfire had worked and burned up enough fuel to prevent the main fire from seeking her out. Hot and almost airless, the sweat running down her neck and back as she pressed her face into the small hollow she'd carved out in the dirt. Amazing what a difference a few degrees made. She prayed and held on, helpless to do anything but wait and see what happened next, reliving Rio's touch on her shoulder and wondering if that would be the last time he ever touched. Until, finally, the heat had started decreasing and the noise had fallen away.

The fire had moved on.

No sirree. She'd really rather never do that again. She rolled and sat up, shoving the shelter down her legs and looking around. Holy.

Shit. The entire ridge was nothing but smoking charcoal.

Rio's escape fire had worked.

Obviously.

She was here. He was here.

She'd always loved the adrenaline rush of fighting fire, but this hadn't been a fight. This had been a lay-down-and-pray moment.

She looked up. She wouldn't cry, she told herself fiercely. Those tears were just a physical reaction to the adrenaline and stress. They had nothing to do with seeing Rio up and on his feet. He was okay. He grinned down at her, relief and something else on his face. His sweaty, dirt-streaked face had never looked so beautiful. Knocking his helmet back, he scrubbed at his face with his gloved hand.

"You okay?" he asked, his eyes running over her.

She did a quick mental inventory as she stood up. "A-okay."

There was a whole world of relief in that one word. Her ankle throbbed, trying to remind her that it was still there, but after those minutes in the fire shelter? She. Didn't. Care. She was alive. Rio was alive. Everything else could take a number and get in line.

"Good." He looked at her like he wanted to say something else, but then he moved away from her, his head tipped back as he eyeballed the sky. The DC-3 banked overhead, moving away from the jump site. No chutes hung in the sky, so she did the math. They were still on their own here, although being alone with Rio Donovan wasn't hardship. Nope. He was exactly the man she wanted to have at her back on a forced wilderness stay.

He followed the departing plane with his eyes. "They have to bug out. They've only got so much fuel. Plus, we're getting close to cut off and then the Park Service won't let them fly anyhow."

Something in the pit of her stomach lurched at the mere thought of the DC-3 running out of gas and taking a nosedive toward the ground.

"We need to hike out," he continued.

And... there he went. Taking control of the situation. Rio was the senior jumper and she had no issue with that. Some things came down to experience and he'd jumped longer than she had. That was a fact. But she also had a brain in her head, which meant she had thoughts and opinions on their best next steps. She wouldn't let him run roughshod over her.

So she pushed back. "That's your plan?"

He folded his arms over his chest. "That's *our* plan."

"We could stay here," she suggested. "Dig line until the rest of the team comes back."

He looked down the slope and shook his head. "The fire's jumped the ridge. There's no controlling it from this side."

"You don't think digging line here would help?"

He didn't bother with explanations. "No."

Instead he squatted and started rolling up the Mylar cocoon that had probably just saved his life. The shelter wasn't intended for multiple deploys, but it wasn't like they could pop into Walmart right now and pick up a replacement. If they encountered another worse case scenario, they'd be glad enough for used goods.

"Come on." He grabbed his pack and motioned to her, like she was a dog and he expected her to heel. He probably liked leashes and chains as well.

When she didn't move, he sighed. "You don't think leaving's the right approach?"

She made a face. It wasn't a question of right or wrong. It was a question of being *consulted*.

"Talk to me," he snapped.

"Stop giving me orders," she countered. "We're jump partners."

"I'm the senior jumper. I write your paychecks. Take your pick, but I'm getting us both home and keeping you safe."

And that was the problem right there.

"Listen to you. It's not your job to *keep* me safe. I look out for me."

They were partners, that was the truth, but he was treating her like someone to be wrapped up in cotton wool and babied. She didn't want special treatment. She wanted him to look at her and see another smoke jumper. An equal.

Which, apparently, would happen when pigs flew.

He scrubbed a hand over his face. "I don't have time for this, Gia. The safest option is to hike out, so that's what we're doing. The safest option for *both* of us," he emphasized when she opened her mouth.

He made a good point.

When he dropped on his haunches and reached for her ankle, she didn't protest. Now wasn't the time to be stupid. His hands were gentle as he wrapped and taped.

"There," he said finally, slipping her foot back into her boot. "Good as new."

"Promises," she said softly because, no matter how magic his touch felt to her, he couldn't fix a sprained ankle. "Do I get a lollipop?"

"You'll have to raincheck on that until we're back at base camp."

Waiting wasn't something she did any better than she took orders.

"We'll take it slow," he promised and then got on the radio.

Jack was all over the call. Quite possibly the bastard had been sitting there waiting. Rio checked his watch. It had been forty minutes since he and Gia had landed. The longest forty minutes of his life.

"I have a situation." He calmly relayed the chain of events to Jack, from Gia's fall to sending the jump team away.

Jack cursed. "Mack unloaded the team about fifteen miles from your current drop site."

Rio could work with that. "Give me the coordinates. Is there a trail? An access road?"

Beside him, Gia took a test step on her foot. One. Two. If she so much as winced, fuck it. They'd camp here as long as it took for her ankle to heal.

She sucked it up though. Her face didn't show an ounce of the pain she had to be feeling.

He wasn't surprised. She'd insist she was fine even if she was missing the entire foot. He'd have done the same.

On the radio, Jack walked him through the map. The fire road where the team was working was a good fifteen miles away, all cross-country. It would be slow, rough going. Gia's ankle wouldn't take kindly to that kind of stress.

"What about a lift from a chopper?"

"Not possible at the moment unless you're telling me the apocalypse has hit your hillside and you need an immediate extract." Jack sounded regretful. "We've already committed all of our resources and we're close to cut-off. If you want to wait, I'll send a bird as soon as I've got one."

"How long?" He didn't want to sit out the firefight and he understood the Park Service put limits on flying when it was dark, but Gia's ankle was a concern. She turned and headed back toward him. When she spotted him watching, she winked and switched to a high-fashion model walk. Heel-toe-heel and all sashay.

"Three days."

"Jack—"

"It's the best I can do."

Gia hit a runway pose beside him and made a face. "We'll hike it," she said and he nodded. *Time to roll.*

Rio spent the next forty minutes trying to reconcile the hike out with the state of Gia's ankle. And his head. He hated the snail's pace when his boys were out there fighting fire, down two jumpers. He wanted to be there, digging line by their sides. And he wanted to get Gia to a doctor because he was no trained medic. He had basic field training and that was it.

Gia hiked along by his side uncomplaining. She'd fought him—again—when he'd relieved her of her pack. Judging by the way she leaned on the stick she'd snagged at the start of their hike, however, he'd made the right call there. He wanted her to take it as easy as possible.

He'd take the double weight any day for her.

"I'm slowing you down," she pointed out. "You should go ahead. I'll get there when I get there."

Like hell.

"We're partners."

"And we've got three working legs between us," she grumbled. "The sooner you reach the team, the sooner you can be out there with the guys."

"We'll be square," he said. "When we get out of here."

She gave him the look, the one that said she saw right through his line of bullshit.

"You caught me when I fell," he explained, trying to find the right words to explain this. To make it easier for her to accept. He didn't want to trample on that prickly pride of hers but, goddamn it, she'd messed up her ankle bad on that landing and the only way she hiked out was with a helping hand. "You made sure I reached the ground okay when my chute malfunctioned. Now, I'm going to make sure you get back to base okay."

"I don't want your help," she pointed out.

He hadn't wanted hers either, but the alternative had been even grimmer. "You've got it anyhow, like a free gift with purchase."

"I didn't buy anything," she grumbled, but he could see the small smile tugging at the corners of her mouth. Then she stepped on something—loose dirt, a stick or a badger hole—and her face scrunched up in a grimace.

This corner of the National Park wasn't heavily trafficked. He'd spent the first hour of their hike alternating between trying not to hover and gritting his teeth. Gia was prickly. She didn't want his hand beneath her elbow. She didn't want his concern. He was torn between tossing her over his shoulder—although her weight combined with two packs would have been a challenge even for him—and tossing her recalcitrant ass over his knee.

That was a fun fantasy he'd store away for later, but it didn't get him any closer to a solution right now.

The problem was, she needed help and he was the only one here to lend the assist. She was stuck with him whether she liked it or not.

She knew it.

He knew it.

But *she* was still being difficult.

And she probably had a point. He was willing to admit that much to himself. If her name had been Mack or Joey and she'd been a six-foot male with the penis to match, he wouldn't have been hovering by her side. He'd probably have smacked her on the back and told her to suck it up. He'd have watched from the corner of his eye, of course, because having Mack or Joey pass out or permanently cripple their ankle wasn't okay either, but he'd have cut them more slack.

Lost in thought, he almost missed the first oh-shit sign as their day went from bad to worse. PVC piping did not belong in the middle of nowhere. Nor did the empty cans of Campbell's finest. *Shit*. He dropped down fast, taking her with him. His hand clapped over her mouth as he made the Spec Ops sign for silence.

He'd misread the signs. Had thought they were on a game trail.

But fuck. No. Not at all.

He'd jumped into a budding firestorm and Gia had jacked up her ankle.

And now he'd just led them both straight into a drug grow.

It definitely did *not* pay to get out of bed some mornings. He felt Gia stiffen against his chest, but maybe she objected to the unplanned intimacy. His sudden drop had her breasts pressed against his chest and her legs tangled with his. Carefully, he nudged her head until she made eye contact with him and nodded. She was on board with the whole silence mandate.

"We've got a pot grow," he whispered roughly, removing his hand from her mouth. Now that he inhaled, he caught the distinctive smell. That was definitely marijuana up ahead. The earthy, almost incense-y scent was all around them.

She nodded and shifted backward a few inches.

"I'm going to go in," he said, keeping his voice low. "I'll check it out. You stay here."

"Here's another plan," she whispered back, crossing her arms over her chest. "We'll both go. Or, better yet, *neither* of us goes. We mark the coordinates and radio them in to the happy folks at the Park Service."

Over his dead body. He narrowed his eyes and braced his hands on either side of her head. When she rolled left, he was ready for her. He followed easily, keeping her pinned beneath him.

"Grows are dangerous business."

"You have firsthand knowledge of this?" She sounded skeptical.

"You bet." He didn't want to have this conversation now. If their approach had gone unnoticed this long, they might be home free. Keep talking, however, and any alert guard would home in on their location.

"Former military?"

"No." He didn't like the rules, the rigid structure. While Evan and Jack had done their tours of duty with the Marines, Rio had spent those same years working undercover for the DEA and drug enforcement. Alone. In the field. As former covert ops, he'd had a personal introduction to the world of the drug cartel and armed growers. The jungles of South America teemed with the illegal stuff, but drugs crossed the borders easily as well and now illegal drug grows were all too common in U.S. National Parks.

She glared up at him. "That's all you've got for me? One word?"

He gave her three more. "Works for me."

She shook her head. "Donovan, this is a partnership—not a dictatorship. I'm going to need a much better reason than *Because I said so* before I hang back while you skip ahead to check things out."

He forced himself to relax his jaw. "Have you done this before?"

"Sussed out a potential drug grow? No."

"I have." Two words. That should make her happy. "There's going to be someone watching. There always is."

"I can watch your back."

She could, but then who would be watching hers? Instead, he pulled the paycheck card. "But which one of us can run?" he growled low, getting down in her face.

That card worked. She dropped her head back into the ground with an audible thunk. "You win."

She flipped him the bird as he left her tucked in place. He wanted to smile, but that would just be adding fuel to the fire. For the moment, Gia was listening to him, so he needed to leave well enough alone. Five minutes later, he was stepping out of the forest and into marijuana grove. He knew those distinctive leaves, the deep-green buds. With their tufts of fluff. Trees half-screened the clear cut field, but there was no mistaking the dozens of neat rows of marijuana plants with drip irrigation. Steel drums set along the clearing's edge held water. *Shit.* The grow had to be one of the largest he'd uncovered in his years of jumping with Donovan Brothers. Movement on the far side of the clearing announced that the growers were on the scene, ramping up the danger factor another notch.

He took a deep breath and the distinctive musky scent hit him. Wet grass and skunk with an almost citrus edge, there was nothing pleasant about the smell. He had nothing but sympathy for the folks who needed medical marijuana, but a hidden grow deep inside the National Park wasn't meant to take the edge off a chemo treatment. This stuff was destined for the streets.

He'd grown up on those streets.

He'd been one of dozens of kids haunting the dilapidated apartment buildings where social services made sporadic checks with limited resources, probably doing the best they could. Not that those efforts had been enough. By the time he was five, he recognized the smell of weed permeating the hallways. And those had been the good days. When he was six—or maybe seven because, hell, time blurred and no one in his first family had had any desire to celebrate birthdays—he'd moved with his auntie to a crack house. The dirt and filth were the least of it. Skinny bodies piled in corners. Crack pipes. Breakfast, lunch and dinner courtesy of the Wonderbread bag he'd lifted from the local Target because it was steal or starve. He didn't miss it, tried not to remember it.

Until a few years ago, he'd led Spec Ops missions for the U.S. military, going in deep undercover to shut the drug supply off at the source. Walking away from this grow wasn't happening because he knew exactly what would happen when the product left this hillside. Shut down this site and the growers would simply rebuild elsewhere because their pipeline was still in place. The only viable option was taking out the leadership.

He bellycrawled toward the site, evaluating his options. A quick look turned up multiple armed growers, with more likely concealed in the ramshackle shacks dotting the clearing's edges. He'd bet money that there were additional makeshift rooms dug out of ground below his feet and disguised with tarps and foliage. And booby traps in case of uninvited guests.

He dropped back, melting into the undergrowth as a pair of male voices grow closer.

"Fire's on the other side of the ridge, asshole." Guard number one sounded unconcerned, which made him a stupid fuck. Fire always jumped where you least expected it.

"Maybe." The second guy clearly had a few more brain cells to spare. "The Park Service put a plane up."

"They left." The first guard sounded certain, so they were definitely monitoring the airwaves.

Five minutes to recon, because he wasn't leaving Gia alone longer than that. His first pass revealed a dozen out buildings, four visible guards—although he was betting on any hidden number of watchers—and a plant count that translated into a two million dollar bonanza if the plants made it to the street. The surveillance cameras mounted in the trees warned that these guys meant business. If the armed guards didn't pick off uninvited guests, the goons parked in the control room would.

Taking out the two guards was temptingly easy. The problem was: then what? Dropping the men reduced the threat to Gia, but left a telltale sign that someone had spotted the grow and been less than happy with his discovery.

Some days, it sucked to be law abiding. It was also a good thing he didn't have a sniper rifle with him, because he didn't need the temptation of a quick fix. Instead, he slipped out his cell phone and snapped photos, making sure he got each outbuilding and guard station. And each guard he could shoot. When the park rangers arrived, they'd know exactly where to go and what they were facing. The shots wouldn't win the Pulitzer for photography, but the phone did the job and then some. He'd have to wait until he had reception to send anything but, as soon as he did, these growers were out of business.

He waited until the guards disappeared out of earshot on their route and then dropped back. As soon as he'd put some space between him and the grow site, he pulled out the portable radio. All park personnel had a safe word to use if they needed immediate law enforcement backup and the airwaves weren't secure. Since the growers were undoubtedly monitoring the park channels, looking for signs of discovery, it was time to send up the official distress flare.

Jack's voice greeted him over the airwaves, starting with a thundering *Where the fuck are you.*

"Can't talk," Rio said. "But I wanted to let you know that I'll be taking those tickets to the Raiders' game."

"You sure you want those seats?"

"One hundred percent."

"Rio—" Whatever Jack intended to say got lost as the guards

appeared on their return circuit and Rio killed the radio and dropped back to the ground nice and slow.

Boots paused in front of his face.

The guard's radio crackled and man flicked the headset piece. "Come in."

"We've got company." The voice on the airwaves sounded blasé. "You know the drill."

"You sure it's not another goddamned squirrel?" The guard lit a cigarette, clearly in no rush to check out the report. Slowly, carefully, Rio began inching away.

"We got a visual on the camera. Looks like Park Service. Female. She's all tied up, waiting for you."

CHAPTER EIGHT

Rio fell back double-time, racing the guards on ATVs to get back to Gia. He needed to make his few seconds head start count. Mentally, he started the internal countdown that he'd learned on his Spec Ops mission. When he hit zero, he'd be out of time.

Rio sprinted straight up the ridge. The muscles in his thighs burned with each step but stopping wasn't an option. He got to Gia first. It was that simple. He didn't want to imagine what would happen if the growers' muscle got there first. Whatever Gia had done to alert them didn't sound good. She sounded *helpless* and that wasn't a word he'd ever imagined in conjunction with Gia.

When he reached the spot where he'd left her, however, it was clear what had happened. Gia probably hadn't moved much—maybe a few feet to check out the path he'd taken or for a pee break—but it had been enough. She'd tripped a hidden wire and now she hung upside down by her ankle, cursing. Either the growers had a camera on the spot or the wire had a sensor, but now she was on their radar. She'd managed to get her knife free and was curled upward, working on the wire.

Not helpless, but close enough because she couldn't possibly cut fast enough. When he stopped and listened, he could just make out the dull roar of the ATVs headed their way and the primitive response that flooded him shocked him. She was *his*. And she was in danger. He wanted to tear the guards apart with his hands. *Christ.*

He was calm.

In control.

He really, really was. She curled up again, with a little grunt he found endearing. Face flushed, she spun in a small circle as she worked the blade. The move put him face-to-ass with her backside. No complaints from him, because he had great memories of cupping those curves and pulling her to him. *Bad timing, Donovan.*

He didn't have time to cut her down, so he did the next best thing. Moving fast, he swiped her pack from the ground and tossed it into the undergrowth to hide it. They'd need every advantage they could get.

"Hey!" She jabbed an accusing finger in his direction. "You want to lend a hand, Donovan?"

"No time," he grunted, turning towards the trail.

"I need your help." She sounded like the admission was killing her.

Another time, he'd have been happy to gloat. Unfortunately, time was a commodity they were short on and this wasn't about their relationship, whatever that was. Hell if he knew. *Christ.*

"They're coming," he whispered, slicing his finger over his throat in the universal gesture for *cut it out* but she wasn't listening. Which just figured. Nothing about today had gone right.

"Who's coming?" she snarled, muttering curses as she attacked the wire wrapped around her ankle again. He hoped like hell her hands were steady. He didn't need her nicking an artery.

A motor gunned as someone came up the trail.

No, what he *needed* was for her to shut up.

Now.

Palming his utility knife, he sprinted across the clearing.

The muscles in Gia's abs burned as she reached once again for the tripwire snaked around her ankle. The move smacked of the world's worst curl-up, except she didn't need a trainer screaming incentives at her to understand there was plenty on the line here. Worse than the burn in her stomach was the nothing she felt in her ankle. Her ankle should have hurt like hell, so the radio silence likely meant she was in shock. And that, when she *did* feel the pain, that would be all she did. Just in case, she forced herself to look up. At least her ankle was still attached to her leg. That was good. Without her steel-toe, she might not have faired so well.

God. It was going to hurt like a bitch when she got down.

She drew the knife across the wire, but the damned thing remained taut. No give at all. Shit. Her falling into the growers' booby trap was just Exhibit A for the "Gia can't take care of herself" school of thought. She turned her head and looked at Rio.

Who was giving the impression of some Grim Reaper version of a pointer dog. He stood there frozen in place, head at an angle.

"A little help?" she hollered, because she didn't want to ask and none of this should have happened. She was in a pissy mood. She'd own that. If he wanted sweetness and light, he could find himself a new jump partner and, since he cut the damned checks, how hard could that be? He could replace her in a heartbeat—even a heart that beat as fast as hers.

She was fairly certain the grinding noise she heard were her teeth.

"Shut up," he growled and lunged for her.

What. The. Hell.

Big hands cupped her head, dragging her face to his. That was unexpected.

"I don't—" Two words. That was all she got out before his mouth covered hers.

She hadn't seen *that* coming.

His hands pinned her in place for his kiss. She probably could have bucked, used the trip wire's momentum because, God knows, she'd been spinning in nauseating circles for long minutes, but she didn't want to.

No, she wanted Rio.

His mouth sealed over hers, hard and unyielding. His beautiful face was fierce and focused as Rio fixed every inch of his attention on her. *Dear. God.*

She opened her mouth. Not to protest. No, she had no idea why her tall-dark-and-brooding was kissing her, but some things were good and she wouldn't question. Much. Instead, she deepened the kiss, stroking her tongue over his lips and concentrated on not dropping the knife. Accidentally stabbing Rio wasn't in her plans, any more than cutting her down appeared to be in his.

Instead, she concentrated on threading her hands through his short hair, holding him to her. He made another sound, rough and needy. She could work with that. She really, really could, because the masculine noise sent a tsunami of lust through her.

Her hands cupped the back of his neck, angling the blade away from his skin. His skin, silky and hard at the same time, was an erotic treat she had no intention of denying herself. Instead, she ran her hands over his neck and down his shoulders. Rio pulled her toward him hard, his upper body supporting hers and taking the painful weight of the snare for her. He tasted so good, but all she could reach was his mouth. His neck.

More.

He moved, turning them, and she let him maneuver her body because whatever he had in mind, she was so on board with his plans. Just as soon as she got down—unless Rio was into acrobatic sex, which she'd never heard and, God knew, she'd have heard—she wanted him under her. Wanted to take him—

His eyes were open. Which she only knew because her own were open. Hell, the pair of them weren't romantic, but they could work on that too. Or just on the orgasms. That was fine with her. Was that roar the blood in her ears? Because, sweet baby Jesus, Rio made her *feel* things.

His eyes slewed right and she wanted his attention back on her.

An ATV gunned towards them from the undergrowth. *Oh.* This wasn't about sex at all. It was the oldest shut-the-girl-up move in the world.

Rio ripped his mouth away from hers.

"Don't go away," he snapped. "Knife up. Anyone but me comes near you, you punch that blade in his eyes or his gut."

Punch line delivered, he strode towards their unwanted company, leaving her hanging in the air like a birthday piñata.

CHAPTER NINE

Rapidly, Rio weighed options. He doubted the welcoming committee was a coincidence, but he didn't have the proof he needed to justify lethal force. He didn't kill innocent civilians, but no fucking way would he let anyone take Gia Jackson. He calculated how long it would take him to close the space between him and the two ATVs hauling ass towards them. Factored in how many bullets the drivers could pump into him if they were carrying and willing to open fire. He wouldn't be any good to Gia dead.

Snagging a branch from the ground, he pointed his makeshift club at the ATV's driver. Lucky thing for him the bastard hadn't bothered to draw before breeching the clearing—and that made him think the growers had cameras pointed on the trip wire, because the guard's eyes widened almost comically when Rio planted himself in the other man's path.

"She's not alone," Rio snapped.

Then he was moving, following up his advantage, his fists flying even as his steel-toe connected with the driver's groin and knocked the man off the still moving vehicle. He followed with an elbow to the throat, snapping the man's head back with the palm of his other hand. *And... out for the count.*

He removed the man from the ATV—okay, he launched the unconscious body at the second driver because he was working with what he had—and took a second to enjoy the satisfying thump. The second driver was following too hard and fast on his companion's heels and, sure enough, he ran the unlucky bastard over.

The second guard kept right on aiming for them though, clearly unconcerned that he might have injured his co-worker. No, he simply yanked the AR-15 from his shoulder and sighted. Of course. This situation wasn't ending in anything but violence. This wasn't a street mugging where handing over his wallet and cell phone would send the assailant on his way. No, these guys wanted Gia dead because she was the eyewitness to their illegal shit.

Before the gun's muzzle could finish its lazy upward arc, Rio launched himself at the man, straddling the ATV's front and pinning the gun between their bodies. Uncle Sam hadn't trained any fools.

Although the idiot on the ATV hadn't come to that conclusion yet.

"Hands up, dumb ass." The guard stood up on ATV, confidently leveling weapon at Rio like having chambered rounds made him the man in control of the situation. *Mistake.* The bastard should have pointed the weapon at Gia, because then Rio would have had far fewer options. Instead, he now had a personal invitation to move.

Redirect.

"Don't mind if I do." He drove his left hand up, knocking the gun aside. The guard never saw it coming.

Control.

Wrapping his hand around other man's wrist, Rio drove the arm aiming the gun away and down until the muzzle aimed at forest floor.

Attack.

He punched his right hand into the guard's jaw repeatedly. This old dog remembered his tricks. Too bad for grower boy, but Rio was taking Gia out of here and the only people getting hurt today were the bad guys.

Take away.

He twisted the wrist pinned between his fingers. He heard bone snap as the guy's eyes rolled back in his suddenly white face. *Two down.* Dragging the gun strap over the unconscious man's head, he shoved the bastard off the ATV and killed the engine.

And looked up. Gia stared down at him like she'd never seen him before in her life. Which was ridiculous—they'd spent the better part of the summer together and then she'd seen *all* of him that day in her truck. Going Rambo on the guards hadn't been his first choice—it had been his only choice. Surely, she got that. Understood that this violence was for her, because he wasn't letting her get hurt any more on his watch.

She flopped down, like her muscles weren't up to holding her any more. He took a cautious step toward her, pretending he didn't notice when his boot caught one of the downed men in the ribs. No complaint from the fallen, so the guy was still out for the count. Perfect. Gia's short hair was tussled and standing on end. A pink flush stained her cheeks and her chest rose and fell like some kind of fucking hummingbird's wings. Hell. Had he scared her? Because he hadn't known it was possible to scare his tough-as-nails Gia.

He opened his mouth to say something—although he really had no idea what—when the third ATV roared to a halt at the edge of their clearing.

Gia's eyes shot straight to the newcomer just yards away from her. They both knew she was face-to-face with Mr. Death right there.

Hoping like hell the AR-15 had a full cartridge, he flipped off the safety and got his finger on the trigger. "I'm not in the mood for party crashers."

The newcomer's head swiveled toward him—followed by a gun. Which just figured. Nothing about today could possibly be easy. But then the man threw the ATV in reverse and started beating a hasty ass retreat back down the path.

Thanks to the nondescript baseball cap crammed low over the

man's face, Rio couldn't get a good look at the face beneath the visor, although he had a sinking feeling that Gia had. She'd been ringside for this guy's arrival. Otherwise, the man pretty much lacked distinguishing features. A white Caucasian who stood maybe five foot eleven with a solid build and sported a sun-faded L.A. Dodgers T-shirt and faded cargo pants. The army-issue boots could have been a surplus store purchase or a bad, bad sign if someone's military was in play here. In short, there was no fucking way Rio picked this guy out of a line up.

He watched the back of the man's shirt disappearing down the trail and he still had time to pull the trigger. He could get off a shot or several and he'd likely hit his target. But, shit, he'd promised Jack. No more guns. Not unless it was life or death.

And this wasn't life and death.

Not quite.

Not yet.

The third ATV disappeared down the trail, home free.

~~~

Holy. Shit. Gia got busy with her utility knife while Rio's back was still to her. Was he even the same man she'd jumped with just this morning? Because she really didn't recognize this version of Rio. On the outside, he was still hotter than hell, the same sensual, dark-eyed bad boy she'd pretty much attacked in her truck and then again today… but this new Rio 2.0 had a lethal edge she didn't want to tangle with.

Hanging around waiting for Rio to notice her had never seemed like a worse idea. Whatever, whoever Rio Donovan was, Gia realized, he was far more than a brawny M.I.T. programmer. He jogged down the path after the retreating ATV and she did *not* want to think about how comfortably he handled the automatic rifle he'd snagged from one of the growers. He wielded the gun as confidently she did a tooth brush.

The wire snapped.

She hit the ground and not in a graceful landing either—more of a splat-on-her-back plant on the ground. The air whooshed out of her lungs and for a long minute she concentrated on breathing.

Because breathing was important.

Unfortunately, as soon as her brain was satisfied with the oxygen levels in her body, sensation returned to her ankle with a vengeance and it was every bit as bad as she'd feared. Her hands fluttering over the ankle, not sure if pressing down would help or just make her holler. She didn't need an M.D. after her name to know she was absolutely not one hundred percent okay. Running wasn't in her playbook.

Neither, she suspected, was walking.

Damn it.

The universe had terrible timing. Her heartbeat picked up, slamming into overdrive. She took a moment—after all, Rio clearly had matters under control in the fight-to-the-death arena—and let her head hit her knees. Breathed in and out for a count of twenty. Was it just this morning she'd left base camp and boarded the DC-3 for what should have been an adrenaline-pumping typical day at work? Because there was nothing typical about this day so far.

Absolutely nothing.

Rio loomed over and that small shock sent her heart into overtime again. How had she never noticed how silently he moved? Like a big cat. The kind with four-inch canines and a taste for raw meat.

"Hey." He crouched beside her, reaching for her ankle to unwind the wire.

She gestured towards the two men lying motionless on the ground. "They don't teach those kinds of survival skills in smoke jumper training."

Were they dead? She squinted and decided she saw a chest rise and fall. Slightly. If she was being optimistic, which she was. Because she did *not* want to think about how her sensual, playful Rio had morphed into a lean, mean killing machine in the blink of an eye. She'd known that Jack and Evan Donovan were both ex-military, but Rio... that was a surprise.

His eyes didn't move from her face. Was that a hint of a smile she saw there? "Maybe they should."

"You think?" She dropped her head back on the ground, closing her eyes. There really was no point in getting up just yet. "I'll sign up for the remedial course when I get back."

"You did good." He sounded like he meant the words.

She cracked an eye to judge his seriousness. Dirt streaked his formerly white T-shirt, which now sported a rip down the side. His big body radiated tension, the muscles in his forearms flexing as he reached for her. Then stopped. He still looked ready to kill. He also looked like a Navy SEAL or a Green Beret. She'd seen that face on the cover of her favorite romance novels—she just hadn't expected to meet him in the middle of a national park. Over a pile of bodies.

"We need to hit it," he said gently.

"Right behind you." If wishes were horses, she'd do just fine.

"So let's see it." He gestured towards her ankle, while his other hand circled her wrist and found her pulse. Which was banging out of control. She tugged, but he hung on. *Déjà vu*. His lips moved as he counts.

"Everything's going to be fine," he promised finally, setting her wrist back on her thigh.

Great. She opened her mouth to correct him—she wasn't *that* scared—but then realized he'd handed her an out. He thought her too-rapid pulse was because she was frightened and alarmed, about to pull a shrinking maiden hissy fit on him. Which wasn't true, but she'd work with what she had.

It wasn't that she never got scared. Because she did. Imagining the consequences of her PSVT, for example, kept her awake at night more often than she cared to admit. She hadn't told the Donovans about her condition and that was undoubtedly grounds for immediate dismissal from the jump team. Getting fired wasn't her first choice and that possibility scared her.

Being out here in the woods with Rio Donovan didn't. He was a fighter and her partner. She had his back. He had hers. That was how these things worked. Plus, Rio owed her for saving his life and Rio always, always paid his debts.

He reached for her ankle again and she butt-scooted away. No matter how hot he looked fighting, he definitely had some explaining to do before he got his hands anywhere near her.

"Green Beret? Navy SEAL?"

He gave her a small smile. "I did my time."

But he hadn't answered her question. "Is your military status *need to know*? Do you have to finish what these guys started if you tell me?"

He exhaled roughly. "Yes. I've been places, done things for Uncle Sam."

"Infiltration? Covert ops?" Talking took her mind off the vicious throbbing in her ankle, she told herself virtuously. She didn't really have a burning desire to learn exactly where he'd been and what he'd done before he'd arrived in Strong. Of course—she eyed the two bodies on the ground—some things didn't have to be *said*. Rio was all about the show and tell.

"Gia." He pointed at her ankle. "I need to look."

"I think we need to get out of here," she countered. "That guy may come back and bring friends. You can look later."

"I'm looking now," he contradicted. "Suck it up, Jackson."

"There's nothing to see," she said stubbornly. "I'm not a sideshow. You already taped the damned thing and, if you unlace that boot, who knows what happens. You can look later."

Rio being Rio, he insisted on looking, handling her ankle with a careful tenderness she did her best to ignore.

"Still attached," he teased gently before tightening the tape and lacing her boot up tightly. "You're going to want the support."

No, what she *wanted* was a pair of crutches. A wheelchair. Or even a bed with one of those Heavenly Mattresses the mega-star hotel chains boasted about. Instead, she got a ten mile hike through back country on a busted up ankle. Lucky her.

He strode over to the two guards, quickly frisking them for spare ammo clips and snagging their handguns.

She wouldn't ask the question burning on her tongue. Wouldn't ask if they were dead. He'd done what he needed to do to protect them both.

"They're not dead," he said without turning around. She could hear the amusement in his voice as he answered her unasked question. "They might *wish* they were when they wake up, but I'm planning on being far, far away before that happens."

"You're sure?" The words came out and she wanted to face-palm.

"Positive." He straightened and checked the clips on the two handguns he'd lifted. He handled the guns with an easy confidence that bespoke years of practice. He flipped the safety on and then slid the guns into his waistband. "You want one?"

She wasn't sure how to answer that.

When the silence had dragged on and he'd finished his body sweep, he turned to her. "Nothing to say?"

"About?"

He shrugged. "The guns. Want to check the 'dead' guys out for yourself and make sure they haven't bought the farm?"

"You said you didn't kill them."

He shot her a look she couldn't interpret. "And I'm such a good guy that you always believe me."

She shoved up into a crouch and sucked in a breath when her head swam. "You *are* a good guy, Rio."

He strode back and planted himself by her side. "And that's where you're wrong. There's nothing *good* about me."

He was wrong. He was one of the good guys. He'd parachuted

into the heart of countless fires, fighting to preserve their national parks for another generation. To check the fire's advance before it consumed houses or cut off communities. He didn't do it to get rich. He did it because it was the right thing to do and because he had a passion for jumping.

She'd bet his reasons for getting up-close-and-personal with that grow were similar.

"Why did you stop?"

He thrust a hand at her and stood there waiting for her to take it. The shiny pink scar decorating the back of his left hand was a fire scar. They all had them. You took on a wildland fire at close quarters, you came away with more than a few souvenirs.

"Killing them?" He eyed her steadily.

She made a face. "Here. To check out the grow. Why not make a note of the coordinates and keep on hiking?"

When she put her hand in his, he carefully pulled her to her feet and then into his arms, steadying her as she straightened.

"Nice and slow," he said. His arms closed around her, surrounding her with a familiar warm, slightly smoke scent. *Rio*. She put her foot down and, sure enough, the jolt of pain was more than enough to drown out the jolt of lust being this close caused.

"How bad?" His voice rumbles in her ear.

Concerned.

Almost sweet.

"Smoke jumper," she reminded him. "If it's not cut off, I can use it."

"Uh-huh." He sounded skeptical. "What's your policy on really large dangling bits?"

She laughed. "You worried about yours, Donovan?"

Slipping back into jump team camaraderie was almost second nature. She needed that space. A fellow jumper would give her shit about the injury, maybe lend her an arm or an ace bandage. He'd still expect her to pull her weight, however. He wouldn't cut her any slack. That was what she wanted. To be one of the guys, to be equal.

She didn't need or want a lover. Rio might be one hell of a lover—smoking hot with a side of sweet in bed—but the lover wouldn't be as willing to let her shuffle off on a bum foot. She enjoyed that alpha side in bed. Out of bed, however, she was standing on her own two feet.

Or foot.

She eyed the ATV. The key was still in the ignition. "You don't fancy a lift?"

He shook his head. "Not our best option."

"Why not?"

"ATVs are loud, they need gas, and where we're headed, there are no trails wide enough. We take one, we might as well paint a neon 'Come and get us' sign on our asses."

She hated it when he went all logical on her.

Unfortunately, he wasn't done yet.

"You got a good look at our departing friends." A statement, not a question.

"Is that a problem?"

He nudged her gently towards the trail. "You're going to be fine."

"Rio—" Whatever he wasn't telling her, she wanted to know.

"You're the only eye witness," he admitted.

"You kept your eyes shut during that fight?"

He held a branch out of her way. "The guy on the red ATV showed up at the end. He didn't engage and he was behind me. You're the only one who got a good look at him."

The path was too narrow to hike side-by-side. Rio hesitated, then stepped out in front of her. She considered the implications of his words while she fell in behind him. A drug grower's muscle knew she could identify him. She was out in the woods, miles from law enforcement. She had one good foot. She could do the math.

She need to hike faster.

Much, much faster.

CHAPTER TEN

Six miles. That had to be enough, because Gia didn't look capable of more and the sun was going down fast. Not that Gia would admit to any weakness despite the noticeable limp she sported. She was Super Woman and Iron Man rolled into one sexy package. She didn't complain either—except when she believed he was acting *high-handed* and trying to boss her around—but each time he snuck a glance back at her, her face was paler than before. He didn't know if they were on a trail or not and that was another problem. Trails meant company and regular traffic. Which, out here this close to an illegal grow, meant drug traffic.

Which he needed to avoid at all costs.

The handguns tucked into his waistband pressed into his back with each step and he'd slung the AR-15 over his right shoulder. Their combined weight was comforting. If the growers came after them, he was better prepared now. He'd always been a good shot. Handguns, assault rifles, sniper rifles... there wasn't too much he couldn't fire. He'd had his first shooting lesson in a Sacramento alley. The hard way, of course, because he hadn't done anything the easy when he'd been younger. People got shot where he lived, so carrying had seemed like a good idea. For a few years, he'd done so, until Jack had convinced him to leave the guns behind. It was hard to forget those early days, however, when he'd never known who might be coming after him. Afraid to turn his back. Afraid to stand down. The lessons he'd learned on those streets would be keeping Gia safe now, though, so he wouldn't give in to the regrets.

"You can stop looking," she said.

"I'm not."

"You are." She didn't sound mad, just tired.

"Gia?" He really wanted to hear that she was okay.

"Just spit it out," she suggested. "Whatever you're thinking, tell me."

"We're stopping," he decided and that was it.

"Here?"

He eyeballed the small clearing one more time. "Yes."

Gia dropped like a stone to the ground. "Thank God."

He squatted down beside her, close enough that his shoulder brushed hers and he could see that she had dirt on her nose. She carefully stretched her leg out, her hand hovering over the ankle like she didn't know if touching would help or hurt. That was enough for him. He popped his pack open, fishing for his field med kit.

"Next time you need to stop, you tell me. Don't wait." He found the packets of pills and rifled through them. "You got any allergies I should know about?"

"Nope. I'm healthy as a horse. Except for this damned ankle." She closed her eyes and he hoped like hell she wasn't passing out on him. "I'll be fine."

"Liar," he said, almost tenderly. "They shoot horses with bum legs." She needed something stronger than aspirin or Tylenol. Vicodin was just what Dr. Donovan ordered. He tore open the packet and handed her the pill.

"Sweet talker." She took the pill though. "I thought we were in a hurry," she pointed out. "And that you were playing big-man-in-charge."

"We were."

But she also needed to rest. No matter how badly he wanted to cover the twelve miles or so remaining between them and the fire road, Gia had hit her limit for the day. He was fairly certain they'd put enough space between them and the growers to make a rest stop okay. The terrain was certainly rough enough to hide in.

"Change in plan?" She blinked up at him from beneath the ball cap jammed down low over her forehead. Sexy tendrils of hair escaped in a dozen different directions. Her hair curled in the heat. He hadn't known that. Or how the curve of her throat as she leaned her head back on her pack looked both vulnerable and strong. He didn't know how she managed to be both at the same time, although she'd undoubtedly kick his ass if he mentioned any "V" word around her. Virgin. Vulnerable. Those were a definite no fly zone.

Instead, he passed her the canteen and watched to make sure she swallowed. She didn't open her eyes. "What did you give me?"

She trusted him when it counted. He settled in beside her, his shoulder touching hers.

"Vicodin," he said. "Just a small pill. You're going to feel better."

"Is that an order?" He could hear the smile in her voice. Fuck it. He reached his arm around her and pulled her into his side. She didn't protest. Didn't tell him they were jumpers and off-limits. Those things were true, but right now he didn't care.

"Absolutely."

He hooked his pack with his foot and drew it closer.

The day's bad news wasn't over yet.

"We've got a problem," he said.

"Another one?"

"You remember those bullets?"

"It's hard to forget getting shot at. I'm fairly certain I'm going to remember that part of the afternoon for the next ten years at least. Why?"

"We didn't get away clean." He eyed the hole in his pack. He was probably damned lucky he'd been carrying the radio—otherwise he'd be wearing the bullet in his back—but now they were definitely incommunicado.

She jerked up, pushing away from him. "If your ass got shot, I'm going to kill you."

Her hands pulled at him, running over him as she checked out his arms and legs. Gia was no Nurse Florence. And he loved it.

"Gia." He captured her hands in his. "I'm fine."

She frowned.

"Well I know your ass is fine. I've been watching it the last half hour."

Maybe Vicodin made her loopy. That would make the rest of this day interesting. He could pry all her deepest, darkest secrets out of her. Definitely a good plan.

"The radio," he explained, nodding toward his pack, "is toast."

"Appliance casualty. Got it."

She looked unconcerned, which only reaffirmed his assessment of Vicodin's impact on her.

"Not that we could use it," he continued. "Bullet or no bullet, I'm pretty certain those growers are going to be monitoring the airwaves. If we used the radio, we might as well stick a Christmas bow on our asses."

CHAPTER ELEVEN

The night sky in the park was a dark, star-studded bowl. Being so far away from any kind of civilization guaranteed no light pollution, only sky and stars. Even though the fire lay behind them now, the winds pushing the flames in the opposite direction, there was no missing the orange glow on far ridge or the smoky taste to air. Rio drew in a breath and then another. If he thought about the fire line less than a dozen miles to the west, adrenaline pumped through him. He wanted to be out there, fighting shoulder-to-shoulder with his team. Instead, here he was getting ready to camp out in the forest. To go to sleep when there were still miles to cover and line to cut.

He was surprisingly okay with that.

Because he was out here with Gia.

He liked her. He wanted…

Sex.

Sex, and something else. The opportunity to get to know her better, away from base camp and the pressures of the team. Out here, in the dark, they could be themselves, Rio and Gia. She'd made it plenty clear that she wouldn't do anything to jeopardize her spot on the jump team, and he'd already pushed the limits when he'd taken her up on her offer to have sex. With him. In her truck.

He grinned.

Damned if he wasn't going to enjoy that memory for the next twenty or thirty years. Even slouched on the ground, her head tilted back against her pack, she was sex on a stick. He wasn't sure if it was her bold self-confidence, her earthy humor—or those legs. Just to make sure, he started at her feet and worked his way up. Christ, Gia definitely had long, long legs. The Nomex work pants weren't Victoria's Secret and her steel-toes didn't look anything like the hooker stilettos she'd teased them with the other night, but she looked good. He'd had his hands all over her legs—and the rest of her—and that one taste hadn't been enough. He wanted to thread his fingers through her hair and tousle her still more. She always looked like she'd just rolled out of bed—and that was a good look for her.

Gia.

His jump partner.

Who he wasn't supposed to touch.

"You're staring," she said, not opening her eyes.

"How can you tell?"

She snorted. "A woman can always tell, Rio."

She stretched her arms over her head, working out a kink in her back. The move pulled her T-shirt taut over her breasts. Like him, she'd shed her jump suit. Now, with the sun down and the temperatures falling, they might be glad for the extra layers. Or, if the fire changed course.

He wasn't thinking about fire.

Not now.

Because he was fairly certain that was a black bra beneath Gia's pale pink T-shirt. The lacy strap he spotted peeking out from beneath the modest neckline woke up his southern parts. *Be a gentleman*, he reminded himself. Just because he had her out here in the woods alone didn't mean anything was happening between them. In fact, he should absolutely be hands-off. Technically, he was her boss.

Gia loved his orders.

Yeah. *Not* what he needed to remember right now.

"So not only are we stuck here for the night, but we're incommunicado?" Gia's ball cap slid down over her forehead until he couldn't see her face. Unlike him, she looked perfectly relaxed and completely oblivious to the erotic hook-up potential of camping out in the woods for the night.

If he'd been alone, he wouldn't have stopped until he hit the fire road or he fell down a gully, whichever came first. Sometimes, pigheaded stubbornness was its own reward. Maybe, alone, he could have been back on the fire line in time for breakfast and sun up. Or not. She yawned, reaching down to rub her ankle.

"We're done," he decided. "And yeah, we're definitely flying under the radar communications-wise."

"All right." She shoved the cap back and opened her eyes. "What do we have to work with?"

They were definitely short on camping supplies. The jumpers frequently spent a night out in the field, but those were work hours. The plus side of fire was that you always had plenty of light to see where you cut your line. And they'd crash for naps or to take ten. Full blown camping, however, wasn't in the cards and so they weren't supplied for that.

"We've got the Mylar emergency blankets," he admitted. "But give me a few minutes and I'll see what I can do."

"You're going to conjure a tent Hermione Granger-style?" She sat up, clearly ready to jump in and lend a hand whatever his plan was. Her can-do attitude was something else he liked about her. She didn't complain and, once she was on board with a plan, she gave one hundred percent. He brushed her shoulder with his hand.

"You keep an eye on the stuff," he suggested, because if he told her to rest she'd run laps around their impromptu campsite just to prove she could. Which she couldn't. He really didn't want her hurting.

"You're worried about the locals?" Her smile was tired.

"Hey," he said. "If you want to watch our Power Bar supply

disappear with a raccoon, be my guest. But you're the one who's going to have to MacGyver dinner."

Like he'd hoped, she laughed, and settled back, reaching over to snag his pack. Which she promptly propped her ankle on. He wanted to take another look at her injury—although he had no idea what he'd do if it was worse other than curse and worry—but she'd resist. Gia and he had that much in common. Admitting to a weakness or an injury wasn't something they did.

So he left her sitting there and moved off into the nearby trees. He could still make out her shadowed shape if he squinted hard enough. If a mad bear tore through the woods or the growers somehow miraculously caught up with them—which he was betting they wouldn't do until it was light—he could be right there for her. In the meantime, since their campsite was sadly lacking in opportunities to play the white knight, he cut down an armload of pine boughs. The branches were slightly crunchy and definitely on the lumpy side, but they'd keep night damp away and smelled damn good. Probably better than he did because the pines definitely hadn't spent hours slogging through a fire zone.

Circling back to Gia, he dropped the branches by her feet, arranging them into a large mound and then adding the two Mylar emergency blankets. It didn't seem like enough, but it was the best he could do.

"I see we've got reservations at the St. Regis." She grinned up at him, holding up a fistful of Power Bars. "And some raccoon-proof, Michelin-starred cuisine."

He'd refilled their canteens from a stream they'd passed earlier. The water was warm and tasted like the iodine pills he'd used to kill any unwelcome bacterial guests, but wet was better than dry. For long minutes there was nothing but chewing—he was pretty certain that if he checked the expiration dates on the Power Bars he'd find they were past their "good by" date—and swallowing.

"No fire?" she asked eventually.

He shook his head. "We don't need to hang out a welcome sign for the growers."

"We probably shouldn't be setting fires anyhow." She waved a hand towards the orange glow on the ridge. "There's enough in these parts."

She laughed and the happy, husky sound shot straight to his groin. *Hands off*, he reminded himself. Again. The problem was, being out here alone with her in the woods made him focus on the *alone* part. He knew what Jack would tell him to do. Hell, what any of their friends, family or jump team members would say. Well, maybe not their fellow jumpers. He had a feeling Mack and Joey would be all *go for it*.

"You think we'll have pursuers?"

And there went the happiness in her voice. Reality check.

"It's likely," he said gruffly. "Two million bucks worth of pot plants and two eye witnesses? The way I see it, we're worth a million each."

He didn't want to see her gunned down. He'd witnessed a few street shootings growing up, both of drug dealers and of innocent bystanders. He wasn't sure which was worse—knowing the dead man had chosen to squander his life for a handful of dollars and the opportunity to rule a block of urban turf or that the dead man had simply picked the wrong sidewalk at the wrong time and walked into a bullet. Dead was dead.

"Maybe I should trade you in," she mused.

"I run faster," he pointed out. "We'll sit tight until sun up and then we'll move fast." He laid out the plan. If she had objections, he wanted to hear them now. "And we'll take turns keeping watch tonight. I don't think anyone's catching up with us in the dark—and I didn't see or hear dogs—but I don't want to take the chance."

"Got it."

"So one of us should turn in now." Christ. Did she feel as awkward as he did? He didn't want her worrying about their sleeping arrangements, so he twitched his

Mylar bag to the far side of the pine bough bed and piled their packs in the middle for good measure.

"Wow," she said. "Someone's afraid for his virtue."

Before he could rethink his action plan, he took his spot on their impromptu bed. He had two feet and forty pounds of gear between him and temptation. Surely, that was enough.

"I'm your boss," he said and he could have sworn that she growled. "I don't want you to think—"

"What?" she interrupted. "That you wanted a repeat of what happened in my truck?"

"You said you didn't want anything to change the team," he pointed out.

"Right. Because sex changes everything. Bad sex maybe," she said and gave him a sweet smile that had him backing up a step. She had her pissed off on all right. "But would you say we had bad sex, Rio?"

Danger. Flash fire ahead.

"There's a chance someone on the team finds out," he said carefully. "Jack already suspects."

"And we wouldn't want to take a chance," she said sarcastically. "That would be too fucking bad."

Jesus Christ. He was too tired for this. When had their conversation taken a 180?

"Don't worry," she continued, "I promise not to cross this Great Wall of China you've constructed and assault you in your sleep. Hands off. Message received."

"Gia—" he growled, frustrated. He had pine branches poking him in the ass and a dinner that tasted like week-old sawdust in his stomach. He didn't need her gunning for him as well.

"In fact," she continued, "why don't I take first watch? You can catch up on your beauty sleep, *Mr. Donovan*."

"I don't want to be your boss," he growled. "I didn't ask for this attraction."

"Well neither did I," she snapped.

"You're the one who acted on it first," he pointed out. If he ignored their late night kiss action—which he had initiated, if he was being fair—she'd come on to him. Pulled *him* into her truck and had her way with him.

God, he wanted her to do it again.

Her eyes flashed. "It takes two and I didn't hear you complaining. It's a little late for morning after regrets. Plus, *you* kissed *me* first, so that counts for something."

"I'm going to bed," he said, before he said something he regretted even more. He set the borrowed guns beside him on the ground where he'd be able to grab them quickly if he had to. "Wake me in two hours."

He set his watch anyhow because he didn't trust her not to let him sleep on, probably just to prove some convoluted idea she had in her head about how she was independent and could do everything on her own. Christ. Would it kill her to accept a helping hand once in a while?

You don't like asking for help, a little voice in his head said as he laid down and dragged the Mylar around his shoulders.

Ironic, that she was more scared of opening up to Rio than she was of facing down twenty feet of flame.

Or going ass over tea kettle out of a plane bay four thousand feet above the ground.

It was true though.

Gia's ankle throbbed, reminding her that Vicodin, like so many things, didn't last forever. She didn't want to take anything while she was on watch though. Two hours. One hundred twenty minutes. Which was… she had no idea how many seconds. She'd take them one by one and the pill at the end could be her reward. Since Rio didn't seem interested in a repeat of their earlier encounter.

She alternated between scanning the dark woods and watching Rio sleep. He slept like he did everything, neat and tidy. She hadn't missed how he liked everything put away and in its place. Maybe it was his military training. Maybe it was just him. He lay on his stomach, his right arm pillowing his forehead, his face turned away from her. His left arm was free to reach the small arsenal he'd parked by his bedside.

Hell.

He was relaxed and she was tense. Sometimes life wasn't fair.

She'd known that for years though. Her PSVT was a big serving of unfair, but she'd also had plenty of good things happen to her unexpectedly and undeservedly. Rio was one of those things. She certainly hadn't done anything to earn her taste of him or his bone-deep loyalty. He'd stuck by her today, far beyond the call of duty. She thought about that and counted stars. Stared at Rio's gorgeous face some more because she loved looking at him and what he didn't know couldn't hurt him.

As the night wore on, the temperature dropped steadily—as it always did at night in the woods—and she tucked her hands beneath her armpits. Funny how there could be a fire burning so close and yet here they were, freezing.

Rio would have changed that if he could. He was all about the protect and defend. She eyed the handgun by her side. The safety was on, but one quick flick of her thumb and that would change. She knew how to fire a gun. Anyone who worked the backwoods in a national park learned how to shoot a rifle. While the odds of a bear attack were low, being prepared made those odds even better.

Rio, however, had taken on their attackers like a trained pro. Which he was, if she thought about it. She was the only member of the jump team without a military background but, even so, there was far more to Rio than met the eye. She'd watched him all summer, drinking in the playboy smiles and laughter. He gave good game and she'd wondered if maybe that was all there was to him, good looks and sensual charm. She'd been okay with that, too, which made her feel shallow now.

Her heart was at serious risk.

CHAPTER TWELVE

A stick cracked. A raccoon wandering by, looking for a late night snack. That was all the sudden noise was. Gia was almost certain. Almost. Automatically, she swept her hand over the ground beside her, raising the handgun in the direction of the noise. She kept her thumb on the safety but she was ready. Just in case the cause of the noise had two legs and not four.

Beside her, Rio sat up smoothly like he hadn't been dead asleep just seconds ago, his left hand palming a gun as he kicked away the sleeping bag soundlessly. Flowing to his feet, he pressed two fingers against her lips in the universal gesture for silence. No worries. She had no intention of hollering a welcome if they had unexpected company.

He obviously assumed she was good with his sit-and-wait strategy because he promptly scanned the trees and then disappeared into the woods, gun out in front of him. Following him meant running the risk he'd accidentally open fire on her, not knowing she was on his tail. Plus, her ankle hadn't miraculously improved after a couple hours of rest and it would take her at least five minutes to work her boots back on. She wasn't stupid. She'd stay put, even if it was tempting to shoot his ass when he returned.

She stared at the shadowy patch of trees where he'd disappeared.

It was darker than hell out here. The full moon helped some, lighting up their small clearing and the surrounding trees. The smoke from the wildland fire, however, cut down on the amount of available light as the wind shifted again, casting a pall over what had been a clear night sky.

She didn't see him come back. One minute she was alone, and the next he was standing a few yards behind her, his face expressionless. He looked at her and she had no idea what he was thinking. She knew what her body was thinking however: Welcome home. Parts of her were really, really glad to see him.

"We're clear," was all he said.

"I should shoot you," she said. "Just so we're clear."

"Really? Why?" He didn't seem concerned. Maybe it was because she'd never taken the safety off the gun or maybe it was the business end of the gun pointing a careful forty-five degrees west of him. He came towards her and tonight he definitely earned a ten on the sexy scale. He was so big and in control—and on edge. There might not be anyone out there now, but he'd wondered. He'd thought an attack was a possibility and he'd reacted accordingly. She had no problem imagining him moving through some South American jungle in military camo.

Playing the little woman and hanging back while he checked out the scary noise still didn't sit well with her, but she could admit that he had the skills and the experience in that arena that she lacked. She liked being in charge. Or, okay, she *insisted* on it. Her PSVT had taught her that much. Control what she could. Live with the rest of it.

Rio was a whole other kind of brave.

He was the kind of brave she wished, in her heart, she could be. Genuinely fearless. He did whatever needed doing and he didn't hesitate. Like tonight. He'd grabbed a gun and stalked off towards the trees. Someone had to go, so he did. No questions asked, no hesitation. She had a feeling she would have thought first when faced with that first step into the dark woods.

"Nobody calling?" she asked.

He grinned down at her, standing beside her sleeping bag like some kind of conquering hero. "Wood rat. I think. It turned tail and ran."

He gave the woods one final scan, however, so she wondered if he was one hundred percent sure or just telling her what she needed to hear. Which would be so like him.

"Not my favorite animal," she agreed, "but probably better than the alternative."

He hesitated, then dropped back down on their makeshift pallet. "You should get some sleep."

"Not yet." She exhaled. "You're sure we're alone?"

He nodded. "There's no one else out there. And, if there were, they'd have moved in by now. The growers don't gain any advantage by waiting until morning. For all they know, we've already radioed in our coordinates and the park rangers are en route."

"Are they?" Color her optimistic, but she'd rather trained professionals dealt with those armed guards. She wasn't stupid, but she was definitely out of her league there. Unfortunately, Rio was already shaking his head, ringing the death knell for those hopes.

"I doubt it. I raised Jack on the radio and gave him the code word."

She nodded. So far, so good.

"Unfortunately, the guards interrupted me at that point, so I had to sign off. He's got the coordinates for the grow, but we're no longer there. If and when law enforcement reaches the site—and I'm betting that will take a while because not only is there a wildland fire blocking access to many of the roads, but the terrain is damned rough—they're not going to find much. The growers will dismantle the site and move on."

"And?" She could hear the unspoken word tacked on to the end of his sentence.

"And we're the only ones who can tie faces to said grow."

He didn't have to say more.

"So if they're not too concerned about sticking to the letter of the law, they just might be hightailing it after us to take care of that particular problem."

Rio shrugged, like being chased by armed assailants through a national forest was just part of a day's work. Maybe it was for him.

She shivered and he misread the reason.

"Cold?" He sank down on the pallet and opened his arms.

She had no problem taking advantage of him. After all, she'd already done it once. She didn't think twice before she crawled into his arms. He was every bit as warm and solid as she remembered. She liked to think that no one and nothing was getting through Rio. Bear, thug or wood rat—she was safe. Laying her cheek on his chest, she savored the feel of his cotton T-shirt and the warmth of his skin beneath that thin layer. Thanks to the flannel shirt he'd snagged from his pack but hadn't bothered buttoning, his broad chest had plenty of room for her. She dug in and relaxed.

His hand cupped the back of her head, massaging her neck. That felt so good she had to moan. Just a little. He didn't say anything, just dug in to the knots, working them out. He had magic hands, but she'd already known that.

"You should try to get some sleep," he said softly.

"I'm not tired." Or she was too tired. He could take his pick. Her mind was going sixty, unable to turn off the day's images. "Besides, you might want the company. Just in case the wood rat pays us a return visit."

She liked to think they made a good team.

"I could lie here, watching you." He sounded absolutely serious.

"You'd get real bored real fast," she teased.

"Never," he said and she let it go. She didn't want to win that battle anyhow.

"You, me and the fire." She leaned into his touch.

"You think it's going to get worse tomorrow?"

"We've got strong surface pressure forcing the winds through the canyons. Add in low humidity and," she shrugged, "voilà. Escalating fire danger."

"Wow." He hadn't expected that.

Gia grimaced. "You didn't want to hear that. Sorry. Too long in grad school."

Part of him wanted to smile. The part that wasn't seizing up in his chest. "Don't apologize for getting an education. Ever. You worked hard for that knowledge."

Her self-confidence was sexy as hell even—if he was being completely honest—he didn't always understand what she was saying. He got the gist though. In layman's terms, the weather sucked and they ran the risk of a bigger, badder fire chasing them through the woods.

She murmured something and, while he didn't catch the words, he understood the sentiment.

He tipped her head back, his fingers cupping her chin. "You worked hard for that degree. I'm proud of you."

"Six months," she said. She didn't move away from his touch. "I won't have my PhD before the end of January."

She'd leave at the end of fire season, go back to Davis and her classes and whatever else it was she did there. He was used to jumpers coming and going, and what his guys did in the off-season was their business. He supposed he hadn't thought about Gia riding off into the sunset quite the same way. She'd go and he wouldn't see her again, unless he made the trip out to Davis. That would be weekend work, though, since Davis was several hours from Strong. Plus, he doubted she stuck around after she actually had the degree. There must be some PhD-y thing for her to do elsewhere.

"What then? You read the weather on the evening news?"

He kind of liked that idea. He could see her, even if it was on his flat screen. Whatever reasons drove her to jump, brought her out here in the field where the working conditions were brutal and the money shit, she probably had other plans for her future. He'd stay, because Donovan Brothers was his life and he and his brothers had built the business from the ground up. He had a good thing and knocking down fire was important.

She punched him in the shoulder.

"What was that for?"

He removed his hand from her person and stared at her.

She stared right back, arms crossed over her chest. "I'm not the weatherman."

"Okay." Agreement seemed like the safest course of action. "I've just heard it mentioned," he pointed out. "A time or two."

She snorted. "Try one or two hundred times."

"You don't want to do that. Read the weather on TV."

She shook her head. "Absolutely not."

"I wouldn't either," he admitted and she laughed. The mental image of him all suited up and staring at a teleprompter while he mimed the week's weather was pretty funny.

"You've got the face for it." She grinned at him.

"But not the PhD."

She shrugged. "It's hardly obligatory. You went to school, right?"

Fucking bastard. Come on over here so I can teach you a lesson.

Yeah. That particular temporary stepdad had been big on educating Rio with his fists. Or the belt. Whatever the man could find. Rio had spent most of *his* time making sure he was out of arms reach. Funny how the bruises faded, but the words stuck to him.

"MIT," he said, because now she was staring at him.

She whistled. "Impressive."

"I didn't like my options. And Uncle Sam picked up the tab."

In retrospect, it had been lucky. He'd left home as soon as he could and had met up with Evan and Jack. Together the three of them had been Lost Boy wanna-bes, carving out a life for themselves, first on the Sacramento streets and then south in San Francisco. Beachfront real estate, Jack had announced the first night they'd camped on the beach fronting the Pacific Ocean. The strip of sand was a long, thin piece of wild fringing a wilder, rougher city. They'd had hotdogs, sleeping bags, and a mindless determination to *not* go home.

Rio was the one to push his brothers to get themselves an education. Knowledge was power and he wouldn't be someone's punching bag again. Even as a ten year-old boy, he'd known that hitting back might stop the beatings short-term, but that forced you down a violent path that couldn't end well. He didn't want to see the inside of San Quentin.

"I grew up rough."

The woods were too dark to see her face clearly. She didn't shove away or act surprised, so the Strong grapevine had probably done its job. He didn't want her sympathy. He wasn't that on-the-skids boy anymore.

She rested her head against his chest, her fingers pressed against his heart. He breathed in and she smelled just as good as she had that first afternoon in her truck. Sweet and citrus and something that was simply, wonderfully Gia.

"Uncle Sam, huh?"

Her fingers traced a circle over his shirt.

"Nonna gave me my second chance. Uncle Sam was my third."

"Did you need it?" She tilted her head back against his shoulder, looking up at him.

"What?"

"After you moved to Strong, did you screw up? Did you need that third chance?"

He shook his head. "I had a hell of a lot to make up for. I wasn't an angel and I got up to plenty before Strong."

"You were a child."

"I knew better." Some rules were black and white. He'd fucked up, so he'd paid back. No matter how desperate or well-intentioned or just plain stupid he'd been, he'd broken those rules. He'd stolen stuff. He'd run, both his mouth and his legs. He didn't like that kid and he sure as hell wouldn't be him now. "And you think too much." He rolled her beneath him. Apparently they really were alone out here.

"So make me stop, Rio." She stared up at him with eyes full of feminine challenge. "You want me to shut up and stop thinking, then you do something about it. Tell me what you want from me. *Show me.*"

The knowing smile curling her lips was pure trouble.

"You're playing with fire, baby," he growled and drew her towards him.

Oh, she was.

She definitely, definitely was.

It had been far too long since she'd had her way with Rio in her truck and she'd missed this. His face was fierce, his eyes intent on hers as he closed his hands around her shoulders and tugged. She toppled into him willingly. It was like facing down the best kind of predator. He was beautiful, although she'd bet he'd cut off a leg rather than use that word. Guys were funny that way.

She looked at him or he looked at her. That was all it took. She forgot about arguing or worrying about who was in charge. Because, if she was being honest, her body was. The zing of heat looking at him generated low in her belly exploded into a wildfire of lust as soon as he had her body pressed up against his. Full-body contact, oh the sweet perfection. Her thighs rubbed against his hard, Nomex-clad ones and her nipples did a little happy-to-see-you thing of their own when she landed against his chest.

Then he kissed her and her brain shut down, her body coming alive as he slanted his mouth over hers in a take-no-prisoners action. *Please don't let him stop.* He groaned, a harsh, masculine sound. *Good sign.*

She slid her hands up his back, tracing the muscles through the cotton, enjoying the smooth bunch and release as he lowered himself onto her. Her hips cradled his, her legs wrapped around his ass and his penis tucked against her mound. She rocked appreciatively and he groaned.

"Gia." That was all. One harsh, desperate word as he lifted his mouth from hers.

It didn't matter. She wasn't done with him yet.

"Come back." She pulled at his shoulders, making her point. Placing him where she wanted him. "Right here."

He groaned, but he did as she said. *Perfect.* Rio Donovan taking orders was the sexiest thing she'd ever seen. Was that how he felt, when he gave orders and she followed? If so, damn... she needed to rethink her no-taking-orders policy. Starting now.

He came down on top of her and that was good too. If she opened her eyes, his face and shoulders filled up her vision. Otherwise, it was just the night sky, the stars, and the two of them.

He distracted her by kissing her, his mouth moving over hers until all she saw was him.

Eventually, he lifted his head.

"Is that what you wanted?"

It was a start.

"What happens if I say no?"

She loved how his eyes darkened with passion. "Then I'd have to try something else. Like this."

He slid his hands beneath the hem of her T-shirt and pushed up until he was cupping her cotton-covered breast. She wasn't a peek-a-boo lace kind of girl and a forest fire was no place for La Perla but she wished... she wished she could knock his socks off. Be more than a one night quickie in the woods. When she and Rio walked away from each other at the end of the summer, she wanted him to remember her.

"Gia?"

He stroked a thumb over her nipple and she arched into his touch.

"I think you like this." The rough satisfaction in his voice just made her wetter, because there was no missing that the raw hunger on his face. For her. She might not be sporting satin and lace, but he was *looking* and she was pretty certain he liked what he saw. He looked at her like she was an all-you-can-eat buffet and he was a starving man.

Her own hands get busy beneath his shirt, skimming up his chest. The man had fantastic abs. She shoved the cotton up and he laughed, the warm, low sound that she loved.

"You're greedy." He didn't sound like he minded. Instead, he leaned up so all those delicious ridges bunch and tighten. Yep. Definitely a lucky woman tonight.

"Equal opportunity. Off," she demanded, tugging, and he pulled the shirt over his head in one, smooth move. Holy. Smokes.

"My turn." She wriggled and he pulled, and then he had her pants and panties off, carefully working the fabric over her ankle.

He tucked them inside his sleeping bag. "You can have them back tomorrow."

Again. *So* on board with that plan.

She shifted, landing on a stick and mumbled. He must have heard, because he rolled and pulled her on top of him. Ooh. Cowgirl style.

"Ride 'em, cowboy." She grinned down at him.

She expected him to pull her down on him—his erection was nudging her in all the best spots and damned if she wasn't ready—but instead he pulled her forward. To her eternal embarrassment, she shrieked.

"Shhh," he whispers against her folds. "We're figuring out what you like here."

Off-balance, she slapped her hands on the ground on either side of his head and tried to find her footing. Something to hang on to. Anything. Thank God it was dark because he could see *everything*. She'd been out in the woods fighting fire, for God's sake. She certainly hadn't planned for this.

"You're beautiful." Two words that meant so much. "Absolutely perfect," he promised.

So. Okay.

She relaxed just a little, letting his hands cup and hold her ass. Then he leaned up and licked her. *Holy. Jesus.* He did it again and she forgot all about the embarrassment, losing herself in the sweet, hot pleasure spearing through her.

"Gia?" She felt his question right there, where the sensation coiled and she was so, so close to coming apart. "You definitely like this."

"If you stop," she said, her voice rough and husky, "I'm going to kill you. Just saying."

He laughed. "You're in charge."

"Tell me you have a condom."

He grinned. "Part of every good survival kit, although I was hoping to use it for something other than carrying water. If you'll let me."

"You bet." She leaned into him and he kissed her again, his tongue exploring her folds in the most delicious way and she didn't care. When he had her right on the edge, whimpering and hollering, he slid her down his body and kept right on going. There was a brief pause while he rolled on a condom but she didn't mind because his fingers were busy stroking her.

"Fast or slow?" he growled and, God, both ways worked for her.

The broad tip of him pushed against her entrance and she made up her mind. "Fast," she growled right back, sinking down onto him. Curling her fingers into his shoulder and hanging on because the orgasm train was speeding her way, the sweet, tight pressure taking her closer and closer to that edge of no return until she barreled over and he followed her.

"Shit." Rio pulled back, lifting Gia off him.

She blinked up at him. "That move's guaranteed to *not* win a girl's heart."

She got the message that they were done though, sitting up and crossing her arms over her chest. Plus, she got the cutest pouty expression on her face, like she'd been denied a treat she really, really wanted. *Him.* That made him want to smile. Fist pump. Go all caveman and thump his chest, because his prickly, snarky Gia wanted him and was okay with letting him know. Still, if he hadn't just caused a fuck-up of epic proportions, he'd have enjoyed teasing her about that look.

"Condom," he muttered, because he owed her the truth. "Hell. The condom broke."

"Oh." She chewed her lip and eyed his dick for far too long. Despite the rude exit and ruder shock of the latex snapping, parts of him were clearly more than ready to offer her a repeat.

Reaching out, she stroked a finger down the length of him. "You're sure?"

Unfortunately, he was.

"The condom broke," he repeated as he rolled the offender up and off. He eyed the remnants, but a second look only confirmed what he'd felt and seen the first time. He had a malfunction of epic proportions.

"Okay." She curled into him, making his good intentions—and other parts—harder to keep. Sitting upright like a medieval virgin all hands-off on her wedding night wasn't his MO, so he slid an arm around her and pulled her into his side.

That felt good too. Not as good as being deep inside her—that was the closest a male like him would ever get to heaven—but pretty damned fine. He liked holding her.

"Okay?" Maybe she hadn't heard him. Because she was the one who'd been so concerned about not screwing up her place on the jump team—and a pregnancy would definitely put an end to that.

She patted him on the arm. *Jesus Christ.* "One broken condom doesn't a pregnancy make. We're probably fine. Fifty-fifty odds."

She sounded matter-of-fact, while he? He wanted to punch something. Go for a ten mile run. Climb a cliff bare-handed. Anything to get moving, because he suddenly felt like he was suffocating. Worse, this was his fault. That had been his condom and his job.

And he'd failed.

Spectacularly.

He'd been—as his teenage mother had emphasized repeatedly—the result of an unplanned pregnancy. The words *condom* and *birth control* had not been part of his mother's vocabulary. She'd made a half-hearted stab at parenting him, which was more than his father had done. The man had been a name on Rio's birth certificate and nothing more.

That cold dose of reality deflated him on the spot. *Great.* Now she'd think he had a performance issue to go with the hardware issue.

"Rio?" She twisted to get a better view of his face. *Busted.*

He dropped onto his back and covered his face with his arm. Christ. Maybe he could fall down a hill or get overrun by fire. Anything as long as it didn't involve him being here.

"Are you okay?" She rubbed her hand over his chest. It was probably a good sign she hadn't run screaming into the woods. Or threatened to shoot his ass. After all, he'd armed her.

"I'm fine." He exhaled roughly. *Man up.* "How about you?"

She blinked. "I'm fine."

When he placed his hand on her belly, he nearly lost it. Her skin was taut and firm, but imagining a mini-Gia tucked inside those curves wreaked havoc with his equilibrium. He was never careless. Ever. And yet now the possibility was here. Inches from his palm.

"It's just a possibility," she said, as if she'd read his mind. "And probably a remote one. Right now, I'm more worried about getting out of these woods without taking a bullet in my back, okay?"

"Where are you in your cycle?" There were better and worse times for getting pregnant, right? Maybe they'd win the fertility lottery and the broken condom wouldn't matter.

"Rio." She sounded amused. And very, very not serious.

"Tell me."

She thought for a minute. "I had my period about two weeks ago, okay?"

Well. Shit. He was fairly certain that made tonight the worst *possible* timing.

"If there's a baby," he began roughly, because some things had to be said, "I'm going to be there for the two of you."

There was nothing he could do to fix this mistake right now, other than get Gia out of the woods and to safety. When he got her back to Strong, then he could do something.

"Got it," she murmured, her lashes drifting down. Between the Vicodin-fueled hike and his ill-timed seduction, he'd worn her out. Her sleepiness bought him the temporary reprieve he wanted. In seconds, she was down and out for the count.

His turn to watch the woods.

Cradling Gia against his chest, he stared into the dark. The dark was nothing new. As a kid, he'd spent plenty of nights curled up, listening for unfriendly footsteps. He'd slept in all sorts of places, avoided all kinds of trouble.

But avoiding a baby? If it came to it, that was a line he wouldn't cross. Somehow, he'd figure out how to make it work even if he was best at moving on. *You're nothing, boy.* Stepfather number three's daily line. Along with *Get your ass over here now* and *Don't make me come over there.* Which had usually been his cue to run until, one day, he'd just kept on running and hadn't ever come back.

He knew running away from home usually didn't work out well for the kids involved. Evan had mentioned wanting to get involved in a charity project for runaways, a group that ran a safe home, and that seemed like a good idea. Most kids didn't end up with Nonna Donovans. Instead, they slept in parks and in bus shelters, hoping they avoided the pimps and the violence. He'd been damned lucky.

All that running had taught him was how to go faster and further. He didn't know a damned thing about sticking things out. About being a father and a partner. And there were worse things than leaving. What if he stayed out and *then* he screwed it up? Words could cut worse than fists.

He ran a hand down Gia's back, savoring the gentle rise and fall.

Tomorrow.

They'd talk tomorrow.

CHAPTER THIRTEEN

Gia woke up with sticks poking her in unmentionable places and a stone-cold ass, but her front was toasty warm. The heat was because she was plastered against a warm male body. *Rio.* Her brain was happy to auto-rewind and re-play last night. She and Rio had had sex. Sex that was sure to figure prominently in her fantasies for years to come—except for that moment when the condom had broken.

Well, shoot.

Broken condoms were no guaranty of pregnancy, but she'd have been a whole lot happier if they'd finished the act without that particular twist. Rio's concern had been sweet and more than a little frantic. Since he wasn't the one who'd have to carry a baby around for nine months—and that was just for starters—she had more to worry about than he did.

She wasn't thinking about this. Not today. She already had a long list of problems demanding attention. Potential baby could take a number and get in the queue.

Rio ran a hand down over her hair, interrupting her thoughts.

"We need to get going," he said quietly. "Five minutes, okay? Do what you need to do, we'll check your ankle and then we'll move out."

She took that as her cue to head into the bushes because there were some things she wasn't doing in front of him. The air was still dark, but tinged with that lighter grey color that came right before sunrise. She did a mental inventory and discovered a very personal twinge deep inside where Rio had been, plus a large collection of bruises from her slide downhill. But her ankle… clearly, an overnight rest hadn't been enough. No such luck. A throb of pain warned that forcing her foot back inside the boot was a bad idea, so she settled for lurching to her feet. Socks it was for her visit to the bushes.

When she limped her way back, Rio was waiting for her. He handed her a Power bar while he packed up their campsite, disassembling their impromptu bed and erasing any trace of their presence.

"So," he said and she'd had no idea such a small word could pack a world of meaning. "Your ankle isn't better."

It wasn't worse. By much. "I'll be fine."

He raised an eyebrow. "Color me unconvinced. Can you even lace that boot?"

She eyed the boot she'd just snagged from the ground. She probably *could*. She just didn't *want* to. Somehow, though, she thought that distinction would be lost on Rio.

"I didn't sprout wings during the night. Hiking out is my only option. That, or staying put while you go for help."

Staying out here alone in the woods wasn't her first choice, but it was logical. She could hide and loneliness wouldn't kill her.

Rio, however, was already shaking his head. His complete authority should have bothered her, but this time she was in agreement with him. She'd give him a pass. "I hiked up to the ridge. The wind shifted last night and the fire's headed back this way. Staying put definitely isn't an option.

She slid her foot into the boot and reached for the laces. "So I hike."

He reached out a hand and covered hers, tugging the laces away, his fingers warm and reassuring as he took over the job. Usually, she would have batted his hand away because she could take care of herself. This time, however, it felt good to let him... Let him whatever. This was just about her bootlaces. She wasn't waving the white flag on any other aspect of her life.

He loosely laced the boot, just enough to keep the thing from falling off her foot. Then he looked up at her. Sexy determination was a good look for him. She could feel her face flushing.

He grinned. "I'm going to carry you. We'll leave the packs here, well hidden, and I'll come back for them later."

Gia gave him a look that told him all too clearly what she thought of his plan. Even if she was blushing and he had to wonder what thoughts had put that color in her face.

Then she put the look into words.

"You're crazy."

"No," he countered. "Staying here is crazy, as is wrecking your ankle to make a point. Goddamn it, Gia, let me help you."

They were already burning daylight. The rising sun filtered through the smoky pall, creating one hell of an orange and gold sunrise. Color banded the sky where the early morning light hit the smoke, but there was still a layer of pale blue above all the rest.

He pulled on his jumpsuit, tying it around his waist. It was time to get Gia out of the woods and back to base. That was what he needed to focus on—not last night or how sexy she looked, glaring up at him. Forcing his mind away from his memories—and he had a feeling last night would be one of his favorite fantasies for a long, long time—he turned his attention to their packs. The two handguns were definite keepers. The semi-automatic would have to go, because he couldn't carry both the weapon and Gia. He'd take the clip, though, and mark the spot for a return trip. Even without ammo, leaving a weapon behind went against the grain. He didn't want it falling into the wrong hands.

He sorted rapidly through the packs, keeping food, water and the bare essentials for the day. Gia continued to stare at him.

"You're going to carry me eight miles, give or take, through rugged terrain," she finally said.

She sounded skeptical, but, he noted, she hadn't said no. Or *over my dead body*. Clearly, she was thinking about it.

He shot her an apologetic grin. "Actually, I was thinking piggyback."

She shook her head. "Glamorous, Donovan."

They were back to last name basis. That was fine. He didn't care what she called him and if using his last name made her feel better about hitching a ride on his back, that worked for him. He'd still be touching her. Holding her.

And getting her to safety.

She nodded, like they'd agreed on something, and shoved carefully to her feet. He kept an eye on her, when he really wanted to lend her a hand. He wasn't stupid, though. While he finished up with the packs, she pulled on her jumpsuit, following his lead and getting ready to move out. The warmth building inside him had nothing to do with the fire creeping closer or the rising sun. No, that heat had everything to do with Gia herself. Maybe she did trust him. He might have screwed up big time last night, but this he could do.

While he thought that over, he grabbed the packs and strode off into the woods. He'd hide their stuff and come back for it later, because he couldn't afford the extra weight now. Gia was hardly a large person, but she still weighed substantially more than a pack and he didn't kid himself. Today's hike would be hard going.

A little quick spotting and he found a likely candidate, a deeper depression beneath a gangly pine. Dropping the packs into the hollow, he carefully shifted a pile of branches over the spot. That was the best he could do. He didn't think the growers had any backwoods specialists in their ranks, but it didn't hurt to be too careful. Plus, if their pursuers did find the packs, they'd start to wonder why the jumpers had abandoned them—and they'd find the busted up radio, which would add a whole new level of urgency to their search. They'd know that Rio hadn't been able to broadcast much information if any. Stop them now and maybe the whole thing went away.

That was a whole new level of trouble right there.

When he returned to their campsite, Gia was waiting for him. On her feet. The tilt of her chin warned him she planned on being stubborn. He could out-stubborn her, though, so this would be interesting.

"Look," she said. "I can walk."

Maybe she wasn't reconciled to the idea of him carrying her out.

"Probably." He didn't like the faint lines of pain carved around her mouth and he wasn't letting her hurt herself just to prove a point. "The real question, however, is how *fast* can you walk?"

She bit her lip. Point to him.

Turning, he gave her his back and slapped a hand on his shoulder. "Climb on, Jackson."

"Shit," she mumbled.

But she came closer. Again, point to him.

Her hands closed over his shoulders. Her fingers were sun-tanned, the nails short and buffed nails because the woods was no place for polish or length. Still, her hands were graceful and unmistakably feminine. He loved the way she married practicality with femininity.

He held out a hand behind him. "Mount up."

She slapped a booted foot into his palm. Her good foot, he noted. He boosted and she swung up and just like that she was pressed against his back. And, hell. They had to try this again when they weren't hiking for their lives in the woods, because she felt fantastic. Gia was all toned muscle and long legs, and there wasn't an inch of space between them. If they'd been face-to-face, he would have come on the spot. She adjusted her position, resettling her weight on his back and he sucked in a breath at the way her knees hug his hips. Okay, not quite perfect. Pulling her legs around his waist, he shifted her heels away from his dick. Getting kicked wouldn't improve his day.

"This is ridiculous." Her breath huffed in his ear as she made her complaint.

"Says you." He grinned. God, she felt good.

She was game, too. She always had been. Her ankle had to be swollen and painful, plus he was fairly certain they had hostiles dogging their asses. Worse, he'd bet the growers knew all about the access road the hotshots were working from—so they'd also have a real good idea of where Rio and Gia were headed. It would be a race to the road.

He'd never lost before.

He wouldn't now.

He opened the compass, got his bearings, and got started. One step at a time. That's how he'd take today.

"This is not in your job description."

She still wasn't on board with his plan.

"You can make it up to me later." He had plenty of ideas of how. He entertained himself with those fantasies for a few minutes before that started to make walking difficult.

"Be serious, Rio." She leaned forward as she spoke.

"You carried me when my chute malfunctioned," he pointed out. "How is this any different?"

She was silent for a moment, although he could practically hear the thoughts whirring in her head. Gia didn't like accepting help. Which was too fucking bad, as she needed it.

"I still think—" she said, circling back for another attempt, but he'd had enough.

"Gia?"

"What?" She twisted her head to meet his sideways gaze straight on. Her mistake.

"Shut up," he said.

He took a hand off her thigh and cupped the back of her head. Pressed a hard kiss against her lips. Since she'd opened her mouth—undoubtedly to ream him a new one—the kiss got deeper and hotter than he'd planned.

He adapted.

He slid his tongue deep into her mouth, tasting and exploring. Gia was sweet and hold, her tongue stroking his in a way that got his blood pumping and his body primed to put out a very different kind of fire. When he finally pulled back, she was flushed, her breath coming faster.

"We're done discussing."

She didn't say anything, which was a win for him. Settling into a steady stride, he took them both down the faint trail. The fire road was roughly eight miles in front of them. The sooner he reached it, the better.

CHAPTER FOURTEEN

They'd been hiking for three hours when Rio knew for certain they'd acquired a tail. He'd stopped to take ten. The terrain now was too rough to make any kind of time, the waist-high chaparral pulling at his thighs and waist like greedy fingers. If they'd been alone out here, he'd have gone for the machete and forced a passage through, but he didn't want to leave that kind of *escaping smoke jumpers here* sign for anyone following them.

Unfortunately, his caution seemed well placed.

"Shhh." He dropped to the ground and rolled, tucking Gia against his chest. Pain lanced through his shoulder at the hit but he held on.

Her question-filled eyes met his, but there was nothing he could do. Instead he pressed his fingers against her mouth. Any sound now could get them killed. There was no chance their company wasn't packing and he estimated they had three more miles to the road. Every step he took here was clearly visible to the trained eye, but they needed to make good time. Good men had died in this kind of chaparral-filled wash and, if the fire caught them here, they'd be just as dead. Thank God, the fire was still safely in the distance.

He only needed to deal with the near-by assholes.

Palming the handgun, he thumbed the safety off.

Do or die.

Shoot first and he had a chance to get Gia to safety.

So fucking close. A chopper swung by overhead, the bucket suspended beneath slopping water as the bird returned from a water run. If he stood up and waved, it might be possible to get the pilot's attention. There wasn't much the pilot could do, however, and that was *if* the pilot even realized Rio wasn't part of the authorized ground crew. Yeah. Tipping his hand like that was out of the question.

Sticks cracked as their company caught up with them. There was plenty of bitching going on, the two men not bothering to conceal their approach. And, sure enough, they spotted where Rio and Gia had entered the wash. *Fuck.* Rio had hoped that his head start would win the day.

Nope.

Too bad, so sad.

"You see them?" The snick of a lighter and the smell of a cigarette followed the question. The man had to be a first class idiot because everything around them was tinder dry and the little shower of sparks as the man ashed was pure trouble.

"Jesus, Carl. Be a little careful. You want to kill us all?"

"Nope." Oh, hell. Rio didn't like the new note in the man's voice. Maybe Carl wasn't a moron after all. "You see an exit trail?"

Sunlight glinted on a pair of binoculars.

Rio silently pulled Gia further into the chaparral, looking for more cover. Instinct and experience both screamed this situation wouldn't end well.

"Then we're golden. We know they went in here." The smoker gestured with his cigarette. "And we're certain they didn't come out."

"They could have." The second man sounded doubtful.

"If they grew wings." The smart one eyed his cigarette. "No, they're in there. Aren't you?" He raised his voice. "Hiding from us. Thinking you're going to get away."

Gia tensed and Rio rubbed his thumb against his cheek. He'd keep her safe. She had to know that.

He silently swung the handgun towards the voices, but, wouldn't you know it, he had a tree trunk in the way. He kept his finger on the trigger, considering the best way to draw the man out.

"You messed with the wrong operation." The smoker flicked his cigarette into the grass. "But now it's game over."

Fuck.

Small flames flickered to life as the lit tip did its thing. As long as the wind didn't shift, smoking man had just pulled a damned clever move in this game they were playing.

The other guard started cursing, clearly not with the program. "You wanna kills us all?"

"Relax. Wind's blowing south. We'll light us a little line and we're golden."

Tilting Gia's head so he could see her eyes, he pressed a finger against his lips. He waited until she nods her agreement, then he released her. She didn't move. *Good girl.* He gestured her forward, pointing to the other side of the gully.

She nodded silent agreement and they started crawling. He covered her, keeping his body between hers and the two men. Mentally, he calculated how fast he could stand and get a bead on the two men. Quick enough if the bastards stood in the open. When he silently rose to a crouch and assessed, however, the men were still standing behind a screen of trees. No clear shot. *Fuck.*

The bastard was right about the wind too. The afternoon wind had picked up just enough to jumpstart the new fire lickety-split. Already smoke hung over the gully, the snap-crackle-pop of the fire all too loud.

"Going to be over real fast." Rio heard that mocking call loud and clear.

He double-checked—still no clear shot—and spotted the guard standing near the top of the gully behind a large tree, flicking a Bick and lighting new fires. *Shit.* The man wasn't even going to waste the bullets.

Time to call for reinforcements. Rio angled off from Gia, getting as much space as he could between the two of them. Which wasn't much. The gully was a Br'er Rabbit's patch of sticks and dense undergrowth. He quickly popped off three shots. Counted two seconds. Fired three times again, methodically emptying the clip before reloading.

And... cue the firestorm. The growers' guards unloaded on him. Bullets bit the ground and bush around him, but he'd picked his spot and fate was apparently in a kind mood. Nothing hit and, soon enough, the growers' men disappeared back into the woods. Sticking around until the gory end was apparently not in their job description. *Thank fuck.*

Getting out of the burn zone was priority number one. Rio pushed through the thick chaparral until he was back by Gia's side. If he looked behind him, he could see the first thin line of flames aiming for his boots. *Not good.*

"Can we deploy?" She didn't stop crawling, but their progress wasn't good, the gully too overgrown for speed.

He didn't know how the shelters' glue would hold up to a second round of heat but, even if the seams were good, this wasn't a deploy situation and they both knew it. Gia was simply checking her facts.

"Too much fuel. The fire's going to sit in the gully and not pass through." They were out of viable options. "We've got to make a run for it."

"That's what I figured." She coughed, a rough, hacking sound that shot straight to his gut as new smoke billowed around them. "I got the memo."

He wrapped an arm around her waist, keeping low in case the guards doubled back but Jesus... given the smoke, he didn't think anyone could aim a shot worth a damn now. Hand wrapped around his utility knife, he cut and slashed, pushing them forward a foot at a time. By his side, Gia wielded her own blade with ferocious intensity. Four hundred yards to the trees.

There was no warning over the noise of the fire. One minute he was listening to the hungry roar of the fire on his heels and, the next moment, the heavy whup-whup-whup of a chopper overhead surrounded them, pressing down the grasses in a sudden blast of air.

"Shit." Gia's hands yanked him down, her arms over their heads. "Incoming."

The whole world went a welcome red as the chopper overhead dropped its load of retardant.

Eight hundred gallons of slurry coated the gully, the mix of water and fertilizer clinging to the chaparral. Rio focused on not inhaling, waiting for the powder to settle. The slurry wasn't supposed to be poisonous but no firefighter he knew wanted to take the chance of inhaling a lungful. Safe. Not sorry. And the red line between them and the flames was a welcome sight.

Although not as welcome as the grimy, gloved hand that appeared out of the pink cloud followed by a grinning face above a bright yellow shirt. *Hotshot*. The broad-shouldered guy lugging a chainsaw was more welcome than Santa Claus. "Welcome to the party."

Thank. Fuck. They'd found the hotshots or the hotshots had found them. Either way worked for Rio. Better yet was the narrow trail through the chaparral behind him, a trail rapidly filling with other Nomex-clad bodies.

Beside him, Gia laughed hoarsely, pink from head to foot. "I don't recall RSVP-ing for this."

An ash-streaked face grinned at her above a T-shirt that read *Big Bear Rogues*. "You must be Gia and Rio. We got a call from Jack to keep an eye out for you."

CHAPTER FIFTEEN

Each mile in the fire truck took them further away from the fire and closer to base camp and the Donovan hangar. Rio itched to get back out there, to join the hotshots on the line, but instead they were sidelined and parked in the truck's backseat. Along for the ride and not much more. Plus, Gia needed the medical attention. Rio wanted her ankle looked at. The ace bandage and elevation prescribed by the hotshots' team medic were great, but he wanted an M.D., someone with formal training and a string of letters after his name. Or hers. Gender didn't matter squat when it came to being good at your job. Gia was living proof of that.

Screw their audience in the truck's front seat. He put an arm around her. She promptly wriggled away.

"Gia—"

He wanted to hold her. No, scratch that. He *needed* to hold her.

"No," she whispered, pressing her fingers against his lips. *Shut up.* He got the message loud and clear, although the music pumping from the front was loud enough to drown out a dozen conversations. "No one has to know. What happened out there in the woods? That stays between us. You keep touching me now and the whole world knows. You might as well rent a billboard."

"We didn't go to Vegas." He ran his hands down her side, curling his fingers into her hips. Christ. She felt so right. "What happened out there can't stay out there."

"Because of a broken condom?" She shook her head. "If and when something comes of that, I'll let you know."

She was pushing him away again. Gia was good at keeping people at arm's length. There might not be an inch of space between them physically, but her head was miles and miles away.

When the fire truck finally pulled up at the Donovan hangar, it seemed like a million years since she'd been here. The welcoming committee surging out of the door wasn't her first choice however, or even a familiar occurrence. Jack Donovan strode toward the truck, concern and relief written all over his face. He wasn't afraid to let his brother know how he felt and she respected that. The bunch of people following behind him exhibited similar emotions. Rio's mother. Jack's fiancée. Evan's fiancée. The whole clan had come out to welcome home their missing member.

Rio popped his door and hopped down, calling thanks to the driver for the lift. She reached for her own handle, but he was waiting for her when she opened the door. Reaching up to guide her down and make sure her foot doesn't hit the ground. She appreciated the thought. Maybe. Or she would have, if that hadn't been a look of pure possessiveness in his eyes. Another time—a time when his entire family and her boss hadn't been watching—that look might have made her shiver. Because the thought of being *possessed* by Rio Donovan? Was delicious.

The welcoming horde surrounded Rio and Gia hung back, leaning against the truck. This was Rio's family. His welcoming committee, not hers. They were thrilled he was okay and they'd clearly spent the better part of Rio's absence hoping and praying for that outcome. Part of her wanted to be right there next to him, while another part wondered if her own family would have been so unconditional in their belief that she'd make it back in one piece. Her family loved her. She'd never doubted that. But they also worried about her PSVT, insisting that she limit what she did, and spending the night outrunning a forest fire and a bunch of drug thugs would have been justification in their eyes for taking it easier.

When Rio finally broke free, he turned towards her. So, of course, all those faces shifted her way as well, filled with emotions. Curiosity. Concern. Pride—that was Jack. She'd always liked him.

Rio looked at Jack. "Gia got busted up some. I'll drive her in to the hospital."

Orders. Just like that.

"I'm fine," she snapped. "Nothing a day off my feet won't fix."

Jack came forward, yanking her into a hard, quick hug. "We'll get you checked out anyhow."

And there it was again. The royal *we*. Right now, she didn't give a damn that the three Donovan brothers were technically her bosses and ran the jump team. She was tired of being told what to do. She got that the orders came from a good place. These men had hearts of gold and were concerned she might be injured. Those were fine sentiments—it was just the delivery mechanism that had her pissed off.

"*I'll* get myself checked out," she countered. "No worries. I'll be ready to jump when it's my turn on the rotation."

Beside her, Rio cursed. "The duty roster isn't the problem here."

No. She was. And she was tired of being someone else's problem.

"Nope." She was in full agreement with him there.

"Gia—" He sounded tired. Exasperated. One hundred percent male.

Jack watched them thoughtfully. Rio's mom focused on their exchange. Gia could practically hear the wheels turning in the other woman's brain as she added up two and two. And came to the correct conclusion of *four*.

He towered over her, big and frustrated. "I'm taking you to the doctor. We'll get you checked out. Then we'll talk."

Rio was rumpled and tired. A quick hose off on the fire road had removed the top layer of ash and grime, but his T-shirt was still candy pink from their earlier slurry shower. Forearms bare, he exuded a masculine power and confidence that definitely wasn't fair because he looked hot while she looked—not. She was tired, her hair standing on end and she had ash in places ash had no business being. Her ankle hurt like a bitch and what she really wanted was a shower with hot water and soap. Followed by a month of Sundays in bed.

"I'm not your problem, Donovan," she said, shoving off the truck. She tested her ankle and it held. Bonus points for her. She started limping towards the hangar. She'd snag her keys from her locker and then she'd get in her truck and go home. Alone. That plan worked for her.

A big hand closed gently around her arm, swinging her gently to a halt. She glares at the offender and wondered just how many years she'd do for assaulting her boss.

"Gia—" Funny how Jack could sound so much like his brother.

"I'm off the clock," she said. "I'm going home."

He nodded reluctantly. "We care, Gia, okay? You're team and we look out for each other."

Rio cleared his throat. "She's more than team," he said gruffly.

Her oh-shit meter started ringing but she was surrounded by Donovans, with nowhere to go. Rio's mother perked up, looking interested. Jack just looked pained. He opened his mouth to say something, but Rio beat him to the punch.

"Gia and I need to talk," he announced, radiating sexy determination, "but she's more than just team."

Great.

She fought the urge to close her eyes and thunk her head against the truck. Or Rio's own hard head. Way to go keeping them below the radar. In twenty minutes—thirty tops—everyone in Strong was going to know that the two of them were an item. Which wasn't true. Not really. They were a temporary hook-up with possible long-term consequences.

Nothing more.

No matter how much her heart perked up at that possessive note in Rio's voice. So she played it off, laughing.

"What Rio's saying is that facing down death and drug dealers together has brought us closer together and he's considering couples therapy." Oops. She'd forgotten that not everyone was in on the drug grow business. Lily's eyes widened and she was pretty sure Rio's mother cursed. Which explained a lot about where her son had acquired his potty mouth.

"Not quite." Rio's growly voice made it plenty clear that she'd pissed him off. Nothing new there.

She headed for the hangar, because she was done here. Was this close to lying down on the ground and sneaking in that nap she was jonesing for. Instead, she slammed into a familiar male chest. She lurched, landing hard on her ankle, and cursed at the bright lance of pain. Dear God, that hurt. Arms came around her, steadying her.

Then his mouth came down on hers and Rio Donovan kissed her right there in front of his whole world. A sweetly possessive kiss, his hands cupping her head, his thumbs stroking over her temples as he tipped her face up into his. She loved his kisses. That was the only reason she stood still, pausing her mad retreat to the hangar. She hadn't thought beyond her shower and her nap and getting the hell away from this man before he could do any more damage to her. To her heart.

Shit.

And now she was standing here, letting him—*letting*—kiss her. She slapped a palm on his chest and shoved. Hard. He put a few inches between them and smile at her.

God, she was in so much trouble.

She looked over Rio's shoulder and, sure enough, here came all the female members of the Donovan can. She liked these women—but she knew exactly what their happy welcome meant. In their eyes, she was no longer a jumper. Nope. Now she was a jumper girlfriend. Sure, it would be special to have a big, tough Donovan male decide she was the center of his universe—to have all that fierce love and protection behind her. All that sensual alpha male wrapped around her at night. It wasn't the nights she worried about, though—it was the days. After all, she'd seen firsthand just how stifling love can be.

She'd stand on her own, thank you very much.

"Touché," he whispered and swept her up in his arms. "Doctor time."

So much for talking, she thought, and slugged him in the jaw.

CHAPTER SIXTEEN

Rio didn't do waiting.

He also didn't do sitting back, relaxing or letting someone else take charge. This was his Gia they were talking about. He wanted to shield her from the danger of the grow they'd stumbled upon but, to do that, he had to bring others. Which was, shit… taking more time than he'd thought it would.

Determined, he turned a steely-eyed gaze on his present company. The hangar was fucking crowded. Both Jack and Evan had insisted on being present and the determined looks on their faces said they had no intention of taking shit from anyone—either the DEA or Rio. As Jack had pointed out, Gia was part of the team—and that made her theirs as well.

Today's new discovery? Rio didn't share when it came to Gia.

"We're all here now." Jack leveled a grim stare at the assembled uniforms. "So it run it by us one more time."

Rio did. He gave them the blow-by-blow account of finding the hidden grow, the guards' reaction, and the chase. He left out exactly how he'd taken down their pursuers and his temporary acquisition of various unlicensed weapons, because he didn't need to borrow that kind of trouble. Besides, his brothers knew him. They'd know exactly what he'd done out there in the woods.

"So Ms. Jackson got a good look at at least one suspect?" The DEA agent nodded thoughtfully, clearly already working out how best to exploit that particular angle.

"She'll meet with a sketch artist," Rio said, not pointing out that they'd already had this conversation. "She should be able to come up with a decent visual on the guy."

"I'm more concerned that this guy saw her," Evan snapped. "He saw her, they followed you, and then you hooked up with the hotshot team working on the fire access road. It's not going to take them too long to put two and two together that their shot at attempted murder failed and figure out that you're firefighters. If they coming gunning for her, how do we keep her safe?"

"That's my job," Rio growled. "No one gets to Gia."

The DEA agent picked that moment to start troubleshooting. "We can move her into witness protection until we've got this case closed."

Gia would hate that. Not only would she be off the jump team, but she'd be under lock and key and close supervision wasn't her thing. Hell. Their possible unplanned pregnancy was bad enough and that was his fault.

He kept those details to himself though. "I'll watch out for her."

Jack scowled. "Like you did out there in the woods?"

DEA wonder boy tapped his fingers on the table. "With all due respect, Mr. Donovan, what makes you think you're capable of acting as Ms. Jackson's bodyguard?"

Jack and Evan both looked at him. *Fuck*.

"Three tours of duty with Spec Ops," he snapped. "That's what. I'm licensed to carry and Uncle Sam made damn sure I knew how to infiltrate and how to kill. Anything else you want to know, you'll have to get clearance from my former superiors, but let's just say that this drug grow isn't my first dance at the ball. What matters here is keeping Gia safe, and I'm the man who's going to do it."

"So how do we do that?" Evan's slow rumble was a welcome

distraction. "She's a smoke jumper, Rio. She goes out in the field."

"And she's a grown woman." That was Jack. The bastard knew Rio had been touching where he shouldn't and know he was going to make Rio pay. "She'll be making her own decisions."

"Not if those decisions jeopardize her safety." That was non-negotiable.

Imagining Gia in the hands of a drug runner made Rio's blood ran cold. He'd seen firsthand what happened to drug trade informants and it wasn't pretty. Nope. Adjectives like brutal, violent and lethal came to mind. Those men would take a knife, a gun, their fists and cocks—whatever it took—to get the information they wanted from Gia and then they'd kill her anyhow. There was no unseeing what she'd seen.

"So we take the grow out fast." Jack sounded positively cheerful at the thought of violence. "And eliminate the threat there."

The DEA agent nodded slowly. "We've got the coordinates Mr. Donovan provided and, as soon as the fire is under control, we'll get a team airborne to check the site out."

"If the wind doesn't shift again, we'll have the fire knocked down in another twenty-four, forty-eight hours." Jack launched into the fire update, quick, succinct, and to the point. His steel-toes stretched in front of him, Rio tuned out briefly, wondering how Gia was doing. He rubbed his jaw and winced. She packed a hell of a right hook.

He'd deserved it too.

After he'd dropped her—which hadn't been his plan at all, but her punch had surprised him—she'd calmed down enough to agree that Nonna could drive her in for a check up. That was something.

"The bad guys aren't going to sit around and wait for your RSVP," Rio pointed out. "The site's been compromised and they know it. They'll have shut down and moved out. They could be anywhere by now."

The DEA agent didn't look terribly concerned. More resigned and matter-of-face like this was a common outcome in his war on drugs.

"That product won't reach the street."

Shutting down one pipeline wasn't enough.

"The site was pretty well concealed." Rio had done this before. He knew the drill. Whoever had laid out that site had made sure the plants had plenty of cover from the air. Otherwise, someone would have spotted the grow months ago.

The DEA agent leaned forward. Maybe his nonchalance had been bait in a trap. Mentally, Rio tipped his hat to the guy. "What do you suggest?"

"If you can't find the site, I'll lead the way in. I've got the coordinates and I've been there before."

A few minutes later, the hangar office emptied out. Checking in on Gia was high on Rio's to do list, but he needed to ask Evan something first. Hell. He'd have asked Jack too, but the man was always first out of a meeting. Jack was long gone.

Evan raised a brow when Rio closed the door. "Question?"

"You worry about it?"

Evan eyed him. The look on his brother's face said he had no idea where Rio was headed with the question. Honestly, Rio didn't know himself. The words had popped out before he could think about them.

"You're going to have to be more specific."

"About getting married. About not getting it right with Faye."

Evan nodded slowly. "All the time," he admitted.

"But that's not stopping you."

Evan shook his head. "I worry about fire burning my ass or overrunning my team, but that doesn't stop me from jumping out of the plane. Same thing, really."

How was it the same thing? Fire was an act of nature. You jumped. You kicked its ass. Or you didn't, but you went in armed with Pulaskis and water and with your guys at your back. So he stared back at Evan, waiting for the explanation.

Nothing scared Evan. Rio wished to God his brother could teach him that trick.

"You just got to trust your instincts," he said finally. "Got to love what you do. And then you jump."

The sudden warmth in his brother's eyes said Evan loved what he did with Faye a whole lot. Christ. "So sex is the answer?"

Evan looked at him. "You really want to talk about this?"

Hell, no. "Is it?"

"Fuck." Evan scrubbed a hand over his forehead, leaving behind a streak of soot from an early morning training exercise. "This had better be for a personal reason, Rio. Sometimes, sure. Sex helps a whole lot. But Faye and I talk, too. In bed. Out of bed."

Evan had never been much of a talker, so clearly Faye had worked miracles.

"I love her," Evan said, "and that's what makes the difference."

"Between?"

Evan winced. "Between having sex and having a relationship, okay? Why don't you ask Jack about Lily? Why me?"

"You're here." He paused. "You don't worry that you're going to screw it up?"

"I do." Evan didn't sound horribly concerned.

"Badly?"

"There are some things I'm not telling you but, yeah. On a scale of one to ten, I've hit all the numbers. We work it out. Is this about Gia?"

Was it? He flattened his hand on the desk. Yeah. Probably. But he was worried he'd pull a ten on Evan's scale. Do something, say something worthy of the stepdads yammering away in his head.

"We didn't get the best start in life," he said instead, because Evan's question about Gia was a landmine.

Evan just looked at him. "You think we're going to repeat those mistakes?"

Well.

Yeah.

Not on purpose and maybe not as badly, but what experience did he have with being a family guy, the kind of guy who stuck? Not much at all.

"Huh," Evan said.

"What?"

Evan slapped him on the back. "You're going to figure it out just fine."

CHAPTER SEVENTEEN

After his meet-and-greet with the DEA wound up, Rio knocked on Gia's cabin door. Knocking felt wrong, but so did opening the door without an invitation. After making love to her in the back of her truck and then out in the woods, he should have felt comfortable entering her place. But he didn't. Not without her saying the words. So he stood there on her porch, waiting for her to answer the door like he was selling newspapers or wrapping paper.

He didn't know what he wanted.

That was the problem.

Sex. Or something else.

Something *more*.

His head and his dick—and maybe something halfway between the two—kept tugging him in two opposing directions. Gia opened the door, yawning as she leaned on her crutches. She'd probably been catching up on her sleep and he'd woken her up. Good going.

"Hey." She blinked up at him like he was the last person she'd expected to see on her porch. She'd get used to having him around. He planned on sticking real close.

She was dressed for bed in a faded T-shirt that made her bra-less state perfectly clear and a pair of shorts that clung to her in all the right places. He immediately lost his train of thought. Hell, all thinking went straight off the tracks and right into fantasyland. Gia was all long, bare legs and his head reminded his dick what those legs of hers felt like wrapped around his hips. His shoulders. The sweet, slick feel of her when he touched her. Kissed her...

Jesus Christ.

He braced an arm against her doorframe. Maybe he should have brought flowers. Or asked his brothers' fiancées for advice. Lily and Faye clearly had plenty of experience of dealing with Donovans. Maybe they could have helped him out here because showing up without a game plan suddenly seemed like a recipe for disaster.

"Can I come in?"

She actually looked like she was considering saying no. He took a step closer, ready to shove his foot in the door because he wasn't letting her shut him out.

"Fine," she said finally, turning and limping away from the door.

He followed her inside, shutting the screen door carefully behind him. The cabins were pretty much standard issue. One main room with a fireplace, a sleeping loft, and a bathroom. Gia had put her own stamp on the place, decorating with stacks of books and some little fluffy throw pillows. She flopped down on the couch, dropping the crutches and pulling the fleece blanket around her even though it was summer, and stared expectantly at him.

Her eyes went to the faint purple bruise on his jaw and winced.

"If you're looking for apologies, come back tomorrow. I'm not in the mood right now."

He suspected she was, but he'd also deserved what he got, so he shrugged. "We're good."

"Uh-huh." She didn't look like she believed him but that was her problem, not his. The pillow on couch sported a visible dent from her head. She'd definitely been napping. She tucked her feet up beneath the blanket, bad ankle propped on a pile of pillows, looking like she might just pick up with the nap where she'd left off when he came knocking. He eyeballed the place, not sure where to park his own ass. Since he might as well be where he wanted to be, he sat down on the couch beside her.

"How's the ankle?" he asked.

She made a face. "I've got a professional wrap job, a pair of loaner crutches, two weeks unplanned vacation, and a medical bill that would cover the price of a small couch. I'd rather be back on a plane getting ready to jump."

"Off-limits?" He was careful to make his words a question and not a statement.

"For now." She grinned. "Until I can convince Jack otherwise or he's short-handed."

He wasn't going to think about her going back out in the field or about how close he'd come to losing her.

"I gave my statement to the DEA."

She yawned and he fights back a smile. She was goddamned beautiful.

"Me too. They say anything about when they're planning on taking out the grow?"

"As soon as the smoke clears, they'll put a plan up." He shook his head. They'd be too late.

"You disagree with their plan?"

He looked at her.

She sighed, pulling the edges of the blanket close. "It's written all over your face. And you get this little crinkle right between your eyes."

She reached out and traced the space. Even that little touch worked wonders on him. He could feel himself settling back on her couch, soaking up the pleasure of being near her.

"You can read me like a book?"

She snorted. "As if. It would be handy though."

"The growers will have dismantled the site by now. By the time the DEA gets out there, there's not going to be much of anything left other than a hell of a trash pile. All the incriminating stuff will be gone. The guys, the guns—they'll be gone too."

"You've seen this before."

Her eyes looked at him knowingly. Not judging, just accepting. He liked the interest and concern, so much so that his mouth opened up and started talking.

"Part of what I did for Uncle Sam," he said carefully, because so much of his job with the military had been classified and that meant radio silence, even for her, "was shutting down drug grows in South America. We flew in, busted shit up, and then left."

"I'm sitting next to a bona fide hero."

He was no hero. "I did my job," he said gruffly.

"Uh-huh. Which took you halfway around the globe and put your life in danger countless times."

That much was true. The thing was, his life wasn't worth all that much. "I'm not a hero," he said because it needed saying. "No," he said, pressing a finger against her mouth when she started to protest. "I'm not. I did more than my share of crap growing up. Doing something to stop the drug trade seemed only fair."

"You grew up rough." She sounded certain. The Strong grapevine was clearly still working overtime.

"It wasn't pretty. "He hesitated. "You've heard how Nonna took me, Jack and Evan in. Before that, though, we made our own way. The streets of Sacramento weren't always rainbows and light. I saw some stuff there and I learned my lessons."

She laughed softly. "What doesn't kill you..."

It was official. He loved her attitude towards life. She didn't wallow in self-pity, didn't waste time on regrets.

"I'll bet you were daddy's little princess." He liked that image, almost as much as the sudden mental image he got of a little girl who looked like Gia. *His* daughter. Huh. Who would have thought it? He'd never thought he was cut out to be anyone's father, but Gia made him want to try.

She grinned, clearly unaware of his mental dreamfest. "You bet.

But it wasn't all fun and games. I had to argue to do anything on my own."

Something dark flashed in her eyes. She had her own demons and bad memories. If she'd been daddy's little princess, that hadn't been all she'd been. He pulled her closer.

"And you like taking care of yourself," he said carefully. *Treading on thin ice, Donovan.*

"Absolutely." She met his gaze head on. "That's non-negotiable."

And there it was. The problem *du jour*.

"You talked to the DEA," he said. "And I think you got the same speech I did. The DEA's going to go after the grow, but it will be on their own timeframe and there's no guarantee that the guys who tried to take us down in the woods don't follow us here. That being said, the security here is unacceptable."

She shook her head. "There's a lock on the door and on the windows. And it's not like we don't notice strangers poking around here."

"The cabin is too exposed," he growled. "You have windows facing the woods. There's no alarm, no security lights. Until we get this case wrapped up with the DEA, you need to move. You'll be safer."

"This is my place." Her eyes flashed. "I'm not going to just pick up and relocate."

"I'm not losing you. That's my non-negotiable."

She eyed him calmly. "You're overreacting."

"You're the eyes on this op. Eliminate you, eliminate the only witness."

"Are you trying to scare the shit out of me, Rio?" Now she sounded pissed. She leaned forward, stabbing a finger into his chest. "Because this is a great conversation."

"I'm stating facts."

"According to you."

"And you might be pregnant."

It was a low blow, but he'd use whatever weapons he had here. She needed to move somewhere safer.

She opened her mouth. Shut it.

He pressed his advantage. "Until you can tell me that you're *not* pregnant, we act like you are."

He'd pulled the pregnancy card. Gia had known it was coming the minute she'd pulled open her door and seen him standing there on her porch—after all, why else would he have come by?—but knowing and hearing were apparently two different things.

Because he was right.

She *could* be having their baby. The condom had broken out there in the field and sperm swam, making their happy, baby-making way to whatever egg her body had on offer. So pregnancy was definitely a possibility, however unwelcome. He watched her now, his face fierce and focused. Yesterday's laughing, sensual lover was nowhere in sight. Instead he was all stern and determined.

Pure trouble.

Because when he looked at her like that she wanted to give him whatever he wanted.

She'd jumped with him for almost two months and then they'd each saved the other. On the life saving front, they were square. And, if she was being honest, she'd rather spend what was left of the summer without that life-and-death adrenaline rush. She'd be heading back to grad school and her last semester there all too soon. Right now, she wanted...

Rio.

He wasn't the kind of man who settled down and she'd been fine with that. She'd wanted a hot summer fling and to indulge her curiosity about her jump partner. She looked at him, sprawled on her loveseat. Worn denim showcased his muscled legs and ended in yet another pair of work boots. Rio wasn't an ironed-and-buttoned kind of man. Nope. He'd changed into another faded cotton T-shirt, this one from a fire department fundraiser for the rundown historic firehouse Jack had bought in Strong with the intention of pulling a rehab. The shirt exposed his powerful forearms and the intriguing tattoo on the inside of his wrist. Rio was big and strong and so very, very focused on the moment.

He was gorgeous.

And he looked uncomfortable.

She got that the possibility of an unplanned pregnancy scared the hell out of him. She wasn't particularly thrilled by the possibility either.

"When do you think you'll know?" Gruff concern filled his voice.

She did some mental counting and then gave up. Her cycles had never been particularly regular and this was foreign territory to her. "Two weeks?"

That was a guess, but Rio liked numbers and specifics.

"Strong doesn't have a doctor. I could drive you into Sacramento."

"I can drive myself," she pointed out. "And I think one of those boxed tests would do for starters."

He looked at her and grimaced. "I think Lily has some."

That was interesting.

"Not that I wanted or needed to know that," he continued. "But I was at their place and the sink was backing up, so I gave the pipes a glance and... yeah. She'd pretty much cornered the market on EPT."

"Maybe they're planning on trying?" she offered, biting back a grin. Imagining Rio coming face-to-face with Lily's secret stash was too funny.

"I didn't ask." He stretched out his arm along the back of the loveseat. His fingers grazed the back of her neck and settled in. "Jack will tell me if and when there's something to tell."

"Did you tell him..."

"About us?"

Were they officially an *us*?

"Not the details." He slanted a look at her. "He saw me kiss you, so he'll have the general idea."

Right. Like whether or not she was actually pregnant.

"Some of those tests are supposed to be pretty sensitive." She'd done her Google-fu as soon as she'd reached the cabin. Before long, she'd have her first shot at an answer.

"Can I—" He hesitated. "I'd like to be there."

"You want to watch me pee on a stick?"

A slow smile tugged at the corner of his mouth. "Are you offering?"

"Some things," she said fervently, "don't need to be shared."

"Just outside the door," he suggested.

His desire to be involved made her feel warm inside. "That works for me."

"And, in the meantime," he said, "I'd like you to move into town. Be close to other people."

"Be close to you and your guard dogs," she groused. He wasn't letting go of the safety issue.

"I want you to stay safe."

She looked around her cabin. The place was cozy, but it was just her here. She wasn't stupid. And she might be lonely. Keeping her PSVT a secret would be a little more difficult in a public setting, but she'd managed on the jump team so far.

"What did you have in mind?"

He took a deep breath. "I want you to stay with my mother."

"Rio..."

"My mother has room. She lives smack in the middle on Strong." He ticked the plusses off on his fingers. "I can have eyes on you twenty-four/seven."

That was so *not* a mark in the plus column.

"I'm not moving in with your mom." She paused. "Did you even ask her?"

"I did. You're more than welcome," he said. "You'll like her."

"I'm sure I would. That's not the point." She hesitated. "But what kind of message does it send?"

Gossip traveled faster than light in a place this small—so their kiss would already have made the rounds and his mother would have plenty of ideas. Bringing a girl home wasn't casual. She and Rio were a summer hook-up with potential side effects. That was all. As long as Gia remembered that, she'd be fine. If she moved into his mother's house, however, she might start thinking about having more.

About keeping Rio.

And he wasn't the kind of guy a woman kept.

"Rio?" she prompted when he didn't answer. She couldn't interpret the look on his face. Part discomfort, part something—else. She didn't know what.

"I'd like you to consider staying at my mom's," he repeated. "This isn't between us and Strong or us and the jump team. Even Jack and Evan are going to have to butt out of our business."

She liked the way he said *our*.

But what would it be like to spend time with Rio's *mother*, of all people? She'd seen Mary Ellen Donovan around Strong and the base camp. It was hard not to know who she was because she was an integral part of Strong and they'd been briefly introduced when Gia had joined the jump team. The older woman had hair that was more grey than brown, twisted up in a loose bun and pinned with whatever was handy. Energetic. Smiling eyes. Those had been Gia's takeaway from their brief meet and greet at the beginning of summer. Oh, and Gia was also fairly certain that the Donovan brothers, the fire chief, and probably a half-dozen other members of the jump team would gladly kill to protect her.

She wanted a chance at that for herself.

With Rio.

And he wanted this for her. For them. She thought about it for a moment.

"Okay."

He stared at her. "Okay?"

"Yes, Rio. Okay.

Gia packed a bag. Her crutches meant she also accepted a ride. She'd have preferred to followed Rio in her own truck to keep her escape route open in case the whole situation backfired. Unfortunately, her ankle still wasn't cooperating.

The drive was all too short. There wasn't much to Strong. She'd be walking distance to Ma's, although alcohol was clearly out for her until she knew whether or not she was pregnant.

Pregnant.

That word was alien as *us*.

Which was the word Rio had used to describe their... relationship. Which was also something she wasn't certain that they had. But she wanted to try. Rio signaled and parked, before swinging down and heading for her, sex on a stick. Of course. His determined stride ate up the distance between them and he had his hand on the door, opening it, before she'd got the thing halfway open.

He met her with his familiar slow smile, wrapping his fingers around hers as she jumped down. Into his arms. Naturally. For a moment, with her body pressed against his, she lost her breath.

"You ready?" He reached into the truck bed and pulled out her crutches.

For early evening, it was still mind-numbingly hot even beneath the shadowy elms lining the sidewalk. Mary Ellen's home was a laidback California bungalow. Powder blue with white trim and a sweet wrap-around porch sporting two fire-engine red Adirondack chairs drawn up with a ringside seat for whatever happened in Strong. Gia could easily imagine spending evenings there with Rio as she limped up the walk.

Mary Ellen met them at the door and they exchanged the usual pleasantries. Not asking and answering the real questions. Just *how's your day been?* and *thanks for the place to crash.* No one mentioned the kiss or Gia's popping Rio in the jaw. Thank God for manners.

Mary Ellen pushed open a door at the end of the hall. The guest bedroom was done in yellows and white with an adjoining bath. The place definitely sported more space than the cabin, that was for sure. Rio followed right on their heels, carrying her duffel bag.

"Go," Mary Ellen said as soon he'd dumped his load, waving him back down the hall. "It's girl time now. You've done your part."

Rio shot his mother a look, clearly wanting to stay right where he was, but she looked back. And he went. Holy moly, alpha male Rio Donovan backed down and left.

"Teach me that."

"What?"

"Getting Rio to obey."

Mary Ellen gave a snort of laughter. "Practice, honey. Practice and desperation. I had three of those boys."

The smile in her voice said she wouldn't have traded any one of them.

"Don't believe a word she says," Rio hollered from the kitchen. A moment later, she heard the front door shut and his truck start up.

Uh-huh. This should be good.

"You should get off your feet." Concern filled Mary Ellen's eyes as she eyed Gia's ankle. She fought the instinctive urge to say she was fine.

"Are you going to tell me embarrassing stories about Rio?" *Please?* She sat on the bed and swung her ankle up. God. That did feel good.

Mary Ellen smiled and settled in the chair near by. "I sure could."

"But will you?"

"I guess that depends," the other woman said slowly, "on why you need to hear these stories."

"Rio's my jump partner."

Mary Ellen just nodded. "And?"

And—what?

"Are you together?"

"We're jump partners," she repeated. *Definitely* not thinking about their very public last kiss. "And he was worried about my safety."

"He's brought jumpers home before," Mary Ellen agreed, warmth and concern filling her eyes. "But I'm thinking you're different. He's certainly never carried in a bag before. Or worried about what I might say."

Holding out on the older woman seemed wrong, but what was she supposed to say? We had wild monkey sex—twice—and the condom broke? There were things you just didn't tell a man's mother.

"I'm a girl?" she suggested finally, when the silence had stretched on for too long. Mary Ellen Donovan could give the U.S. military lessons in interrogation.

"You are," Mary Ellen said agreeably. "And I raised him to have manners. But he looks at you differently."

Honestly.

He *looked* at her?

That was ridiculous evidence to base a relationship on. Even if she liked the sounds of it. Rio's mother clearly wanted him to have a girlfriend. That was all. Gia had to wonder what the older woman would say or do if she knew about the potential grandbaby.

"Ben warned me not to pry," Mary Ellen confessed. "But I've never been good at taking orders."

"Me neither." She grinned at the other woman. So they had two things in common: Rio. And a dislike of orders.

"Well, there's that." Mary Ellen sighed. "We'll work the rest of it out. You'll tell me when you're good and ready, or I'll drive you crazy prying. You take your pick but, in the meantime, I owe you a story."

Rio stayed out as late as he could, working around the hangar and then going for a run. Ten miles hadn't been enough to knock any sense in him however. Nope. His head still went a million miles a minute thinking about the woman he was running from.

So here he was.

Hovering in his mother's hallway. *Man up*. He knocked softly on the bedroom door and then opened it. Gia was curled up in bed, reading. She stuck her finger in her book and looked up at him. Her face was scrubbed clean, but her hair was mussed like she'd been running her fingers through it. She was pretty as hell and he ached to climb in bed beside her.

She watched him for a moment.

And then she smiled.

"Hey," she said.

"Just checking in." Not *on*, he thought. *In*. "How's the ankle?"

"Good as new."

Which was a lie, but maybe more of a white lie now. He eyed her ankle, propped up on a pillow. Maybe he should take a look.

"Stop it," she said.

"Stop what?" Staring at her? Because he didn't think he could do that. Hell, he'd happily look at her for the next five, ten or maybe fifty years.

He thought about that for a moment while she set the book on the bedside table and shook her head.

"Stop thinking you need to see my ankle for yourself. I've been to the doctor and all I need now is some time. A couple of days and we'll be running again. I want back on the roster."

"We'll see," he said because *over my dead body* wouldn't come out right.

She sighed. "You're going to make sure Jack forgets to add me back in, aren't you?"

"Maybe," he admitted.

"Are you jumping?"

"We're short-handed," he pointed out. "If the call comes in, I go up."

There was a moment of silence while he hovered in the door.

"Can I come in?" he said finally. Nonna's guest bedroom had a queen-sized bed and the spot to Gia's right looked pretty damned good.

She looked at him like she was deciding something. "All right."

He wasn't sure why she was being so hesitant. This was Gia. She'd never had a problem asking for what she wanted. Hell, she'd demanded he get into bed with her. The sex had been fantastic. So why did she seem to be having second thoughts now?

He stepped into the room before she could change her mind, leaving the door cracked. She promptly craned her neck, trying to see around him into the hall.

"Ben convinced Nonna to take a walk."

"Oh." She looked relieved. He didn't blame her for not wanting an audience. Even if they weren't going to do anything—and they *weren't*, he reminded himself, because she was exhausted and recuperating.

Not to mention possibly pregnant.

She eyed the duffel bag in his hand, but she didn't say anything. Base camp now had two vacancies. He set the bag down on the floor and moved towards the bed.

"I'm staying down the hall," he said. "Just in case." *And... surprise.* Maybe he should have mentioned his plans earlier.

He sat down on the empty side of the bed, eying the white chenille spread.

The plastic bookstore bag crinkled in his hand as he dropped it beside him. He'd get to that in a minute.

"You got everything you need?" He unlaced his boots and toed them off. If he put dirty boots on the bed, Nonna would kill him. Stretching out beside Gia, he rolled onto his side until he could see her face. She smelled good, like some kind of fruity shampoo. His favorite scent in the world.

"I'm set." She hesitated. "Your mother's fantastic."

"The best." He meant it too. Nonna had singlehandedly rescued him and he wouldn't forget that.

This was a damned awkward position to have a conversation in. Reaching out, he pulled her onto his chest. She wasn't reading anyhow. She stiffened for a moment, then relaxed into him. He cupped the back of her neck and rubbed.

"Magic hands," she murmured. "That's what you have."

"How do you feel?"

"Fine."

Her hand slipped between them, finding his chest. And his nipple. She stroked and, damn, did she have any idea where her fingers had strayed?

She looked up at him and ginned. "And you?"

She knew.

So he dipped his head and kissed her. A quick, soft, hi-there-you-are kiss while he slid a hand over her belly. Hard to believe that beneath all that toned sexy there could be a very small, almost not there baby.

"I meant this," he said.

"Oh." She dropped her head back onto his chest. "It's still too soon, Rio."

Weren't women supposed to have a second sense about these things? Because what he still didn't know about pregnancy could fill a book. Which reminded him. Shifting her into his left arm, he reached behind him and snagged the plastic bag.

"I brought you something. Just in case."

He sat up, pulling her into his lap, and handed her a small stack of books from the bag. The lady at the bookstore had been really happy to help him pick out a few titles. She'd assured him that *What to Expect* was practically a must-read. Hell if he knew.

"You don't think this is jumping the gun a little?"

He liked being prepared.

So shoot him.

And so maybe he'd read the first one sitting in his truck. He wanted to be there for her, but he didn't know anything about pregnancy other than the basic mechanics. Which was enough, if he thought about *Gia* popping out a baby, enough to scare him shitless. Moe information couldn't hurt, so he'd bought the books.

"If I am pregnant, there are options," she said carefully. "We don't have to have this baby."

The fierce protectiveness that swept him was both old and new. He rubbed his palm gently over her belly because that could be the newest member of the family. Strange and scary, sure. But not unwelcome. Family was family, no matter how small.

"Is that what you want?" He held his breath like a first class idiot waiting for her answer. His brothers would laugh their collective asses off. Rio had never pulled his punches, ever, and now here he was, dancing around the elephant in the room.

She pulled away from him slightly, angling her head to see his face. "I want to hear what *you* want."

Busted.

He'd imagined Gia, round and waddling with their baby, and he was... curious. That was all. He'd seen women, at the grocery story and in town and they looked like they'd swallowed a damned watermelon. He sure as hell wasn't thinking about how they got the watermelon *out*. But they'd be a family. He'd be adding two to the happy threesome of Jack, Evan and Nonna.

"If there's a baby," he said roughly, "I'm seeing this through, okay? He or she is going to be family. *Our* family."

He didn't know what that meant, but he'd figure it out.

When she didn't answer right away, he gently nudged her chin up with his thumb so he could see her face. "Gia? What do you want?"

She hesitated. "Rio—"

"Whatever you need," he promised. "I'm going to give you that. If I don't do something, you tell me."

"Rio—" This time, his name came out as a laugh. "You don't take orders. We both know that."

"I'll learn. I'm serious, Gia. Whatever you need, it's yours."

He felt rather than saw her nod against his chest. He was still holding her when he drifted off to sleep.

Mary Ellen tiptoed down the hall. Ben had coaxed her out for a walk. Exercise was good, but the company was better. He wanted a relationship. He'd made that plenty clear in the last year and had even kissed her. Once. He hadn't repeated the attempt, but she had a feeling he was waiting for some kind of a sign from her.

Which was the problem, wasn't it?

She didn't know what she wanted.

She paused outside door of Gia's room. Gia was an interesting conundrum. When Rio had asked if Gia could stay with her for a few weeks, he'd presented her as a fellow smoke jumper who'd taken a nasty tumble—and who'd witnessed a drug grow firsthand. The ankle she could certainly help with, and the drug dealers didn't worry her. Between Ben and her boys, she had four potential bodyguards. The president of the United States couldn't have better or more dedicated security. Anyone who tried to get to Gia or into the house wouldn't get far.

What she hadn't figured out yet was what else there was between Rio and Gia. Because there was definitely something and she didn't think it was just chemistry. Oh, that was there. She didn't fool herself. She'd raised three good-looking alpha male sons. They'd had lovers, but she'd taught them to respect women and she trusted they weren't careless.

Gia had the potential to be something more.

And Mary Ellen wanted Rio to be happy.

On the surface, he was the most laidback, happy-go-lucky of her sons already. That was the surface though. Underneath he still hadn't dealt with all of the baggage he'd picked up as a child before she'd got him. His sensual charm and playful demeanor were weapons he wielded with deadly accuracy. No one outside of the family got close to him.

He'd dated. Often. She'd never worried about him being lonely. Just the happy part of the equation. Jack and Evan were settling down, which made her want the same thing for Rio.

And now he'd brought Gia here.

Gia's door was cracked, but the room was dark. She shouldn't look in.

She really, really shouldn't.

Thank God Ben wasn't here to bust her.

Carefully, she nudged the door just a little wider.

Payday. Gia slept on Rio's chest, her fingers curled into his T-shirt. And her Rio had his arms wrapped around her like she was someone precious. Like they belonged together. Their feelings for each other could be platonic. God knew, she and Ben had slept together on more than one occasion and there hadn't been any sex involved. Yet. And that was the key, wasn't it?

She retreated down the hall to her own room. She and Ben had a relationship. She still wasn't certain exactly *what* that relationship was, but they were friends—and something more. They cared about each other.

Maybe, just maybe, her Rio had found his someone.

CHAPTER EIGHTEEN

A week into her enforced vacation and day seven was the same as days one through six. Gia had her ass parked on the porch, her ankle elevated. She could practically feel the eyes boring into her from the fire station. Rio was out, training with the jump team, but she was under no illusions.

He'd simply handed off the babysitting detail to someone else.

She was bored, she was alone and she wanted to scream.

The car that pulled up in front was unexpected. Gia hadn't made too many friends in Strong outside of the jump team, which was a not unexpected side effect of forty-eight hour shifts and little down time. The beat-up import looked like someone had drag-raced the poor car up and down the mountain roads and, once upon a time, might have been fire engine red. Now the paint was more pink than night-on-the-town and the purple flowers hanging from the rearview mirror were both a disgrace and a distraction. Definitely not the kind of car you took on a fire road or even on the freeway. The car couldn't have seen fifty miles an hour this decade.

Gia wouldn't have been caught driving it.

The driver was familiar however. Lily Cortez was Jack Donovan's fiancée and genuinely nice.

Jack was a damned lucky guy.

Even if Lily's parking skills were as suspect as her car's paint job. The car protested as Lily carefully edged the car into the open spot in front of Nonna's bungalow. Lily had Faye riding shotgun, so apparently it was meet-the-other- fiancées day. Except, of course, that Gia wasn't a fiancée. More of a baby momma, although even that was still up in the air. She'd liked the two women when they'd met, but they were hardly close.

The two women got out of the car, juggling bags. Gia watched them come since it wasn't like she could duck inside and pretend no one was at home.

Damned ankle.

"Girl therapy." Faye waggled her eyebrows at Gia when she reached the porch.

"That sounds positively kinky." Lily didn't sound deterred, however.

"She's practically under house arrest," Faye pointed out. "So this is more like a jail visit."

Lily ignored her and turned to Gia. "We've brought chocolate."

Chocolate was definitely an incentive. Curiosity might have been enough however. Lily sported the most outlandish pair of flip-flops Gia had ever seen. The enormous daisies with diamond sparkles made it downright impossible to miss her.

"And chips." Faye grinned. "I voted for ice cream, but Lily pointed out that it's pushing ninety-five today and we'd arrive here with soup instead."

"We're going to pig out and watch the show."

"The show?" She wasn't firing on all cylinders today, but the lethargy crawling through her body had to be due to the heat. Nope. There was no other possible explanation at all.

Lily waved a hand toward the fire station. "The guys always wash the trucks on Tuesdays."

"Unless there's a fire," Faye announced, plopping down onto the porch by Gia's feet. "Then we're out of luck."

"Okay." Gia eyed her two companions. Nope. She still didn't follow.

Across the street, the door on the firehouse rolled up with a noisy clang. Engines revved as the firemen began backing out the two trucks.

"Right on schedule." Faye rummaged happily in the bag and produced a plastic baggie. "Best. Brownies. Ever."

When Gia cracked the Ziploc, the heavenly aroma certainly gave credence to Faye's claim. Better yet, the guys hopped off the trucks, unrolled the hoses and got busy with the soap and water. That was definitely worth watching. Plus, Faye and Lily turned out to be good company, trading teasing comments that had them all in stitches.

"So," Lily said, when the firehouse hotties finally began to wind down the action. "You and Rio."

That topic was off-limits. She reached for her crutches, but Faye snagged them.

"Uh-uh. Answer the question."

"That wasn't a question." Gia narrowed her eyes. "And this is an ambush."

"Pretty much." Lily grinned. "But you're bored. You like us. And we have inside information about Rio Donovan. Take your pick."

Gia thought about that while the firemen finished rolling up their hoses. "It wasn't a question," she said finally.

"I'll rephrase. What's up between you and Rio? And don't give me this 'We're just friends' crap. You might be friends—"

"*First*," Faye emphasized.

"But we saw the kiss he laid on you when you reached base camp after your campout," Lily finished.

"Evan has never kissed one of his teammates like that." Faye sounded damned certain. And like she was trying not to laugh.

Lily nodded solemnly. "I'm fairly certain I can say the same for Jack."

"How do I know that whatever I tell you doesn't go straight back to Jack and Evan?"

"She's going to spill," Lily said, her eyes sparkling.

"Scout's honor." Faye held up two fingers. "Shit. Is that the right gesture?"

"I don't know." Lily leaned forward. "But you can trust us. We're all girls here."

They were. That was true. Why *not* talk to them? Maybe they really did have the inside scoop on Rio Donovan. And, even if they didn't, she was tired of sitting by herself and the silence bothered her. If she had to guess, they'd want to know if she was getting any and, if so, if the sex was worth the hassle of house-training Rio. Damned if she knew, but maybe they could shed some light on her situation.

"We're having sex," she announced.

"Blunt. I knew I liked her for a reason," Faye said.

"Before or after the kiss?"

"Yes and yes."

Lily choked on her chocolate. Of course, that might have had something to do with the firefighter who had just climbed on top of the truck. His wet T-shirt clung to washboard abs and, despite the ball cap jammed down over his head, Gia was pretty certain that was Jack. Jack and Lily must have mastered the silent communication thingie, because he definitely had Lily's attention.

"He knows about the Tuesdays," Gia guessed.

Lily shrugged, but she didn't take her gaze off her firefighter. "He objected and claimed we were objectifying the guys. I told him to put out or shut up."

"Not that there's more than one way to interpret that," Faye teased. "But your secret plan to get him half-naked and wet appears to be working."

"He takes his job very seriously." Lily grinned. "I'm a lucky woman he decided to take one for the team."

Her engagement ring flashed as she raised her hand waved energetically. "But you and Rio..." She looked sideways at Gia.

"Wow."

Rio was definitely all about the wow.

"Explain," Faye demanded. "This is going to be good."

"There's not much to tell." *Unfortunately.*

"You had sex with Rio Donovan." Lily sounded impressed.

"You're having sex with Jack," she pointed out.

"True, but Rio's in a whole different league. The man is a legend."

Faye snorted. "That just means he's used."

They all thought about that for a minute and then they started laughing.

"But more than once?" Lily sucked in a breath

Jesus. "Yes. More than once."

Lily nodded slowly. "That's almost a record for Rio. No offense." She looked apologetically at Gia. "But he's all about the moving on. Mimi had him for three weeks and that was *definitely* a record."

She winced.

"I probably shouldn't mention formers."

"No. It's okay." She'd already heard all about that relationship. And she liked Mimi. She really did. She was the only one who'd played the V-card. So maybe Rio was a lot less picky than she was.

Faye raised a brow. "And you're seeing him now?"

"Define *see*." She saw Rio every day because they were both living in his mother's house. It was driving her crazy, if she was being honest.

"Are you dating?" Faye narrowed her eyes. "Because if you're having sex and he's parked you in Mary Ellen's house, I'm going to vote *yes*."

"It's complicated."

Lily sighed. "It's been a while since I dated, but how can that not have a *yes* or *no* answer?"

"We don't go out." She shrugged.

"You just have sex and share a roof?" Faye's eyes widened. "That's a little modern for me."

She hadn't thought about it. Probably because she was too busy taking advantage of Rio and wondering if she just possibly might be pregnant. Her plate was full. Now that she did, however, she could see that Faye had a point. Rio hadn't taken her out on anything remotely resembling a date. . Their overnight campout definitely didn't count.

Lily nodded, reaching into her bag and pulling out a stack of magazines. "You should definitely make him take you out."

Gia waved at her foot. "I'm grounded."

"And you have crutches. Rio's positively yummy. Hey," she said when Lily elbowed her, "I have eyes in my head. Getting engaged didn't blind me. You known and I know that Rio's gorgeous. And, if he's anything like his brothers, he's really, really hot in bed. Of course Gia took advantage of any opportunities that presented themselves."

"I took advantage of him," she pointed out in the interest of being fair. "I put him in my truck and—I believe the words you used were *told him to put out or shut up.*"

"Good for you." Lily sighed. "I should try that."

Faye just grinned.

"What is it with you and cars?" Lily groaned. "No. Don't tell me. Evan's going to be my brother-in-law. I do *not* want to know."

Gia didn't particularly want to hear about Evan's sex life either, so she brought the conversation back around to Rio. "Having sex was my idea. Maybe he wouldn't have done anything if I hadn't pushed him."

Lily snorted. "He's a Donovan. Making him do anything he doesn't want to do is downright impossible. Trust me."

Maybe he didn't want to date her. Disappointment washed through her. She was a checkmark in the potential responsibility column with a side of hot sex. That wasn't attractive forever-and-ever materials.

"Unhappy thought?" Faye guessed.

"What if he isn't interested in dating me?"

"You're living together," Faye pointed out. "So what if you skipped a step?"

"But—"

"This is going to be good," Lily observed.

"What I say doesn't get repeated, right?"

"Definitely good," Faye said happily. Then, more seriously, "Absolute discretion. The guys will never hear a word of it from us."

"The condom broke," she said miserably. "When we were out in the woods. So, between that and the possibility that the drug growers come after me as a potential eye witness, Rio wanted me here where he could keep an eye on me."

Lily's eyes widened. "You're pregnant?"

"You skipped *every* step." Faye sounded impressed.

Gia thunked her head back against the chair and closes her eyes. "We're not dating because we don't have a relationship. We had sex and then he would have walked. Except the condom broke and now he's worried that I'm pregnant."

"Are you?" Lily stared at her. At least she wasn't eying her stomach.

"No idea yet. Ask me in about a week."

"How do you feel about it?" Faye sounded curious, but she didn't sound horrified. That had to be a good sign.

"I don't know," she said honestly. "I certainly hadn't planned on having a baby *now*. I mean, maybe some day in the future, but I'm finishing my degree and I love jumping. A baby complicates all that."

Some of the funny went out of the afternoon when she thought about the baby. Because that was something she hadn't really done yet. This wasn't about a broken condom anymore. The little pulse of warmth somewhere low in her belly made her smile. This was about a baby. A small person who would, some day, become a bigger person. Her eyes teared up. Damn it. She wasn't a crier.

"Sometimes complications can be good," Lily said softly, bumping her shoulder against Gia's good leg. "Maybe this is one of those times?"

"Could be," she agreed. To her surprise, she didn't choke on the words.

"Doing everything in order is over-rated." Faye handed her more chocolate. "Date. Sex. Ring. Wedding. Baby. I mean, you've cut the line and gone straight for the good stuff."

"Because we don't really have a relationship." Rio had promised he'd be there for her and their baby and she believed him. He was an honorable guy. No matter how many sensual games he'd played in the past, he'd never walk away from his child. And he'd always treat her with respect and look out for her as the mother of that child. She knew that.

It was her problem if she wanted more.

"You do." Lily handed her a magazine. "You absolutely do."

"It's just a little hard to label." Faye curled up in the chair next to hers. "And that's okay. You and Rio will figure it out, although, if he's anything like his brothers, you're going to what to give him plenty of hints and provide some direction."

"Donovan men can be clueless," Lily agreed.

"All men can be." Faye snorted and that set them off on another round of laughter.

While they discreetly gave Gia time to wipe her eyes—and, yep, she used the hem of her T-shirt, sue her—Lily produced a stack of bridal magazines and post-it notes and talk shifted to the double wedding Lily and Faye were planning for October, after fire season was safely over. They spent the next half hour laughing and dreaming about dresses and flowers. Gia didn't know if she'd still be here to see the wedding, but she could imagine it.

Lily and Faye would make beautiful brides.

"We weren't going to do the whole bridesmaid thing." Faye eyed her speculatively. "But I think we should rethink that."

Lily nodded. "We'd love for you to be our maid of honor, Gia."

Oh, God. She felt that seductive stab of belonging. Of hope.

"I'd love to," she said, when what she meant was *If I'm here, yes, please. Absolutely.*

As soon as the girls cleared her porch, climbing back into Lily's POS beater and waving as they drove off to do God knew what somewhere else, Gia grabbed her cellphone. Texting was both a cop-out—and one hundred percent, bona fide dating behavior.

She tapped the message into her phone and eyed it. *You wanna go on a date?*

Thought about it a minute and added *with me* to the end of the sentence.

Just in case Rio thought she was setting him up with a girlfriend. Or was trying for some kind of strange heart-to-heart.

Across the street, the firefighters backed the last truck into the bay, the door rolling shut with an impressive clang. If her hostess had slept through a single fire in the last ten years, color her surprised. On the other hand, she had a feeling Mary Ellen wanted to know *every* time the firefighters took off for a job. She hadn't missed the chemistry between the other woman and the fire chief.

Not really her business.

Even if she and Rio worked something out between themselves.

She eyed the phone but, nope. Her message hadn't magically sent itself. She had to tap Send for that to happen. And she was a chicken.

Maybe Rio was out on a training run. Or packing gear. He could be jumping out of the DC-13 for all she knew, because Jack had decreed shop talk off-limits for her. She appreciated his concern—she really did—but she was going stir-crazy stuck here on Mary Ellen's porch while fire season rolled on without her.

And, like it not, they were both part of this half-assed, part-time relationship.

A date.

How hard could it be to ask a man she'd already slept with out on a date?

If she was very lucky, she might even get him naked at the end of the night. Or before. Even during. She apparently wasn't very picky when it came to Rio Donovan. She'd take him however and whenever she could.

Huh. She thought about that for a moment. She probably should have minded more that she looked at him and started thinking wicked thoughts about his big, gorgeous body. Rio probably wouldn't care. He'd had women chasing him for years and she'd seen the easy familiarity with which he treated Mimi. He liked women. Women liked him. In Rio's world, it was that simple. She was the one who wanted to change the rules and take their relationship somewhere other than fun land.

Starting with a date.

She eyed the phone.

"Wish me luck," she muttered to no one because, that's right, she was alone. Before she could have more second thoughts—or third, fourth or fifth thoughts—she tapped Send.

When Rio texted back five minutes, she didn't know whether she was happy or just plain scared. Because she had a date. For tonight.

Peeing on the stick now was cheating.

Plus, the marketing copy on the back of the box said she needed to wait another week if she wanted reliable results—and who wanted *unreliable* test results?

And yet she wanted to know.

Right now, damn it.

Fuck it. No one needed to know what she'd done and the test wouldn't be accurate anyhow. Probably. Even if there was a baby, there was probably nowhere near enough hormone running around her body to register two pink lines.

Which was why she'd bought not one, not two, but *three* kits.

Target offered a discount on multiples anyhow. She wasn't sure if the store catered to the trying-to-get-pregnant crowd or the truly desperate, but she'd bit. And bought.

She hid the surplus boxes behind a stack of Always. Hopefully, that was deterrent enough. Not that she expected people snooping in her bathroom, but it paid to be careful.

She'd also bought a new box of condoms.

Wishful thinking on her part since Rio had been hands off.

Taking the test required the coordination of a gymnast, but she managed to aim where she needed to aim and then laid the stick out on a piece of toilet paper on the counter. All the better to hide the evidence with afterwards. One quick wad and toss and voila. No more evidence.

While her iPhone counted down the seconds, she kept busy, reorganizing the contents of the bathroom cupboard. When the phone beeped, looking was harder than she'd thought it be.

This test didn't count, she reminded herself.

It was far too early.

She looked and, wouldn't you know it?

Two pink lines.

Two lines that didn't, couldn't count.

By the time Rio brought her home—and she really shouldn't think of Mary Ellen's place as home—it was late. Well past midnight and creeping closer and closer to those smudgy grey hours between late night and really, really early morning. Mary Ellen had left the porch light on for them.

The movie had been good. Sitting next to Rio in the darkened theater, bumping fingers and elbows with him as they went after the popcorn in the enormous tub he'd bought? That was even better.

The movie had been an action flick, all car chases and explosions paired with a few hot bedroom scenes. She and Rio had laughed and talked.

About the movie.

He'd been fun. Polite. And all hands-off.

His hand cupped her elbow, helping her negotiate the stairs with her crutches.

She hesitated. "Rio?"

"Yeah?" He turned his head and look at her and, nope, she couldn't read a thing on his face. She needed something… but she had no idea what. The date had been fun, but it hadn't filled the funny ache and void she was growing.

"Never mind," she said and turned away.

She got her hand on the knob, but a big, masculine hand slapped the wood above hers, holding the door shut.

"Wait up," he growled.

Like she was going through that door until he let her.

"We're done."

"Not yet."

He grabbed her crutches and tossed them onto Mary Ellen's Adirondack chair.

"I need those," she protested.

"Not for this. Stand on one foot." Turning her around, he got her back right against the wall. "You're skipping the best part of date night."

"Which would be?"

"I walked you to your door." He paused, dragging a thumb down her cheek and over her jaw. His touch caused a shiver she felt in all her good parts. "Now I get the goodnight kiss. If I do it right, you might invite me in."

"Is that how it works?" She was breathless, but not due to her PSVT. Nope, the hitch in her breathing was all due to the man pinning her in place. She ran herhands up his arms, loving the way his eyes darkened.

He lowered his head until his mouth almost touched hers. "It's been a while since I dated, but I have it on good authority."

"Really? Because, technically, this is your mother's door."

The kiss, when it came, was quick and sweet, a simple brush of his lips over hers. "Jack swears it works."

He swallowed her laugh with his second kiss.

"Wow. I should probably tell Jack *thank you*."

When he lifted his head, her dazed look was impossibly sweet. And sexy. Christ, he touched her and he wanted her beneath him. On top of him. With her, he wanted to act out the entire fucking Kama Sutra.

He probably didn't need to tell her that. "You could say *thank you* to me."

"You did walk me to the door." She leaned her head back against the door and he wanted to kiss her again, just because he could and she'd let him. Gia in an accommodating mood was sexier than any fantasy his brain had come up with in years.

So he did.

Their third kiss was hotter and wilder than their first. Except that they were still standing on his mother's porch, in full view of the entire town of Strong and the firefighters he'd told to keep eyes on the house. *Hell*. He reached behind her for the knob. Before this summer, that door had never been locked. Strong wasn't that kind of place. After the trouble Gia had run into, however, that had changed. He slipped the key into the lock, turning the knob with a quick flick of his wrist.

A truck backfired somewhere in the distance, followed by a faint wash of sound from Ma's as the bar door opened and closed. There was a shitload of crickets too, the insect chatter part and parcel of being home. Strong's night song was real peaceful and definitely calmer than the angry noise of a fire chewing up the mountainside.

"You're thinking again," Gia said.

That was a no brainer. He wanted to make her happy. They still had four days until she took the pregnancy test, but he was suddenly certain. They'd be starting a family together. Whatever it took, he needed to keep her content and by his side. For the baby.

For him, if he was being honest.

"I'm thinking that I love you."

Those three words were the right words to say. Those words fix things, mean things, and any baby of his would have a family full of love. That was non-negotiable.

She slapped a hand on his chest and shoved him away.

"Is that part of the date night walk to the door?"

"I love you," he repeated.

"Uh-huh." She stared up at him, clearly skeptical. "I'm going to kick Jack when I see him next. His relationship advice sucks. It's a miracle he got Lily to agree to marry him."

Well. Hell.

He went on the offensive.

"When someone tells you that he loves you, calling bullshit isn't the appropriate response."

"Move," she snapped. "I'm doing playing games, Rio. Dating was a bad idea."

"I'm not playing." He was deadly serious.

"You love me." She shook her head. "I don't think so. Give me one reason."

"You want a reason?"

"I'd prefer more than one."

"I've got plenty of reasons. You're loyal to the core. You know how to laugh when life pisses all over you." He didn't do words. Compliments, sure. But he was so far out of his league that it wasn't funny.

"You're stuck on number three," she pointed out.

He figured telling her she was the sexiest woman he'd ever laid eyes on wouldn't up his believability quotient.

"So what if I don't have a laundry list of reasons? It doesn't make my feelings for you any less true."

Because those words were true. He tested that idea and—wasn't that a shocker? He meant every word. He threaded his fingers through her short hair, cupping her head and holding her in place. She didn't get out of this so easily. He loved Gia.

Unfortunately, it appeared his feelings were one-sided.

"Whatever." She reached behind her and opened the door, hopping under his arm to retreat inside. "I assume you're locking up?"

He followed, grabbing her crutches from the chair. "We're not done here."

"And I say we are," she insisted stubbornly.

In answer, he flipped the lock. Big mistake on her part—now she was trapped inside with him and working on one good foot—but it worked to his advantage. He kept right on coming towards her too, until they were chest to chest.

"Rio?" That note of sexy hesitation was back in her voice. Yeah, she knew she was in trouble. She didn't sound like she minded much either.

"No more talking," he growled. "I can work with that, Gia."

Her bedroom or his? His, he decided, although he'd be happy to move right in with her. He didn't like having separate rooms. Or separate lives. When he held her in his arms, everyone was happy. Right?

Bending down, he scooped her off her feet and brought her where he wanted her. His bed. One gentle bounce and she was dead center.

"You just want to get into bed with me. I can work with that." Gia shifted backwards and patted the side of the bed. Then she tugged—hard—on his wrist for good measure. As big as he was, she wouldn't move him much, but she wanted to make her point perfectly clear. He let her, his jean-covered thighs bumping against her side of the bed. That put her on eye level with his belt buckle. She figured it would take her four seconds to undo that buckle and get her hands on him—which might be three seconds too long. She wanted him undone and exposed, wanted him panting and begging for her. Instead, she had Stoic Soldier standing beside her bed, all hands-off like he thought a bottle of cold water was enough to solve her problems.

Like hell. She blamed him for a good share of the mess she was in, she realized. Which was fine, because he was also more than capable of making it up to her. The sensual fire lighting her up from the inside out shot to volcanic proportions. Licking dry lips, she dropped her hand to his thigh. His muscles tensed, and she was fairly certain he growled. Or cursed. She didn't care which. Thank God he was fighting for control too.

There was no arguing Rio was a sexy, creative lover—it was just that some part of her—her *heart*—wanted more. And she wasn't convinced Rio had it to give, despite the words he'd said.

So she'd make do with sex for tonight.

"Now, damn it," she said and palmed his erection.

Christ. There was nothing subtle about Gia's touch. She pushed her palm over the denim, rubbing the fabric over his dick, and he hardened more. When she shaped him through the cloth, he bit back a groan. Gia out of control was a sight to see.

Gia's face was pale everywhere except the pink flush staining her pretty cheekbones. Her eyes glittered as she stared up at him. He wanted to scoop her into his arms and…she was possibly pregnant. With his baby.

Probably.

He was fairly certain he shouldn't be standing here, even if she did have one hand on his dick and the other yanking at heartstrings he hadn't known he possessed. She squeezed, and he bit back a groan

She leaned so far forward he was sure she was about to tumble out of the bed. He had a feeling that he'd just follow her to the floor, and when she repeated her earlier demand, he was sure of it.

"Get in the bed." Her fingers found him through the gaps between the buttons of his fly. That soft butterfly stroke on his bare dick was the most erotic thing he'd ever felt. She could take charge here if that's what she needed.

Her other hand cupped his balls through the worn denim, and his desire for this woman exploded. She'd said *yes*. She was as all in as he was, so he didn't need to wait. Stepping back, biting back a groan as her fingers slid off his dick, he hauled his T-shirt over his head and shucked his jeans. He probably beat one or two known speed records for undressing, but Christ, she was waiting and she'd invited him in and he was so done resisting. If she wanted to have her way with him, he'd let her.

And then he'd have his way with her.

Sliding an arm beneath her back, he covered her and took her down to the bed.

He caged her head between his arms, pressing her down into the mattress. Reminding her who was in control. She wouldn't get away from him now. He had her at his mercy, and they both knew it. He could feel the slow grin splitting his face, because, hell, he liked having her spread out beneath him.

All *his*.

She looked up at him, all wide, brown eyes and sexy need. Wanting him. Wanting this. He was naked. She had too many clothes on, but he'd fix that.

He ran a hand along the vee of her T-shirt. The dark pink cotton was a fiery contrast to her sun-kissed skin. She'd skipped the bra, and her nipples pebbled beneath the cotton. Yeah. She wanted this all right. He was one hell of a lucky man.

"You're a pretty sight," he said.

He didn't give her a chance to answer. Instead, he pushed her T-shirt up with one hand and, Christ, she was so pretty. Her breasts were a handful he couldn't wait to palm, all soft skin and the sweetest pair of nipples begging for his kiss. He trailed one calloused finger over the white marks from her summer bikini, down and over the sensitive tips. She squirmed, and he liked that too. He liked everything about her, and that was the truth.

"Lose the shirt," he growled, because he wanted her naked, *now*, and she seemed to be of the same mind. Thank God. Together, they yanked the shirt over her head, their fingers meeting at the hem, palms brushing as the cotton went up. Her long, blessedly bare legs wrapped around his, her hips rocking into his erection as she shimmied to get the shirt over her head. He didn't help her with those last few inches. Hell no. He held her and enjoyed every second of her effort.

He dropped the shirt on the floor and kissed her as her reward. She kissed him right back, all hot need and fiery passion. He gave, she took, and gave right back in a hot tangle of lips. He pressed, licked the soft seam. Nipped her lush lower lip and about groaned when she opened up. *Christ.* She touched him back, her tongue meeting his, and he knew, just knew, there'd be nothing polished or refined in what they did here in this bed tonight. Raw, hot sex, he thought, as his head shut down and his body took over. That's what he had to give her tonight. He hoped like hell she was ready for him.

He cupped her breast, feeling the satiny softness as she pressed into his hold. She moaned, her hands making demands of their own as she traced the lines of his abdomen down, down, down, her fingers wrapping around him again. Oh hell yeah. She held on to his dick, squeezing and tormenting him.

He ran a finger over her pretty pink nipple. She whimpered, hungry-like, and her grip on his dick tightened. That was his clue right there. She liked that. So he repeated the slow stroke again and again. Teasing her. Plumping the little nub and squeezing lightly. Then lowered his head and sucked her into his mouth like the sweetest of cherries. His Gia was damned perfect. He switched, kissing his way over to her other breast, because no way he didn't get himself a taste there too. She whimpered, her legs moving restlessly, brushing his. But he had her pinned wide, and there wasn't much she could do but ride out the sweet ache.

He trailed a hand down over her stomach. He could feel the heat and damp of her through the fabric. He hadn't thought he could get any harder, but that did the trick. Her wanting him was the sexiest thing he'd ever felt. He tugged her shorts down, rolling to the side so she could toe them off and he could shift his hand down and touch her where she was all slick heat and luscious wet. Christ, he loved learning what made her gasp, what made her shiver.

"Rio—" She bucked hard, but he had her.

"Right here," he promised and touched her again. His mouth grazed her ear.

He circled his thumb and forefinger around her clit, plumping her, and that sent her over the edge. She throbbed and pushed against his touch, coming in a short, hard burst. Primal satisfaction filled him. *His.* She was his. He'd given her this, done this for her. He'd do it over and over, make her come on his fingers and his mouth. Just as soon as he'd had her.

He reached for her.

Rio.

She shouldn't, he shouldn't, but they *would*. She liked how out of control this too-in-control man was around her. She also had plenty of plans to make him still crazier. After all, she was one up on the orgasm count, so she definitely owed him.

Plus, he was watching her again. "I think I like that look on your face," he said, stroking a finger over her as she caught her breath and came back to earth.

"Just wait," she promised and slid down his big body. The muscles in his stomach twitched when she touched and licked her way lower. She liked that. A lot. Rio had a reputation, and she'd worried she wouldn't stack up with the other women in his past, but he didn't seem to care, so she let go of those fears and just enjoyed him. Drank him in as she ran her hands down the cut lines of his abdomen and farther south. He was glorious. There was no other word for it other than *mine* because, right now, he was all hers, and she didn't have to share.

His erection was thick and hard, the tip of him damp. She wrapped her hands around him, savoring the hot, delicious heat of him.

"Touch me," he demanded, and she gently dragged a thumb over the crown, stroking the velvety skin.

He groaned. "Just like that. Take me into your mouth, baby. I want that tongue of yours on me." She didn't hesitate, his rough plea making her pussy spasm.

Acting on pure instinct, she let her head drop forward and wrapped her hands around his thick length. Her hands guided him toward her. He was too big for her to take all of him easily, so she suckled just the tip, swiping her tongue over the crown. Exploring him like he'd explored her. Her pussy clenched, remembering, as Rio groaned in her ear.

His big hands tangled in her hair, guiding her, holding her. She gave him more, took more, loving this new power over him.

"Gia." He growled her name, clearly near the edge. Good. She licked her way up, swirling her tongue at the top. Then sank back down. Did it again because she loved touching him like this.

"Let me inside you. Please?" The rough demand and the hoarser please undid her.

She rolled onto her back. He looked down at her and hesitated—a small beat of time so quick she almost missed it in the haze of need and lust—but then he followed her. His powerful biceps braced on either side of her head, his big body pressed hers down into the mattress.

She smiled up at him. "Wish granted."

"Thank Jesus." He fished in the bedside drawer, producing a condom.

"Just in case," he said, rolling down the condom.

Don't ruin the moment, Jackson. Don't tell him he doesn't need a condom anymore, not with you.

So when he tucked himself against her opening and pushed steadily in, she held on and enjoyed the ride, drawing his mouth down to hers. No questions. No words. Just hot sex and heated promises that had nothing to do with *forevers* and everything to do with *right nows*.

Inhaling, Gia took stock. She was in Rio's big bed, the sheets tangled around her waist and six-plus feet of male temptation pressed against her back. He was here now, one arm snagged around her waist. The clock on the bedside table read four a.m. which made this getaway time. When she tried to pull away, however, his grip tightened. Sprawled on his back, he consumed most of the available space in the bed—that figured—his head turned away from hers. Stubble roughened his jaw. He screamed pirate. Six-plus feet of bronzed, muscled, *naked* pirate.

Was she the luckiest girl in the world—or the unluckiest?

Rio Donovan was overwhelming. He was sensual and demanding, with a side of arrogance that she should *not* have found so appealing. He wouldn't let her hide from what he made her feel. He was the drug, and already she craved more of his touch. That was definitely her cue to hit the road. Wrapping her fingers around his wrist, she tugged.

"Let go," she whispered.

Leave. Stay. Both options were equally impossible. And both required buy-in from the soldier lying there in the bed, fully aware that she was walking out of his room and out of his life. She didn't have super Ninja stealth skills, and she'd never make the door without his knowledge. They both knew that, like they both knew he was letting her go.

Sometimes words just weren't enough. *I love you.*

Grabbing her clothes from the floor, she dressed quickly. She was so not going out into that hallway half-dressed. Knowing her luck, she'd run into his mother or both of his brothers.

"Gia—" He rolled over, propping his head up on one powerful arm as he watched her. She didn't want to talk, and she wasn't staying. To be on the safe side, she added another five feet of space between them. The man was too damned sexy for her own good.

"You want to come back over here?" He growled the words, and damned if she could tell if they were a question or a statement. Unfortunately for her, both worked. Clearly, she'd underestimated Rio's sex appeal. That, or what had happened in his bed was about more than just the sex. It was a definite possibility, she decided as she hopped on her good foot, tugged her shorts up, his gaze burning her. Maybe she'd gotten a touch emotionally involved.

So fine.

She'd get uninvolved, starting right now.

Snagging her shoes with a finger—there was no dignified way to beat a hasty, morning-after retreat hopping away on one foot—she made for the door. So what if they'd had sex? They were both unmarried, consenting adults. She'd come. He'd come. No problems there. It had definitely been one hell of a date.

"Thanks," she said flippantly.

The muttered curse behind her made Rio's opinion perfectly clear.

What she didn't expect was the way he shot out of bed and came after her. With one smooth move, he snatched her up and deposited her on the bed.

Oh happy day. Her caveman was back.

"Time to talk," he growled.

Her pulse picks up like a runaway fire, banging out a staccato rhythm that was no shade of normal. Nope. Her heart had the beat of a sixty year-old, three hundred pound man confronted with cardio for the first time in his life.

Ah, hell.

CHAPTER NINETEEN

"Jesus Christ, Gia."

Rio shot up and flipped on the bedside light.

Gia was visibly short of breath, fighting for each hit of air. She ignored him, leaning over to swipe her purse from the floor and then rummage through the contents for something.

Fuck this. He yanked the bag away from her, upending the contents on the bed. She didn't have that much crap stowed in the half-dozen pockets but whatever she wanted, she got. *Now.* He needed to fix this. Stat.

She picked a brown pharma bottle out of the mess on her lap. The amber plastic kind with one of those child-proof caps. When she didn't get the cap off the first time, he took it and popped the lid. Digitek. Whatever the fuck that was. He was no pharmacist

While she downed the pill, he grabbed his cell phone.

"I'm calling Ben. We're going to get you in the ambulance and to the hospital."

She shook her head, still sucking in air like she'd been underwater for a century and only just come up. "It's a wiring problem, Rio, not a death sentence."

What. The. Fuck.

He leapt out of bed anyhow, his fingers already punching buttons.

But her color is better. Her lips weren't blue and he couldn't hear her breathing.

"Please?" She leaned back against his pillows, clearly wiped.

That *please* did him in because damned if he didn't take his thumb off the Send button.

"I have PSVT," she said finally. "It's no big deal. I've dealt with it all my life."

"PSVT?" She was speaking a language he didn't understand.

"It's a heart arrhythmia. Paroxysmal supraventricular tachycardia if you want the fifty cent words." She tried to grin at him and all he knew was that something was wrong but damned if he had the knowledge to fix it.

"You have a heart arrythmia."

That hadn't been in any of her application materials. He definitely would have remembered that. His head skipped ahead. "Did I cause this?"

"My episode?" She shrugged casually, but her eyes studied him intently. "It's not simple cause and effect. If I get too tired or too stressed, I'll have an episode. Sometimes, though, the episodes come out of nowhere."

"We had sex. I got you excited."

"We were both excited," she pointed out. "Weren't we?"

"Only one of us has an arrythmic heart," he said grimly. Did she take her life in her hands when they got in bed? Was this his fault? And then they'd argued. *Shit.*

"Sex isn't going to kill me, Rio." She sounded sure. "This is just something I have to watch out for."

He sat down on the side of the bed, setting the cell phone on the bedside table. He could dial in five seconds, but his legs were telegraphing an urgent sit-down-now message to his brain. How had the night gone from hot sex to fighting to this? Wrapping his fingers around her wrist, he found her pulse and counted.

"See? Better."

How could she sound so sure? Her lips had been *blue*.

Before he could answer, however, there was a soft knock on the bedroom door. Perfect. Now his mother was in the mix.

"Rio? Gia?" Nonna's calm voice filtered in from the hallway. "I don't want to intrude, but is everything okay?"

"God." Gia closed her eyes. "This is a nightmare."

He agreed with her there. His mother was concerned enough about the noise coming from his bedroom to come and bang on the door. And, well, shit. He couldn't leave her standing in the hallway, wondering. So he got up and went to the door. Opened it and, sure enough, Nonna was standing there, looking worried. She had the instincts of a firefighter's family for trouble.

"Gia isn't feeling well," he said.

Which was an understatement.

"I'm fine," Gia insisted.

"Are you a doctor now?" He stepped back so Nonna could come in.

She came in, seemingly unfazed by Gia's presence in his bed, although he'd bet he'd hear about it later. *Christ*. He hadn't lived at home since he was a teenager. Nonna didn't beat around the bush any, going straight to Gia's side. "Are you okay?"

"I'm fine." Gia did sound okay. Tired, but like herself. "I have a heart arrythmia. I had an episode. It's over for tonight."

Nonna nodded. "You want me to call someone?"

"Like a doctor? Family?" Gia shook her head. "I'm done for the night. Sorry to have woken you up."

"Honey—" Nonna sounded like she wanted to say something, but settled for fussing instead. The attention made Gia uncomfortable, but what could she say?

His head was stuck on what Gia had said. That Nonna didn't need to call her family. Damn straight. *He* was her family, or he wanted to be. He intended to be the person by her side when this thing hit her. He had a hell of a lot to learn, but he had no doubt that he could do it.

Because she was his everything.

And, shit.

She was.

It was that simple.

He saw Nonna to the door and then turned back to Gia.

"You're really okay?" He needed to hear her say the words. One or two hundred times might be enough.

"Absolutely." She swung her legs over the side of the bed, fishing with her feet for her shoes. He recognized an exit in the making. He'd done the same thing himself, although without the medical drama.

"Stay," he said, really meaning tonight, tomorrow and every day after that.

She shook her head. "I don't think so, Rio."

"Why not?" he asked carefully.

"I need some space." She swiped a hand over her face. "And some sleep."

"You're not one hundred percent."

"So you're volunteering to take care of me? Again? You should buy a lottery ticket, you're so lucky. I can take care of myself, Rio."

But she didn't have to. She had him. He opened his mouth, but she kept right on talking.

"I'm tired of it," she said. "My whole life, everyone has rushed to look after me. To do things *for* me. It's not necessary. I'm not limited."

"Which is why you never mentioned it?" Her color looked good now. Maybe he didn't need to roust Spotted Dick for a hospital run.

Her chin came up. "What would you have said, Rio, if I'd mentioned the PSVT before I joined the jump team? Would you have politely passed?"

He answered her question with one of his own.

"What would have happened if you had one of these attacks out there in the field?"

"I handle it." She glared at him. "Has it happened? Yes. It has. And you didn't notice, Rio. It was no big deal."

Well, hell.

He thought back and, yeah, it didn't take long to remember the episode in his truck. The slow burn of anger followed the memories. She'd been sick. He should be gentle. But—fuck that. She claimed she didn't want special treatment.

"You lied to me." He held a hand up when she would have spoken to me. "You lied to our team. A lie of omission is still a lie, Gia. You didn't tell us about something that could impact every man on that team. We counted on you and you let us down."

She shoved off the bed. "I'm not my PSVT. It doesn't make me weak. It doesn't stop me from doing what needs to be done."

"Unless you can't breathe," he snapped. "Then, it sure seems to me like you've got a problem."

She'd put herself in danger. She'd taken unacceptable chances. He catches her arm, turning her to face him. He didn't know what to say. But part of him apparently had plenty of words, because the words kept on coming out of his mouth.

"You're grounded. Permanently. No more jumping."

"You can't do that." She tugged on her arm.

"I can." For a dozen reasons, starting and ending with the fact that he represented one third of Donovan Brothers, which put him in charge whether she liked it or not.

She froze in the door. "So much for loving me."

"I do love you. And because I do, I'm going to make damned sure you stay safe. And that what I'm doing is best for you and our possible family of three. Don't push me on this, Gia."

She shook her head. "Fuck off."

Two words that summed up the situation perfectly.

Rio's bedroom door slammed closed.

Hell.

Gia had him coming and going. He didn't know what she wanted him to do or to say—and, for the first time ever, he *wanted* to please. What had happened between them here in his bed should have been a step in the right direction.

Wrong.

Shit. He had it bad, and his brothers would be merciless. He'd thought he and Gia had a *thing*, and she'd walked away. Just like a guy, he thought, and wry amusement curved his lips. Except that he wasn't done with her.

And he didn't know how he felt about that.

Sex, he told himself firmly. Their relationship had been about sex and sex only. This business of him loving her was simply a misconception on his part that he'd get past. He didn't know why he'd expected something more, or why he was looking around the room for some kind of sign that she'd been there. Gia wasn't Cinder-fucking-ella, dropping glass slippers on her way out the door. She'd gone.

And, yeah, he still loved her.

So it was plain pathetic that he rolled over, putting himself on her side of the bed, his head on the pillow she'd used. Not, he promised himself, because that side was where she'd slept, but because that was his usual spot. He always got the right side of the bed, and this was definitely his favorite pillow. He was lined up like a soldier on report, hugging one side of his bed, when he usually sprawled all over it.

Absolutely pathetic.

Yet he couldn't bring himself to move away, to *not* lie in the place she'd just vacated. The sheets were still warm from her body and the sweet scent of her perfume drove him nuts. She liked those light floral scents he'd always hated. A fun, flirty scent that clung to her clothes. He'd never walk by the fragrance counter in Macy's again without getting a hard-on.

Again, pathetic.

Instead of getting out of bed, though, he turned his face into her pillow, breathing in her scent. Lowered his hand to his dick and thought about Gia while he took care of business.

CHAPTER TWENTY

Gia still wasn't talking to him the next morning.

Rio didn't know how he felt about that, but she damned certain didn't get to take her pissed-off and drive away on her own, even if she claimed her ankle was better and she was more than capable of driving. He was her eyes for the morning. So here he was, with Mack riding shotgun, trailing her to the jump hangar while she limped ahead on her crutches with Joey for her morning companion.

His truck wasn't the only vehicle on the road, but it was damned close. Rio scanned each passing car in turn. "Did the DEA have any updates?"

"Nope." Mack didn't shift from his post by the passenger-side window. The man looked lazy and relaxed, but Rio knew the other man could kick into action at the slightest hint of trouble.

When they created the road, the road dipped and he could see ahead, around the curve she was taking blind. "We've got more company."

He jerked his head towards the large SUV parked in a pull out intended for runaway vehicles and turn-arounds. Emergency type stuff. None of which—shit—seemed to be in play here. The SUV wasn't familiar. The vehicle could be a local with a new pair of wheels or a tourist. He frowned. Gia'd been living in a fucking fishbowl, so any kind of takedown should not be happening.

"Call Joey. Tell him there could be an SUV on his six in a half mile."

"On it." Mack pulled out his cell and punched a text.

The caution might be unwarranted, but Rio's instincts screamed *trouble*. He wanted Gia within arm's reach now. Even as he thought it, however, she hit the gas, picking up speed. She loved driving. *Fuck.* He hated to rein her in. She'd accuse him of being highhanded and dictatorial, and maybe she was right. Gia didn't take orders well.

"Move, Gia," he growled as Mack looked up from his cell phone.

The SUV pulled out of its hidey-hole as Gia passed, dropping in behind Gia's truck. Not too close, but closer than Rio liked, especially on these roads. Mud covered the plates, obscuring the license number.

It hadn't rained in weeks.

"Who else do we have out here?" he barked, riding the accelerator hard. "Where are the DEA eyes?"

Gia took the next curve beautifully, her truck taking the bend tight and fast. Five miles to base camp. The company would minimize her exposure, but she was still vulnerable. The weight of the gun holstered at his back promised one solution, but only if he could get close enough. Steering his truck along a stretch of flat, he had a bird's eye view of the SUV gunning to life as Gia shot by. The vehicle pulled out, hard and fast, riding Gia's bumper.

Damn it.

"DEA's a mile back. Flat tire." Mack's voice was lethally controlled as he tossed the cell onto the seat, all playfulness gone. "Joey's on speaker." He rolled down the window, palming his own weapon. Mack didn't mess around. He'd been one of the best snipers the military had to offer.

A new curve in the road hid Gia and her tail. He pressed the gas pedal to the floor, looking for more speed but the speedometer already hovered at eighty. Any faster was near suicidal on a rural mountain highway but getting to Gia was paramount.

"Seat belt?" Getting Mack killed wasn't part of his plan.

"Roger that." Mack's hand curled around the oh-shit handle, handgun braced on that arm and ready for business.

They shot out of the curve and Rio pulled on the wheel, hearing gravel spin beneath the tires. And then there was Gia and the assholes riding her.

"Drive, Gia!" Rio bellowed the order.

The pumped up volume on the cell registered Joey's curse, loud and clear, but nothing from Gia. Her truck picked up speed, though. A hundred yards and closing fast. The man riding shotgun in the SUV raised a gun and sighted.

Rio cursed, calling out the obvious. "He's armed."

"On it." Mack unbuckled and hauled himself into the window frame. Rio wanted to be the one in the hot seat, but bitching about his place in this battle wouldn't help Gia any. Instead, he concentrated on keeping Mack's ride smooth and straight. Mack aimed, pulling the trigger as the SUV's passenger fired.

The SUV jerked as the leftmost tire ate the bullet.

Shit was hitting the fan in a spectacular way.

Gia tightened her grip on the wheel and pressed the gas pedal to the floor.

Beside her, Joey cursed. "We've got problems, Gia."

No shit. Her first clue had been the SUV exploding onto the road behind her. Sane people didn't drive mountain highways like that. Thank God for the truck, because anything with balder tires or less pick up and she'd have rolled the truck.

Which might have been the point.

A bullet cracked and she flinched instinctively.

Rio roared orders over the cell phone Joey had tossed on the dashboard. Bossy as hell, but the man knew what he was doing and she felt better just knowing he was there watching her six. The windshield spiderwebbed with the next shot, sporting a round hole in the center.

"Thoughts?" She rammed the accelerator, seeking every bit of speed she could get as the SUV inched closer. If that beast hit her rear bumper, she'd fishtail, go right over the side. She kept her eyes on the asphalt, her senses attuned to the truck and the way the tires rode the road. *Fly for me, baby.*

"I'm out," Joey said. "Just drive like hell and do some praying. Get some distance between us and them so the boys can do their thing."

Base camp was still almost four miles away, which at their current speed put them there in roughly three minutes. There was no time or way to turn around before then, not without slowing down and then she and Joey would be sitting ducks. She wasn't sure what she could do when she hit the parking area and the hangar, but hopefully there'd be some kind of cosmic sign. A neon sign touting *escape route this way* or even another barked command from Rio. She'd take whatever she could get.

Behind them, the SUV swerved before straightening out. She wasn't sure she was a nice person because part of her—a big part—was disappointed the assholes hadn't gone over the side.

"Mack's shooting," Joey said, savage satisfaction filling his voice. "They're gonna be running on rims."

Not fast enough, she thought, as another shot finished their windshield and, holy shit, glass flew everywhere. The truck swung wide and she fought the wheel for control, Joey's hands clamping down on hers as they wrestled the wheel together. The guardrail sprang into her field of vision too close, the beautiful, lethal mountainside not far enough. *God.* That was a long way down with no way back up.

Metal shrieked against metal and then they were shooting straight down the middle again.

"We hit." She tightened her hand on the wheel. Two miles. And then what?

Joey grinned as he shifted back into his seat. "And we're still here, so go you."

The truck shot onto the final straightaway, base camp visible ahead of them as the SUV surged closer in her rearview mirror.

"Brace," Joey snapped, his eyes glued on their tail. "You got airbags?"

"You bet," she said and then the SUV caught up, driving hard into their bumper. The world swung crazily, everything off-kilter, and then everything, everyone and everything went tumbling like she'd cleared the plane bay and only then discovered she hadn't packed a parachute after all.

Free fall.

Rio.

Jesus. Christ.

The SUV slammed into Gia's truck and Rio didn't know if he was praying or cursing. Begging, maybe, because the woman in that truck was his everything and there was nothing—nothing—he could do to help right now. She had to hold on all by herself and all he could do was race to pick up the pieces.

"Come on, baby," he growled, eyes glued to the road and foot to the pedal.

She almost controlled the spin. Almost. The truck shot off the road, narrowly missing the trees, bumping violently into the empty field the Donovans used to park their trucks.

Adrenaline shot through Rio, followed by a protective surge. *I'm coming for you, Gia.* The SUV roared up alongside Gia's truck and Rio knew the next move in this script.

Open fire.

Rake the disabled vehicle with gunfire, making sure whoever survived the crash ate a lethal dose of lead.

Mack's gun cracked beside him again, but Rio was done sitting by. It was time to go all in. To get out of the truck and into the action.

"I'm going in," he barked and Mack dropped back down into his seat and punching the window up. In the rearview mirror, he spotted another vehicle coming up fast behind them. That would be their DEA support, but those guys would never make it in time.

Gunning the motor, he picked his target. One final burst of speed and he drove the truck into the SUV's side. The impact rocketed through the truck, but Rio clamped down on the wheel, fighting the buck and spin. He didn't want to force the SUV into Gia's truck.

Nope.

He just wanted to make sure that the SUV's load of big, bad and dangerous couldn't pop the doors and finish the job.

He slammed on the brakes.

Mack jumped out, gun up as Rio launched himself from the driver's side door, covering the SUV. *Good man.* Sprinting to the SUV, he drew his weapon and leveled the gun on the first face he saw. There was the guy from the trail. Imagine that. The bastard had gone through the windshield headfirst because seatbelts apparently weren't part of his repertoire. Rio tried to feel bad about that, but the man had been gunning for Gia. Now he was twenty feet from the vehicle, doing a face plant in the dirt. Not a threat. No visible weapons.

Hell. No visible breathing.

He looked up and spotted the runners coming in hot from base camp. Jack was in the lead, gun out and running like he means business. His brother would take care of this guy. Would render first aid until the cops arrived if there was a need.

"I'm on point," he growled and headed for the SUV, Mack

guarding his six. This op would turn out okay. Not because he'd performed countless raids and rescues, but because he wasn't letting Gia go. In just a few, he'd have her out of her truck. He'd have her home free.

The approach should have been a walk in the park, a familiar job, but the gut-churning nausea ripping through his stomach was a surprise guest at the party. He sucked in air, forcing himself to breathe evenly. Emotions like *fear* and *worry* got a soldier killed. He wanted to spring for the truck, but first he had to disarm the immediate threat.

He leaned into the SUV.

"Game over. Drop the weapons and hands up."

Gia's hands wouldn't budge. Her fingers had a death grip on the wheel, hanging on for a ride that was over. The truck's motor pinged, starting the cool-down, but her brain wouldn't get with the plan and send the unlock message to her fingers.

"We're not dead," she said, because she wasn't sure she believed it.

"Christ," Joey announced from the passenger seat. She'd never been so glad to hear his voice. "I'm having a come-to-Jesus moment here, Jackson. That was too close. I'm never calling shotgun again."

The rearview mirror had acquired a crazy tilt—she vaguely recalled slamming her head into it as they rock-and-rolled their way to a stop—but Rio was out there, booted feet spread and radiating aggression as he hollered commands into the SUV. *Safe.*

She flipped off the ignition and rested her forehead against the wheel. Holy. Shit. Her truck was definitely headed for the shop, the front crumpled and banged up. Hell, the state of the windshield alone demanded repairs because there was nothing left between her cab and the great outdoors. She considered turning the engine on and moving out because staying put probably wasn't her best option. Nope. Her hands were shaking too badly.

"Gia?" That was Joey's hand carefully coming in to land on her shoulder with a medic's precision. "Talk to me some more. Let me know how you're feeling, okay? I need to hear your voice right now."

"Clear," Mack barked somewhere behind her. She cracked an eye and decided the man showed every inch of his military training as he finished his sweep of the area. "One knocked out, two injured. Our boys here weren't big believers in seatbelts."

The Rio came into view, one big, angry badass man. Coming for her.

Thank God.

"Gia?" Joey shifted, undoing his seatbelt and moving in.

God.

How close had she come to dying?

Get out.

She needed to move. Needed to find a safer position. What if Rio had miscalculated? What if the SUV pulling off the road to join the party wasn't full of the good guys but was instead packing reinforcements for the bad guys? Her body didn't care, giving in to a tsunami-sized series of shakes. Yep. She was in full shut-down-and-reboot mode.

"Hey." Joey's hand touched her arm again. His seatbelt clicked as he unbuckled and leaned toward her. "Jackson? You okay?"

She opened her mouth. No. Not really.

"I think I'm pregnant," she said instead.

There was a moment of silence followed by a particularly vile curse.

"You kiss your mother with your mouth?" she asked.

He ignored her, running his hands gently over her arms and legs as he went all EMT on her. Right. Their Joey often doubled as the team medic. How convenient he'd been the one riding shotgun with her. Couldn't have planned that better.

She fought the urge to giggle hysterically.

Instead, she put a hand out, bracing herself against the steering wheel, like she could hold herself together if she pushed hard enough or got enough distance. *Don't cry.*

She never cried.

"Does it hurt anywhere?" Joey crouched on the seat beside her, assessing.

"I'm fine."

"We're gonna get you a real doctor. See what he says."

Rio opened the door slowly. That made her want to laugh again—God, she wasn't herself, was she?—because he was more of a rip-the-door-off-the-hinges kind of guy than the slow and cautious type. Maybe he thought things were falling apart in here.

Maybe he was right.

"Can I move her?" he asked over her head, going straight to the source.

"No visible injuries." That from Joey. "Get her out of here. Rio—" Joey paused. "She says she's pregnant?"

"Not a newsflash," Rio growled and Joey nodded.

"That's what I thought."

Rio didn't answer, just pulled her carefully into his arms, lifted her out of truck, and started walking. She didn't care where he was going. Her eyelids were too heavy and the world was closing in, narrowing to the worried face watching hers.

"Stay with me," he ordered fiercely.

"Bossy," she whispered. Just this once, she wanted to do what he demanded, but it wasn't going to be possible. She needed a minute. Maybe two. Her eyelids were steel-plated right now, the weight dragging them down and giving her a few blissful seconds of dark and relaxed.

"Gia—"

All hell broke loose behind them as the DEA guys sprang into action. Who knew? The third vehicle had been carrying salvation after all. When she finally managed to crack an eye, she spotted Mack, face down, his gun two feet from his head. Getting shot by accident probably wasn't high on his to do list.

Under control.

Everything was under control.

She broke into sobs.

The EMTs had been on the scene fast, although not quickly enough for him. He'd been arguing for a chopper lift, although Evan had pointed out that it would take more time to get the bird in the air than it would to wait out the ambulance's arrival. Setting Gia down on the gurney and letting go so the trained professionals could do their thing had been almost impossible.

He'd done it though. All the field training in the world wasn't enough. He wasn't the best man for this job.

And he wasn't taking the chance.

Not with Gia. Not with their family.

So what if when he'd held her in his arms, walking them away from the crashed truck, he'd wanted to keep right on going? Away from the cops. Away from the whole world, if he had his way.

"She's pregnant," he said and Gia nodded.

Shit. Did she know for certain?

"We have to work on your delivery," he whispered roughly, leaning in to press a kiss against her temple. "If that's a *Hey Rio, I just took a positive pregnancy test*, you're supposed to make me dinner and light candles or something."

Her eyes closed and her face was still pale. But the shakes were stopping. That was something.

"You volunteered to wait outside the door," she said, not winning any prizes for coherence. Good thing he was sticking by her side in case she needed anything he could provide.

He could have lost her.

Had come real, real close to doing so.

So, nope, not going anywhere. He parked his ass beside her gurney and picked up her hand, threading his fingers through hers.

Thirty minutes later, the EMTs finished their checkout and reluctantly let Gia sit up. She'd refused transport, although she'd agreed that she'd go get an ultrasound. Just to make sure. He'd make sure she did but for now her body just needed time.

She carefully swung her legs off the gurney, grabbed the crutches Joey had produced from her truck and planted her boots on the ground. Stood up steady as a rock. Good as new.

Not.

He sucked in a breath. Some things had to be said and this was one of those things. Says the words to her back wasn't his first plan, but he'd work with what he had. Fuck the fact that they'd acquired an audience in the last thirty minutes. Most of the jump team was hovering nearby, waiting to hear that Gia was fine.

"I love you."

She stopped.

"Our time is up." Her voice was quiet.

Right. The pregnancy test.

"I'm not asking if you know about the baby or not. I'd like to know, but that's not the important thing right now."

"Oh." She sounded uncertain. That had to be a first for his Gia. "You still love me."

She sounded like she was testing the words, trying them on for fit.

He cleared his throat, because there was something in there. "Still. I also loved yesterday and the day before that. And I'm going to love you tomorrow and every day after that, okay?"

He reached out a hand, curls his fingers around her shoulder. "You're the part that matters, Gia. A baby would just be a bonus."

Their onlookers picked that moment to open the floor to

audience participation. Again, not what he'd planned on.

"Didn't you have the safe sex talk with him?" Jack punched Evan in the side. "Because, from what I'm hearing, somebody skipped something important."

Evan said something, but Rio didn't hear because Gia turned around and limped the two steps back into his arms. Her walk was more of a swing and a body slam, because she wasn't that far away, but he liked the effort. And he liked having every inch of her pressed against his body.

Someone whistled—that audience participation thing again—and he flipped the guy the bird with the arm he had around Gia's back. The spectators didn't matter. What mattered was holding onto Gia, no matter what. She didn't get away from him this time, not unless that was really what she wanted. She thunked her forehead onto his chest. He was probably sweaty and more than a little dirty. He was certainly no Prince Charming.

"Rio." She said his name like he was something special though and he'd probably wait fifty years by her side just to hear her say his name like that again.

"Yeah, baby?"

"Say it again."

"As many times as you want," he promised. "I love you."

She grabbed his hand, turned and headed for the hangar. "Let's talk," she said.

Rio let her tow him along even though her grip had his fingers pinned against the crutches. "I thought I was. Talking."

"Absolutely." She grinned at him over her shoulder and his heart turned over. "You talked. I listened. Now it's my turn."

Rio had got her naked in record time. The undressing part would have gone faster, he'd complained, but she'd had *her* hands on him.

Getting in the way. He'd also required convincing that she was up for this after her near-brush with death. She didn't know how to tell him that maybe it was *because* she'd almost died that she needed to remember right now that she was alive.

Very, very much alive and just a little shaken up.

Finally, he'd pulled her onto his lap so that she faced him. They had the storage loft in the hangar to themselves and she was fairly certain this was the best damned use their jump gear had ever been put to.

He kissed her again and touched her with his big, knowing hands and she came unglued. He knew it, too, even before he dipped his fingers between her thighs.

"Rio—"

"I'm listening." He stroked deeper. Oh, God. His fingers were wicked.

"I've got something to tell you." She sounded breathless.

"Uh-huh." He bent his head to her throat, his mouth tracing a pattern over her skin that gave her goose bumps.

"You said you loved me."

His mouth paused. "And I mean it," he growled against her throat. "You don't get to have second thoughts about that, honey. That's gospel truth."

"Mmmm," she breathed, losing her train of thought as one hard finger slid inside her.

"You going to tell me that you reciprocate?"

"I definitely love this." She ran a hand down his stomach. "And this."

When she wrapped her palm around him, he groaned louder.

"How about the whole package?" he asked hoarsely, lifting his head.

"Sure," she whispered, leaning in to kiss him. "The whole package is pretty damn sweet."

"And?"

"And I love you too."

"Thank God," he said, his eyes glinting with familiar mischief, "or this next part would be awkward."

He pressed a thigh between her legs. *Bad boy.*

Oh, please.

"I've been told going down on one knee is obligatory."

Her breath caught, her heart pounding fit to burst. But not because of her PSVT. No, it was her Rio. All him, all the time.

He spread her thighs with his shoulders. God, he was looking at her.

And she loved it.

Loved him.

He slid his hands up, parting her with his thumbs. The first kiss on her inner thigh had her jumping in the best possible way.

"What are we discussing?"

Another kiss, closer and higher to where she burned for him.

"We're not discussing anything, honey. I'm asking."

"Oh." Her answer was more moan than word as he pressed a gentle kiss right there on the sweetest of sweet spots. "With kisses?" She was so on board with that plan.

"Kisses are better than words," he said solemnly. "But a *yes* would be good."

He wasn't waiting around though. No, he kissed her deeper, his tongue sinking into her folds so that she lost her train of thought as pleasure streaked through her.

Right. Questions.

He asked again. "You got a *yes* in you for me?"

His next kiss had her hips bucking, but his hands held her in place.

"Uh-huh. You don't get to go anywhere just yet, honey. Because we're talking." He could call it whatever he wanted.

She felt his smile against her. "You got it."

"What's the question?"

He slid a finger deep inside her, pushing her higher and faster toward the pleasure. Damned if she knew what he was saying. Or if she cared.

"Will you marry me, Gia?"

He had his tongue curled around her clit and she was supposed to answer him? And then he paused.

"Rio," she wailed.

"I'm waiting," he growled. "For my *yes*."

And then he kissed her again. *Oh. My. God.* Heat and sweet pressure built inside her. Once wasn't enough. Or twice even. Forever, however, sounded just about right.

Her *yes* was a long time coming.

CHAPTER TWENTY-ONE

Three days later, Gia was back in the hangar. Mandatory team meeting, her ass. She'd woken up to a male hand slapping said ass. That had been interesting. Rio had claimed he'd just wanted to get her up for work. She'd counterclaimed he was into the kinky stuff.

And then...

He'd insisted she prove her words and now they were both late for work and whatever was really going down in the Donovan hangar today. Or, rather, Rio was late because he drove like a pansy. Her loaner truck had some sweet pick up. She'd made it here with precisely thirty seconds to spare.

The hangar floor was empty of people. Not of stuff though—there were piles of gear everywhere. Rio's brothers definitely hadn't inherited his neatnik gene.

"Incoming," she hollered. "Where do you want me?"

Jack poked his head of the office. "We're in here."

He looked around her. "Did you lose Rio? Already?"

She shrugged. "He drives too slow."

Jack stared at her. "Have you heard of global warning and car pooling? Maybe you could ride in the same truck together?"

"She won't let me drive," Rio called, striding into the hangar. Not too far behind after all. Maybe he did know how to pick up the pace.

Jack shook his head and headed for the office with a wave of his hand. "You two work it out."

Rio caught up with her, sliding his arms around her waist and pulling her back against him. His mouth nuzzled her neck. "You didn't wait for me."

She hadn't waited for him earlier that morning, in their bed, either—but that was definitely his fault. He'd touched and he'd kissed—and she'd left him far, far behind. She'd finished first.

She grinned. "You like that I'm impatient."

"Yeah," he growled, his mouth moving south. She tilted her head to give him better access.

"Hey." Jack popped his head back out. "We're having a meeting here?"

Rio dropped one last kiss on her neck and then started for the office, tugging her gently along. Somehow, he'd switched their positions so that he was leading while she followed. He had a definite talent for that.

When they reached the door, he stopped and looked down at her. "I love you. Remember that, okay, and cut me some slack?"

Definitely an ambush.

And, when she stepped inside, she got the reason for his concern. This was most definitely *not* a team meeting. Nope. The office was currently hosting Jack and Evan. Rio. And her.

"I see why you're asking," she said. "We're short a few members of the jump team."

Evan hooked a chair for her with his foot. "Sit," he suggested.

She sat and eyed her audience. "Gentlemen."

Evan looked uncomfortable. "Shit, Rio. You said you were going to discuss this with her."

"The *her* in question is right here," she pointed out. She tilted the chair back on two legs and stared them down. They were a big, rough bunch of men. She had no idea how Lily and Faye kept their guys in line. Maybe it was the sex.

Or the love.

Because she was fairly certain her newest girlfriends had these guys firmly wrapped around their fingers. She needed pointers. ASAP.

"I got distracted." Rio sounded unapologetic. The already crowded office was out of chairs, so he settled for leaning against the wall by her side. She shifted an inch and her shoulder bumped his blue jeans-covered thigh.

"Jesus." Jack swung his booted feet up onto the desk and winced. "I don't want to know."

Evan just grinned.

"I'm that good," Gia said, just to twist the screws a little. She knew her guys. If she didn't give as good as she got, they'd walk all over her. With the best of intentions, granted, but she'd still be under their very sexy boots. Which wasn't happening.

Rio shook his head. "Play nice with my brothers, okay?"

"You want to cut to the chase here?" She waved a hand around the office. "Because this is a really strange team meeting. I'm not seeing the other jumpers."

"That's because this is a management meeting." Rio watched her carefully, like he was expecting some kind of reaction from her.

Great.

"Are you firing me? Because I think I could sue for sexual harassment," she said flippantly. She loved him, but she wasn't blind or stupid. Rio was alpha to his core—and he didn't like her jumping because it wreaked havoc with his heart.

Or so he claimed.

Maybe women were the tougher sex, because she didn't have that problem. As long as she was by his side, he could jump out of all the planes he wanted. He, on the hand, would absolutely ground her if he thought he could get away with it.

"Gia." Rio scrubbed a hand over his head and looked at his brothers. They just stared back at him doing that silent male communication thing. Or passing the buck. She tilted the chair back further, hooking her feet around the legs. Whatever he had to say, they'd work it out. Somehow.

"We've got a proposal for you." Rio reached out and gently tugged her chair to the ground. "Hear us out?"

She nodded, heart in her throat. The thrum-thrum-thrum half-drowned out his words, but the message was clear. Rio wasn't playing.

"We want to make a change to how Donovan Brothers is run. I can't be your boss."

She was *so* getting fired.

"Donovans," Jack said. "Instead of Donovan Brothers."

Her heartbeat double-timed it as her head struggled to make sense of where Rio was going. He hadn't Donald Trumped her yet. Apparently, she still had a job—and now she had no idea where this conversation was headed.

"We want you to be a part of the business, no matter what name goes on the stationary, but I thought you'd appreciate the new name."

Holy. Moly. "You want me to join you?"

"Is that a *yes*?" Evan asked.

"Us," Rio said, ignoring his brother. "Everyone in the family can and will have a hand in running the company—from the ground or in the air, as part of the jump team. Although," he shot her a wry grin, "I'm begging you to be careful, okay?"

She liked the sound of Rio begging almost as much as the sense of belonging that swept over her. From the way his eyes darkened, he clearly spotted the possibilities as well, but Rio had always been observant.

"You're giving me a promotion? Making me an equal player?"

"You've earned it," Rio said, his dark eyes steady on her face. Watching her. *Believing* in her. "This isn't a gift."

Rio definitely didn't play fair. And… she was so in.

"Count me in," she said.

CHAPTER TWENTY-TWO

The plane banked gently as Rio rand his hands over her gear, gentle and sure. "You're good to go."

As was he. As his jump partner, Gia had made doubly sure of that. Losing him once was enough. Joey nodded from his position as spotter, seconding the motion, and Spotted Dick flashed a thumbs-up from the cockpit.

"Baby's okay?"

"He's doing fine."

Rio rubbed a hand over the almost-invisible swell of her belly. This would be her last jump until after her miniature Donovan made his appearance. Since her pregnancy had been straightforward so far and was low risk, her doctor had cleared her for this afternoon since she'd jumped before and was no novice. She had a feeling, though, that next time he'd be more careful when he cheerfully spotted the well-known line about it being fine for a woman to continue all her usual activities.

She looked out the door. No fire, just clear blue skies and a wide-open landing zone. "This is too easy."

Thirteen thousand feet stood between them and the start of happily ever after. She couldn't wait.

Rio gave her the look. "Next time, I'm arguing harder for a church."

She tugged gently on his hand, pulling him into position in the door. "You don't get a next time, remember? This is it. You can argue against jumping when we're doing our vow renewals at our fiftieth."

His slow answering smile set all the fires she needed. "Right. Remind me why I'm doing this?"

Spotted Dick's voice crackled on the headset as he announced that he was bringing the plane around for the jump pass. It was almost time. She snuck another glance out the open door. Making out individual faces from this height was impossible but she knew they were all down there, waiting for her and Rio.

Leaning up, she planted a kiss on his mouth. "Nervous?"

He grimaced. "This is my first time, Gia. I've never done this before."

"I'll be gentle," she promised, loving his laugh and knowing that she wasn't alone in her nervousness. This was the jump of a lifetime, a leap of faith she knew in her heart she was ready to make... but that didn't stop the butterflies gathering in her stomach.

"Breathe in, breathe out," she reminded him. "Just keep it steady."

A simple lesson she'd learned from PSVT. Breathe in, breathe out. One breath following the other. Together.

The preacher moved closer and started the ceremony. This was what she and Rio had decided on. No big ceremony, just the two of them, the woman uniting them in holy matrimony, and their witnesses. Face-to-face, hand-in-hand. Gia liked the simplicity of it all, followed by the grandiose gesture of literally jumping feet first into marriage. Which would be all the more special because of the welcoming committee waiting for them on the ground and the reminder that they weren't doing this alone.

"Rio Donovan, do you take Gia Jackson to be your wife?"

The fierce look on her Rio's face as he waited for the preacher to finish made her smile. "Hell, I sure do."

"Do you swear to love, honor and cherish her? To protect her and to forsake all others forevermore?"

"I do." His thumb rubbed over the back of her hand, the small circles anchoring her.

Moments later, she made her own vows, repeating the words so many other women had said before her. She loved blazing her own trail, but sometimes it just felt right to take the familiar path. This was one of those times.

Rio raised her hand and tugged off her glove with his teeth, working the diamond band over her finger. The wedding ring was sparkly but nothing to catch on her gloves or when she was out in the field. Beautiful and full of substance—like him. The weight on her finger was unfamiliar but welcome.

The preacher kept right on talking, the beautiful words of the ceremony rolling around them, over the headset and filling the air. Absolutely perfect.

"Rio and Gia, you have promised your love for each other with these vows and these rings. I now pronounce you to be husband and wife."

Joey whooped louder than he ever had going out the plane's bay. "Kiss the groom, honey."

And she did. A sweet kiss, with hot promise of more. Later. Breaking off only because Joey gestured them into the open door. It was time to go. Time to take that leap of faith together.

"Ready?" Rio looked at her and the expression on his face had her heart turning over in her chest. God. She was lucky.

"You bet. I was born ready."

His little growl heated her right up. "You made me chase you, honey. There wasn't anything *ready* about you."

"And you liked it," she countered, drinking in his grin.

"Count it down," he said, tugging her just a little closer, and she did. On three, they were out the bay together. Clearing the plane, they hung in the air for a long moment. Just the two of them, the roar of the wind filling her ears as her eyes locked on Rio and they started the free fall.

Not alone. Never again.

He reached out and she took his hands. For one perfect moment, they hung there in the air together. They'd hit their breakoff altitude soon and then she'd have to let go, but the separation would be only temporary. Rio would be waiting for her on the ground or she'd be waiting for him. Every time.

"I love you," she said, squeezing his hand. "And I'm letting go now, but only temporarily."

"Right back at you," he growled. "Damn straight we're in this together. Forever. I love you," he said and the truth of his words was written on his face. Her big, strong Donovan loved her with all his heart and soul.

She soaked in the jump of a lifetime, the ground spinning closer. No malfunction this time. Just two people moving in unison, soaring towards the wedding drop zone where their jump team, friends and family wait for them.

Feet-first into happily ever after.

BURNS SO BAD

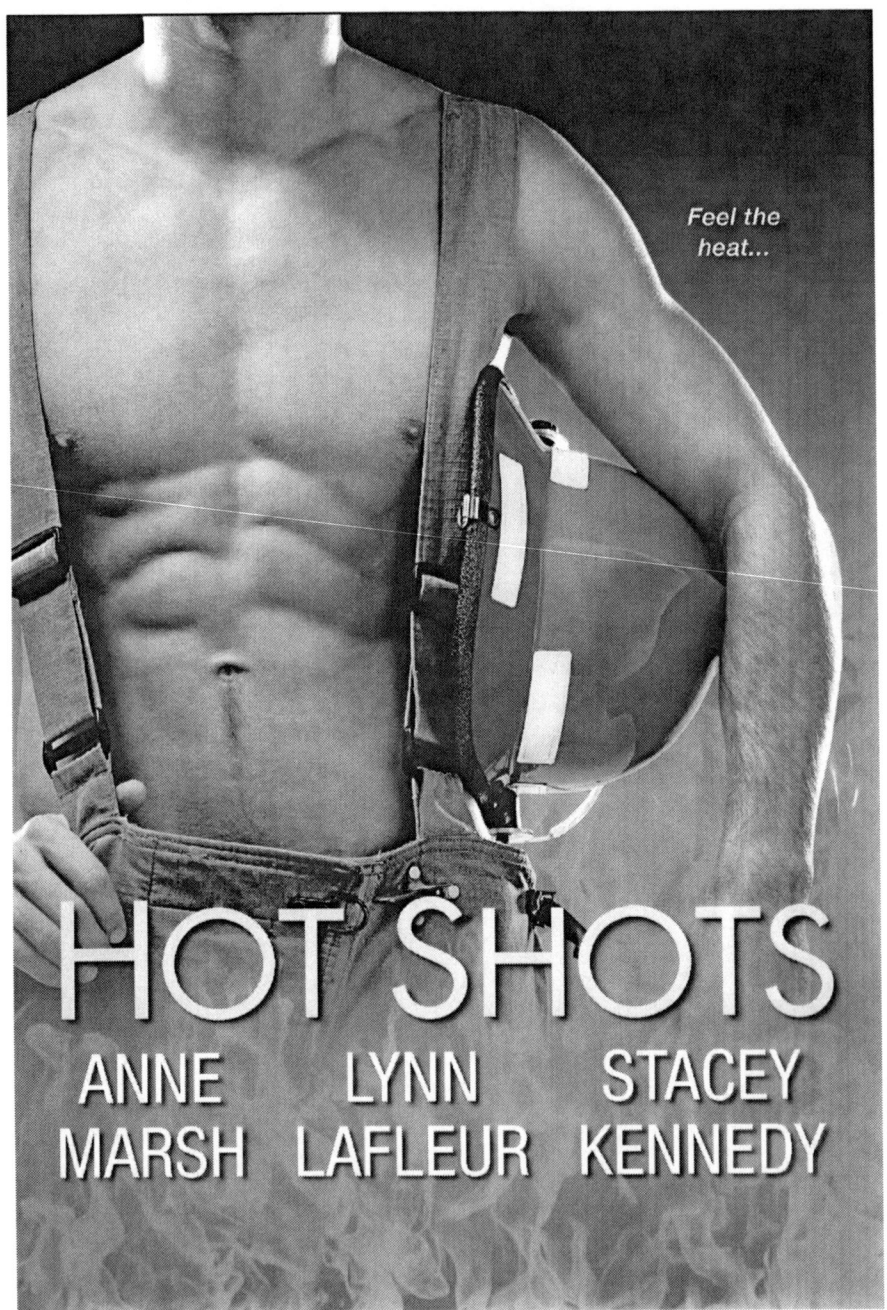

Sexy as sin and hot as hell, these firefighters smolder with passion and burn with desire...

"FIRED UP" BY ANNE MARSH

Hannah Green watches for wildfires from an isolated fire tower in Sequoia National Park by day and radios Cajun firefighter Cole Henry at night to share carnal fantasies hot enough to start a forest fire...

"SIZZLE" BY LYNN LAFLEUR

When photojournalist Maysen Halliday arrives in Lanville to take calendar pictures of the sexiest firefighters in Texas, red hot Fire Chief Clay Spencer makes her want him for her own personal centerfold...

"FIVE-ALARM MASQUERADE" BY STACEY KENNEDY

With her home destroyed in a fire, Abby has only the muscular arms of a rock hard firefighter to hold her up and the dream of blazing hot nights of pure erotic pleasure to keep her going...

It's supposed to be a quick wedding hook-up. She's lonely. He's available. After seeing Rio Donovan and Gia Jackson down the aisle, the sizzling sexual chemistry between Mimi Hart and Mack Johnson has this pair burning up the sheets in a night of no-holds fantasies. One night. No regrets. And no promises.

As Strong's resident bad girl and bartender, Mimi has earned every inch of her reputation. Tattoos, motorcycles and dancing on the bar—Mimi's all in. She's fun and she's tough, a hot sex-on-the-pool-table woman—not a sunset-and-kisses sweetheart. Until her wedding hook-up, Mack Johnson, turns into a man on a sensual mission…and threatens to send her heart into freefall even as her own past threatens to catch up with her.

Mack didn't choose Strong—Strong chose him. Fresh from the warzones of the Middle East and battling PTSD demons, this Spec Ops soldier is most at home on the battlefield. Still, when Jack Donovan calls in a favor, he heads to Strong, California for fire season. Guns. Firefights. And chutes. These things make sense. One summer and then he heads back to the frontlines where he belongs. He never counted on falling in love with Strong—or with Mimi. She's exactly what the doctor ordered. Now he wants all of Mimi—the sweet and the sour, the tough and the loving. And he's ready to convince her one night—and one fire—at a time…

Available March 2014!

SMOKE JUMPERS

ANNE MARSH

Smoking Hot

"White hot suspense and a drop dead sexy hero!"
—*New York Times* bestselling author,
Roxanne St. Claire

Temperatures are rising...

For Navy SEAL Tye Callahan, Strong, California is a debt of honor and temporary detour in his military career. He's fought hard in Afghanistan and he won't stop until the battle is won. When an ambush he should have prevented kills one of his men, however, Tye steps up and steps in to fill the fallen man's obligations. One summer in Strong fighting fires with the smoke jumper team. One sister to look out for and get back on her feet. But the adrenaline rush of fighting fire, of jumping into the heart of the flames and pitting wits and body against the inferno, is nothing compared to the rush of coming face to face with Katie Lawson...

Until there's no beating the heat

Katie can't accept her larger-than-life brother has been killed in action. While she waits for him to come home, she vows to fulfill her brother's bucket list. And who better to help her than Mr. Tall, Dark and Sexy—her brother's commanding officer and substitute smoke jumper? Now, as the summer heats up one sexy task at a time, they must decide if the chemistry burning between them might just be their second chance at living their own lives... together.

Available April 2014!

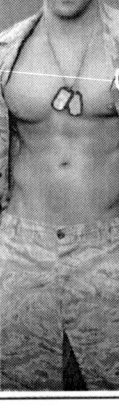

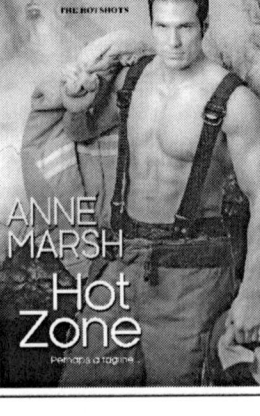

Look for these titles by Anne Marsh

Blue Moon Brides

TEMPTED BY THE PACK
PLEASURED BY THE PACK
CLAIMED BY THE PACK

The Fallen

BOND WITH ME
HIS DARK BOND
SAVAGE BOND

Hunter's Mate

THE HUNT

Smoke Jumpers

BURNING UP
SLOW BURN
BURNS SO BAD

The Hot Shots

REBURN
HOT ZONE
FIRED UP

Dawson Brothers

ONE HOT COWBOY

ABOUT THE AUTHOR

After ten years of graduate school and too many degrees, Anne Marsh escaped to become a technical writer. When not planted firmly in front of the laptop translating Engineering into English, Anne enjoys gardening, running (even if it's just to the 7-11 for Slurpees), and reading books curled up with her kids. The best part of writing romance, however, is finally being able to answer the question: "So… what do you do with a PhD in Slavic languages and literatures?" She lives in Northern California with her husband, two kids and five cats. You can visit her online at www.anne-marsh.com.

CPSIA information can be obtained at www.ICGtesting.com
Printed in the USA
LVOW07s2137280115

424814LV00001B/151/P